Praise for Sister Carol Anne O'Marie and the Sister Mary Helen Mystery Series

"Father Brown, move over . . . tough and compassionate, [Sister Mary Helen] understands the secrets of the human heart."

—Andrew M. Greeley

Requiem at the Refuge

"O'Marie twines the strands of these disparate lives with humor and sympathy."

—Publishers Weekly

"Another first-rate installment in an unfailingly entertaining series."

—Booklist

The Missing Madonna

"The author's handy mix of humor and suspense again proves irresistible."

—Publishers Weekly

Murder in Ordinary Time

"Sister Mary Helen handles her cases with bustling efficiency and an elfin sense of humor."

—The New York Times Book Review

"A tidy mystery . . . a satisfying read."

—Publishers Weekly

A Novena for Murder

"Hair-raising . . . a fast-reading story . . . this is one you won't want to put down."

—West Coast Review of Books

More . . .

"Sister Carol writes with sure knowledge, a deft touch."

—Houston Post

Death Goes on Retreat

"Sister Mary Helen's gentle insights inform this story about age-old prejudices with a quiet wisdom."

—Publishers Weekly

Murder Makes a Pilgrimage

"Neatly plotted, entertaining mystery fare."

—Booklist

The Corporal Works of Murder

"Another suspenseful whodunit . . . in an unfailingly cozy mystery series."

—Library Journal

Death Takes Up a Collection

"Enlivened by its series of incisive character studies—and sure to please the Sister's legion of fans."

—Kirkus Reviews

"An unfailingly cozy mystery."

—Library Journal

Death of an Angel

"O'Marie delivers compelling characters . . . sophisticated plotting."

—Publishers Weekly

"[An] excellent mystery series . . . hard to put down."

—Booklist

Murder
at the
Monks' Table

A Sister Mary Helen Mystery

Sister Carol Anne O'Marie

St. Martin's Paperbacks

This is a work of fiction. All of the characters, organizations and events portrayed in this novel are either products of the author's imagination or are used fictitiously.

MURDER AT THE MONKS' TABLE

Copyright © 2006 by Sister Carol Anne O'Marie.

Library of Congress Catalog Card Number: 2006040365

ISBN: 0-312-35768-0
EAN: 9780312-35768-9

Printed in the United States of America

St. Martin's Press hardcover edition / June 2006
St. Martin's Paperbacks edition / July 2007

St. Martin's Paperbacks are published by St. Martin's Press, 175 Fifth Avenue, New York, NY 10010.

10 9 8 7 6 5 4 3 2 1

For Eva Eulalia Benson,
born on July 26, 2005.
Your arrival has brought
us great joy!

and

Congratulations to
my niece Noelle Benson
on her marriage to
Ryan Sullivan!
February 25, 2006
We thought you'd never ask.

Acknowledgments

Thank you to all who helped and supported me in researching and writing this mystery. I am especially grateful to Sister Maureen O'Connor, former provincial superior, who made my trip to Ireland possible, and to Sister Maureen Lyons, who accompanied me there, helped me get settled, and then filled in for me at my "real job" with homeless women at A Friendly Place. Thanks, too, to Connie and Lee Poldino, who met us early on and brought a touch of home.

I am most grateful to my dear "old" friends, Christina Decker, Jean Walker Lowell, Cynthia and Joe Kelly, and Eileen and Jack Shea. They came to visit and generously showed me much of the magic and magnificence of the west of Ireland.

A special thanks to my sister, Kathleen; my nieces, Caroline and Noelle Benson; and Ryan Sullivan. They arrived with the energy, enthusiasm, and sense of adventure that only they can bring.

Thank you, too, to Brenda Morrissey and her family and the Sisters of Charity in Clarinbridge for their hospitality during my stay in their village.

I am also grateful to Sister Kathleen Kelly, who arrived at the end of my stay to help me pack up and come home, and to Mary Elena Dochterman, who gave me my first experience flying business class.

I cannot thank Steve Danko enough. When my completed manuscript disappeared from the computer, he generously offered to retype it and make the corrections. Without him, I'd still be staring at an empty screen and crying.

Heartfelt thanks go to Rosalie Kelly (may she rest in peace) for her helpful critiques over the years and to Mary Rock, who checked the manuscript for all things Irish.

I appreciate the members of my writing group, Margaret Little, Jil Plummer, Vlasta Turko, Greta Cox, and Ann Damaschino. They listened to my manuscript for months and made many valuable suggestions.

I am grateful to my local community, Sisters Barbara Flannery, Ann Maureen Murphy, and Maureen Lyons for their never-ending interest and encouragement.

Finally, I'd like to thank my agent, Dominick Abel, who has stuck with me all these years. I am convinced that he is the best in the business!

Murder
at the
Monks' Table

Friday, August 29

May the road rise to meet you,
May the wind be ever at your back.
— Irish blessing

The long black hearse came speeding out of the driveway, nearly careening into the hackney. *Don't tell me this is going to be one of those days,* Sister Mary Helen thought, grabbing the car door handle.

"Cheeky get!" she heard the driver mumble. Then, realizing that she might have overheard, he added a quick "Sorry, Sister," turning full around to check her reaction.

"Maybe he's late," she said, wishing the driver would keep his eyes on the road, especially since he was driving on the opposite side, which, of course, wasn't the opposite side here in Ireland.

Ireland, she thought, closing her eyes and wondering if she were dreaming. Her eyelids felt sandy. Why wouldn't they? It was four o'clock in the morning, San Francisco time. And she'd had little sleep since her friend, Sister Eileen, had called less than a week ago, inviting her to come.

"Late for his own funeral!" The driver laughed. "That's a good one, Sister. But if you want to know what I think, I think it is one of his boyos on his way to pick up the pearl of the festivities, the Oyster Queen. Her da owns the funeral parlor. Probably why they chose her," he said, "comes with her own grand car."

The Oyster Festival! Until last week Mary Helen had never heard of the event, but then Eileen had called with the sad news that her sister Molly, whom she had gone to County Galway, Ireland, to nurse through her final illness, had died. Eileen's nieces and nephews were so grateful for her help that they insisted on treating their aunt to a holiday before she returned to her convent in San Francisco. The Oyster Festival was in County Galway, so why not attend that? As an added surprise, they had purchased a ticket so that her good friend, Sister Mary Helen, could join her.

"What about my work at the homeless center?" Mary Helen had asked when Eileen called with the invitation.

"Glory be to God, old dear, you're a volunteer! If the truth be told, you are actually retired. What's the point of being retired if you can't go off once in a while for a little fun?" Eileen asked, and then added as if it were news, "Life is short."

Mary Helen's recent brushes with murder had, if anything, made it clear to her just how short a life can be. So here she was.

Looking out the car window, she watched the green fields and stone fences slipping by. Enormous clouds blew across the bright sky.

Both Sister Anne, whom she helped at the homeless center, and Sister Patricia, the president of Mount St. Francis College, where she lived, were delighted that she had the opportunity to go. Too delighted, in Mary Helen's opinion, but there was no sense getting into that.

After nearly sixty years in the convent, she had learned that there were some things you were better off ignoring.

"We'll be there in no time," the hackney driver called out.

Paul. That was his name, Mary Helen remembered. Paul Glynn. He had introduced himself at the Shannon airport where he had met her, holding a big sign with her name neatly printed on it.

"No hurry, Paul," she answered, closing her eyes again as he passed the hearse.

When she had first spotted him, he had reminded her of pictures she'd seen of the young James Joyce—slight, with straight black hair and rimless glasses on a thin face. Just add a patch on the left eye and a mustache . . .

"Only another thirty or so miles," Paul said, whizzing past a stretch of cars, "and we'll be in Ballyclarin."

Ballyclarin, located on the Clarin River, Mary Helen had discovered on the Internet, was home of the Oyster Festival. In fact, the village slogan was, "The world is your oyster and Ballyclarin is its home."

It seemed that Paul, a distant cousin of Sister Eileen's niece by marriage, had been recruited to be their driver. And zipping along the narrow roads, past signs that warned "loose chippings," and around the roundabouts, Mary Helen was becoming more and more grateful that neither Eileen nor she would be at the wheel.

According to Paul, the family had rented a small mews in the village where the nuns were to stay and enjoy the weeklong festivities. For festival events as well as for any side trips, he was at their service.

Slowing down, Paul entered the village and Mary Helen spotted her friend immediately. Eileen stood in front of an impressive Georgian house, smiling and waving.

After a few hugs and several pats on the back, the two old friends studied one another at arm's length.

"You look none the worse for wear," Mary Helen said.

"Nor you, old dear," Eileen returned. "And we probably both need our glasses changed."

Quickly Paul brought Sister Mary Helen's suitcase into the small, cozy mews in the back of the house, then handed Eileen a card with his name and phone number on it. "Ring when you need me," he said and slipped away, leaving the two old friends to catch up.

And there was a lot of catching up to do. Eileen fixed them each a cup of tea and they settled on the sofa. Mary Helen leaned forward and patted her friend's hand. "I know how hard these last two years must have been for you," she said. "You and Molly were always in my thoughts and prayers."

Eileen's gray eyes suddenly filled with tears. Quietly she began to talk about her sister's death and how difficult it is to suffer with someone you love. Mary Helen listened, knowing that was all she could do, as Eileen poured out her grief and pain.

A long streak of dying sun shot across the carpet of the mews when Eileen finally checked her wristwatch. "You must be exhausted," she said, wiping her eyes. "Do you know what time it is?"

"Don't even go there," Mary Helen said. All she knew was that her head was beginning to ache and that she could scarcely keep her eyelids up.

"Let's pop next door to the Monks' Table for a bite to eat and then it's to bed with you."

"Pop where?" Mary Helen wasn't sure she'd heard correctly.

"The Monks' Table." Eileen smiled. "It's a pub-restaurant and has delicious homemade soup."

Once inside, Mary Helen followed Eileen through a jumble of small, dark rooms and alcoves, past signs cautioning patrons to "Mind Your Step." The only things, in her opinion, that faintly resembled a monk's anything were the high-back benches where the diners were seated. Conceivably they could be recycled choir stalls. Was that why it was called the Monks' Table?

"Is soup enough?" Eileen asked once they were seated in a small room.

"Plenty," Mary Helen said, wondering if she'd even stay awake to finish that.

"Let me tell the waitress, so she doesn't fuss with all the silverware." Eileen excused herself.

Leaning her head back against the bench, Mary Helen closed her eyes. The room was quiet. Only one other couple was nearby. They were seated at the table behind the nuns.

Mary Helen had noticed the pair while the two nuns were being seated. The woman was small and wiry with chestnut brown hair, courtesy, no doubt, of Lady Clairol. The man, on the other hand, was big-boned and ran to fat. A tuft of gray hair formed a ring around his bald pate. *Must be husband and wife,* Mary Helen had thought when she'd seen them.

The woman, whose voice was high and whiney, was obviously complaining about something. Although between her brogue and her whispering, Mary Helen had no idea about what. Then without warning, her words came through loud and strident. "I am surprised someone hasn't killed you already," she said.

Mary Helen's eyes shot open.

"What is it?" Eileen asked, sliding onto her bench.

"Behind us," Mary Helen whispered. "I just overheard the woman say that she was surprised that someone hadn't killed that man already."

Eileen leaned forward. "She was probably joking," she whispered.

"It didn't sound like it."

"You are a little oversensitive to murder," Eileen said. "Not that I blame you," she added quickly, "what with the bad luck you've had stumbling into them. But this is Ireland. There are only about fifty murders a year in the entire country with a population of 5.8 million. What are the odds of one happening in Ballyclarin?"

"About as good as winning the lottery," Mary Helen conceded, adjusting her bifocals, which had slipped down the bridge of her nose.

"Right," Eileen said as the waitress put down two bowls of steaming hot chowder and a basket of fresh, warm soda bread.

"Now eat up, old dear," she said. "Tomorrow we have a big day."

Saturday, August 30

May you always have walls for the wind,
A roof for the rain, tea beside the fire,
Laughter to cheer you, those you love near you,
And all your heart might desire.
                                    —Irish blessing

Sister Mary Helen awoke long before the dawn. As hard as she tried she could not fall back to sleep. *Jet lag, no doubt,* she thought, refusing to even look at her travel clock.

She closed her eyes, still unable to realize that she was actually in Ireland. The mews Eileen's relatives had rented was perfect for them, with two bedrooms, a sitting room, a bathroom, and a small kitchen. Best of all, it was in the heart of the village, across from the parish church and close to all the Oyster Festival activities. She'd just rest until she heard Eileen stir.

Sister Mary Helen smelled the coffee even before she heard her friend whispering her name.

"What time is it?" she asked, opening her eyes. Bright sunlight flooded the room. "I must have fallen back to sleep."

"A little after ten," Eileen said, "and the village market day starts in about an hour. I didn't think you'd want to miss it."

"I don't want to miss a thing," Mary Helen said, pushing herself up.

When the two nuns finally left the mews, the main street of the village was packed with people. The church car park as well as the side streets were full of motorcars. Mary Helen wondered where everyone came from. Ballyclarin must be a great deal bigger than it had looked when she had driven in.

Everyone seemed to be in a festive mood as they moved toward the village green. *What a mixture of people,* she thought, keeping her eye on Eileen, who was being pushed along with the crowd. There were elderly folks and young couples pushing strollers, teenagers and the handicapped, middle-aged men and women, several uniformed gardai on duty, and hundreds of children darting in and out.

The green itself was a large triangular piece of land in the center of the village. A cut stone wall surrounded it. Beech, chestnut, and yew trees grew alongside the wall. There were benches for sitting, a fire pit, and the remnants of what must have once been the village well.

An enormous stone Celtic cross rose from the middle of the green. And a replica, Mary Helen noticed, of the inside of a thatched roof cottage was built for a stage. On it a traditional Irish band was beginning to set up.

Stalls covered the grass. Medieval carts loaded with fruits and vegetables were held to the trees by very modern chains. There were crafts of every kind on display. One woman was churning butter. An older man was thatching a roof while near him a young woman was painting the children's faces.

The farrier, a short stout man who Mary Helen guessed to be in his seventies, was busy at his anvil pounding horseshoes. Behind him was an eye-catching display of handmade kitchen knives. But possibly the chief attraction was a huge pink sow on display with her twelve piglets.

Sister Eileen stopped next to a tall gray-haired man in a black suit and clerical collar. Mary Helen assumed he was the parish priest. "Father Keane," Eileen said, "I'd like you to meet my friend, Sister Mary Helen. She just arrived from San Francisco."

After greeting her graciously, Father Keane could scarcely wait to ask if they had heard all the commotion last night.

"We didn't hear a thing," Eileen said.

"There was a terrible row," he said. "The travelers had a wedding and a fight broke out at the party after."

"Was anyone hurt?" Eileen asked.

"Not that I know of," the priest said. "The worst catastrophe was a broken mirror at the Monks' Table."

"Seven years bad luck," Eileen mumbled.

"Not for the travelers," Father Keane said. "Most of them are gone." He looked up to say something else, but someone called his name and he excused himself.

Travelers, if Sister Mary Helen remembered correctly, was another name for the tinkers, a community that was the butt of much intolerance and prejudice in Ireland. They had been accused of everything from stealing pots to cursing brides and kidnapping babies.

The tolling of the noon Angelus rang out across the village, and all activity stopped while Father Keane reverently led the ancient prayer over the loudspeaker. At its conclusion, he announced, "I now solemnly declare the opening of the Ballyclarin Oyster Festival." He paused. "Let the fun begin!"

To a chorus of cheers, the band struck up a rousing reel. Eileen and Mary Helen began to mill around the booths. They examined the herbal remedies, the spicy vinegar, the hand-stitched tote bags, and finally decided on some homemade black currant jam.

They were so fascinated by the woman at the spinning wheel that they didn't realize that Paul Glynn, their driver, had moved in next to them. "Let me introduce you to my wife and son," he said proudly.

The two nuns spent several minutes chatting with Paul's lovely young wife and his three-year-old son, who had hair as red as his mother's.

"Here comes the Oyster Queen," Paul said, pointing to a young woman dressed in a medieval Irish costume of emerald green taffeta. Her long dark hair was crowned with a rhinestone tiara, and her skin was so white that Mary Helen wondered if she ever saw the sun.

"Tara," he called as she came closer. "Tara O'Dea, may I present you to two nuns from America?"

Tara smiled and did and said all the gracious things a queen should do and say. Mary Helen was impressed.

"How were you chosen for this honor?" she asked. "Was there a competition?"

Tara's white cheeks flamed. "No," she said. "I just met with the festival chairman and answered a few questions." She shrugged. "And I was picked."

"Why is it you ask?" The question came from behind Mary Helen. She thought the sharp voice sounded vaguely familiar. Turning, she recognized the woman with the chestnut hair from the Monks' Table, looking none too friendly.

"This is Tara's mother," Paul said quickly. "Zoë O'Dea."

Sister Mary Helen had just enough time to say, "How do?" when Father Keane's voice came booming out of the loudspeaker again.

"Now, I'd like to introduce our master of ceremonies

for the day," he said. All attention shifted toward the thatched cottage stage.

The master of ceremonies, a television soap opera personality, told a few jokes, then went on to introduce Tara.

"What was that all about?" Mary Helen asked, watching Tara mount the stage, her mother close behind. "I was just curious." She shivered. A sudden wind swept through the village green and dark clouds seemed to be bubbling up from the horizon, threatening the sun.

"Pay her no mind," Paul said. "There was talk of a bit of a fix."

"A fix for the Oyster Queen?" Eileen's gray eyebrows shot up. "You can't mean it!"

"Some say that Carmel Cox should have been chosen. There is Carmel over there." Paul inclined his head toward a lovely young woman with fair skin, large blue eyes, and a full head of curly auburn hair.

"She's beautiful," Mary Helen said. "They are both beautiful. If the queen was picked for her looks alone, it would have been difficult to choose."

"Right you are, but the word is that Zoë had the chairman's ear."

"Who is the chairman?" Mary Helen asked.

"Owen Lynch." Paul indicated the man with horn-rimmed glasses standing near the platform.

Mary Helen adjusted her bifocals. "Who's that next to him?"

Paul strained to see. "The fellow in the tweed cap? That's Willie Ward. Works for the local rag as a reporter, of sorts. If you ask me, he's nothing but a second-rate gossipmonger. Although he takes himself quite seriously."

Mary Helen studied the man. It was hard to tell with his cap on, but she could almost swear he was the man she'd seen having dinner with Zoë O'Dea last night. Today he carried a long narrow notebook and seemed to jot down notes as he listened.

"And the woman who just joined them," Paul said, anticipating Mary Helen's question, "is Owen's wife, Patsy Lynch—Patsy Sweeney, she was. Lucky devil."

"How so?" Eileen asked.

"Patsy is an only child. With Patsy comes a garage in Oranmore."

"What we call a car dealership," Eileen explained.

Mary Helen strained for a better look. Patsy was a large-boned woman with thick graying hair drawn back and held with a tortoiseshell clip. She was attractive in a clean, outdoorsy sort of way. Flanking her were twin girls of about ten or eleven years of age. They were dressed in Irish dancing costumes of a bright royal purple and trimmed with pink. They had inherited their mother's large frame and apparently their father's bad eyesight, for both of them wore horn-rimmed glasses.

By this time the sky had clouded over, and a brisk wind rattled the leaves on the trees and blew over the display of photographs.

"Ladies and gentlemen. May I have your attention, please." The voice of the master of ceremonies echoed from the loudspeaker. "The sun seems to be deserting us, but before it does, may I present the pride of our village, our prizewinning girls' dance team."

Amid clapping and cheering, sixteen young girls, including the Lynch twins, spilled onto the dance floor that was set up below the stage. The band filled the green with music and the youngsters whirled and twirled and leapt and kicked as the audience clapped in time.

A second set had nearly finished when the heavens opened, sending everyone, including the squealing dancers, scurrying for shelter.

"What now?" Mary Helen asked as she and Eileen took refuge under a beech tree.

"If it doesn't let up in a few minutes, I'd suggest it's back to the Monks' Table for more soup."

When they pulled back the door of the pub, the two nuns realized theirs was not an original idea. The place was quickly filling.

Following the waitress to a table, Mary Helen realized how large the Monks' Table really was. More rooms were vacant beyond where they had been seated last night. There were several fireplaces, all roaring, and a potbelly stove was lit. The warmth felt good on the wet afternoon.

Passing a small alcove, Mary Helen noticed the queen's mother already seated. She was with another man, probably Tara's father. What had Paul said when they'd met the hearse on their way into town—that her da was the undertaker?

Mary Helen smiled at Mrs. O'Dea as she passed. But the woman stared straight ahead, pretending not to see her. *Talk about getting off on the wrong foot,* she thought.

Or maybe she was imagining it, since Eileen didn't seem to notice any coldness. "Hello, there, Mr. O'Dea," Eileen said, stopping at the table. "What a lovely girl you have." She smiled. "You must be very proud."

As Mr. O'Dea struggled to get up, Eileen introduced Sister Mary Helen. "Mr. O'Dea gave my sister a lovely send-off," she said.

"No more than she deserved," Mr. O'Dea mumbled, then introduced his wife.

"We've met," Mrs. O'Dea said with a thin smile.

"I didn't realize you knew that woman," Mary Helen said when the two were seated in another wing of the restaurant.

"First I saw her was when you saw her last night. When she said we'd met, she must have meant just now at the village market. I don't know her. It's her husband I dealt with, and he was kindness itself." Suddenly Eileen's eyes filled up, and Mary Helen thought it best to drop the subject.

The village folks were still pouring into the Monks' Table when the nuns rose to leave.

"How about a little nap?" Eileen suggested, her eyes red. "We have a big night tonight and you look tired."

"And what is that?" Mary Helen asked, stifling a yawn. She checked her wristwatch. They must just be getting up in San Francisco.

"It's a wine and cheese tasting," Eileen explained, "and they'll be announcing the winner of the Irish soda bread baking contest."

"That sounds like fun," Mary Helen said, following her friend out of the Monks' Table. "Certainly no one can think that is fixed."

The wine and cheese tasting was scheduled to begin at eight o'clock. Sisters Eileen and Mary Helen were among the first to arrive. The nap had been a good idea. Mary Helen was beginning to feel more like her old self.

She surveyed the large hall into which they were ushered. Amazingly, it was built onto the back of the Monks' Table and was set up as though someone planned to give a lecture.

Each participant received a plastic wineglass and an

emerald green paper napkin and was moved quickly to a seat.

"How many people do you think they are expecting?" Mary Helen asked.

"I'd guess there are about one hundred chairs," Eileen said.

Mary Helen jumped as a disc jockey blasted the room with a lively reel. "Sorry, ladies," he said sheepishly, and he adjusted the volume.

Mary Helen looked around. Surprisingly, there were just ladies present, so far anyway. That is, unless you counted the disc jockey and the two men in the front of the hall, plus Owen Lynch, the chairman of the event.

There was a little stir when Queen Tara arrived in her emerald green costume, her mother right on her heels.

By 8:15 the room was beginning to fill with smartly dressed women who, if the voice volume was any indication, were determined to have a good time.

Finally, about a quarter of nine, when Mary Helen was wondering if it was ever going to start, one of the men who had been standing in front tried to get the group's attention. Most of the women were so busy talking to their friends that they scarcely noticed him.

"May I have your attention, please?" he repeated.

"Good luck," Eileen said under her breath.

Then, he made the fatal mistake of the inexperienced speaker. He tried to talk above the noise.

From what Mary Helen could make out, the poor man was a wine merchant in Ballyvaugh and his name was John something. Because of the din she was unable to catch the last name. His companion was a cheese expert from a specialty shop in Galway City.

The first wine, a sauvignon blanc from New Zealand, was poured and tasted with the accompanying goat-milk cheese. Plates of homemade Irish soda bread were passed down the aisle for anyone who wanted a "blotter." Mary Helen took one. From the looks of the wine table, they had several bottles to go.

The audience seemed to quiet down, at least long enough to swallow. Jumping on the unexpected silence, John Wine Merchant quickly had the second wine served and passed around a creamy cheese. The quiet while the women swallowed this time was even shorter.

By the fifth wine, Asti Spumonte, there wasn't even a pause for swallowing. The ladies of Ballyclarin were mildly snookered.

Mr. Lynch, the chairman, didn't seem to know how to get the audience back under control. Interestingly enough, his wife, Patsy, was among the most rambunctious. She was laughing uproariously at something the lady next to her was saying.

In a desperate attempt to restore order, Mr. Lynch took the microphone from the disc jockey. "Ladies," he said, blinking behind his horn-rimmed glasses, "if I may have your attention, please. It is time to announce the winner of the Irish soda bread baking contest."

His announcement did make some impression on the group, for the noise level lessened a bit. Taking advantage of the lull, he began, "First of all, I'd like to thank John McDonnell and David Gumbleton for their presentation here tonight." There was mild clapping for the two gentlemen whom Mary Helen was beginning to think of as heroic.

A high-pitched voice broke through the applause. "Who is Gumbleton? Never heard of her. Did she win the contest?"

"Bridie, turn up your hearing aid," someone hissed.

"If I may call on Queen Tara O'Dea," Chairman Lynch ignored the interruption, "to present the award."

Tara rose from her seat and stood next to Mr. Lynch.

She took the envelope he handed her, opened it, and pulled out a sheet of paper with as much solemnity as if she were presenting an Academy Award.

"The winner is . . ." She paused, suddenly distracted by some commotion near the entrance to the hall.

Mary Helen turned in time to see Willie Ward enter, his long, thin reporter's notebook in his hand. An angry voice floated in from the outside. "You maggot! You've gone too far this time," a man called.

Willie smiled sheepishly. "Apparently, Jake doesn't think tearing up the Monks' Table last night was newsworthy," he said with a snicker.

"I'd be careful about making the tinkers angry," the woman next to Mary Helen said to no one in particular.

"Can we get on with it?" Bridie's high voice filled the room. "Who won the baking contest?"

"Carmel Cox," Tara announced, looking relieved to get back to the business at hand.

Owen Lynch scanned the room, waiting for the applause to die down. "Carmel Cox doesn't seem to be with us this evening," he said, sounding a little surprised. "But I see that her mother, Oonagh, is."

"Widowed four years now, poor Oonagh," the woman next to Mary Helen lamented.

Heads turned, searching for Mrs. Cox. A small woman raised her hand. Her daughter resembles her, Mary Helen thought, but living had softened and deepened Oonagh's good looks into genuine beauty.

"Ah, Oonagh, will you see to it that Carmel gets her prize," the chairman asked.

"Yes, indeed, I will, Owen," Oonagh said, taking the small package from him. "And in her name I'll say 'Thank you.'"

The room began to buzz again as the wine tasters started for home. As Eileen and Mary Helen passed the chairman, they couldn't help overhearing him say, "I'd be careful if I were you, Willie. Those tinkers can be dangerous if they have a mind to be, especially Jake. He's a trigger temper."

"If I let everyone who threatened me stop me, I wouldn't write a word," Willie replied with a touch of bluster.

"Just exactly what do you mean by that?" Zoë O'Dea asked, her mouth forming a tight, straight line.

"Not a thing, dear Zoë," Ward said with a supercilious grin. "Now who did you say won the baking contest? My readers will want to know all the details."

"What kind of a column does that Willie Ward write?" Mary Helen asked, once Eileen and she were out of earshot.

"As far as I can tell, it's a bit of a local news mixed with a little local gossip," Eileen said.

"An Irish Herb Caen?"

Eileen nodded. "At least a wannabe," she said. "From what I hear, his column is quite popular, even if he himself is not."

"Do you really think he gets many threats?" Mary Helen was finding it hard to believe that anyone would take the man that seriously.

"Doesn't he wish," Eileen said with a smile.

Sunday, August 31

May the neighbors respect you,
Troubles neglect you,
The angels protect you,
And heaven accept you.
— Irish blessing

The full deep tolling of the church bells awakened Sister Mary Helen. She realized with a start that her bedroom was bright. *What time is it?* she wondered, fumbling on the nightstand for her glasses and staring at her travel alarm. Eleven o'clock! She had slept for over twelve hours.

"Eileen," she called softly.

"I'm just putting on the coffee," she heard her friend say.

Struggling up, Mary Helen slipped into her bathrobe and mules and padded into the small kitchen. To her surprise, Eileen was fully dressed.

"What time is Mass?" Mary Helen asked with a yawn.

"Twelve noon," Eileen said, popping sliced soda bread into the toaster. "That bell is a reminder. If you don't hear that, the next thing you'll hear is Gabriel's horn."

Mary Helen laughed. "Just one Mass?" she asked, surprised. The parish Church of the Annunciation was an enormous edifice. Its tower dominated the entire village.

Eileen nodded. "One on Saturday night and one on Sunday. The village has only one priest," she said, "and he has to minister to several other villages, as well."

Even Ireland is having a priest shortage, Mary Helen thought, staring sleepily into the toaster.

Although the country was having a priest shortage, there was no shortage of Catholics. The noon Mass was packed: the nuns were lucky to find a seat. And they had to walk clear to the front of the church to do that.

Mary Helen recognized a number of people she had seen yesterday at the village market. She was not surprised that during his homily, Father Keane urged all the faithful to participate wholeheartedly in the Oyster festivities but to "stay on the dry" if they were driving. Nor was she surprised to find that the parish bulletin listed the events of the week.

The Oyster House Hotel advertised a hearty Irish breakfast for festivalgoers at half its usual price. Since the hotel was within walking distance, the two nuns decided to take advantage of it.

"Hearty" scarcely described the meal. Scrambled eggs, rashers, sausages, grilled tomatoes, Irish soda bread, butter, jam, and a mound of hot toast followed orange juice and coffee.

"I'll never eat again," Mary Helen said, scooping up the last of her eggs.

"Until our next meal," Eileen commented wisely. "What shall we do today?" she asked, reading aloud Sunday's festival schedule. It included a yacht race ending at Moran's Tavern on the Weir, an illustrated lecture on the history of the village at the school hall, and to-night an Oyster Gala at the Monks' Table.

"A yacht race sounds like fun," Mary Helen said. "But what is a weir and how do we get there?"

"It's a small dam," Eileen answered, then dug in her pocket and produced the card Paul Glynn had given them. "And here's how," she said with a delighted grin.

Within minutes after they rang, Paul arrived in his hackney, his straight, dark hair still wet from the shower.

"I hope we didn't interfere with your plans," Sister Eileen said as they climbed into the car.

"No, indeed," Paul assured her with a crooked smile. "The wife and son are going to the lecture at the school. I was happy to have an excuse to get out of it."

Mary Helen couldn't help wondering as he banged the car door shut just how happy his wife must be.

Whistling, Paul zipped along the country road. Tall full bushes of red fuchsias ran along each side, making the road seem narrower yet. Mary Helen was relieved when he finally pulled up behind a line of cars waiting for entrance to Moran's car park.

"Looks like a good crowd," he said, drumming his fingers on the steering wheel. "And up there is your tavern." He pointed ahead to a lemon-colored building with a thatched roof.

It looks like something right out of an oil painting, Mary Helen thought. In the water in front she counted thirty-six swans and a blue heron, all seeming perfectly indifferent to the gathering crowd.

"Why don't you two get a table inside?" Paul suggested when a young lad finally directed them into the crowded car park. "It can get windy and fiercely cold out here." He shivered as if to make his point.

"What about you?" Mary Helen asked.

"Not to worry," Paul assured her. "I'll just stay in front and join a few of the lads for a pint."

Paul pulled back the heavy entrance door and waited for them to step inside. As Mary Helen's eyes adjusted to the sudden darkness, she saw that an ornate mahogany bar ran along one entire wall of the tavern. A dozen or so bar stools were already occupied. Men of all ages clustered around them in small noisy groups. *These must be the lads Paul was talking about,* Mary Helen thought, watching the publican, a large smiling man in a white dress shirt, pull one pint of Guinness after another from the tap.

At the far end, sitting apart from the rest, she noticed a small, wizened figure with a stained tweed cap drawn down over his eyes. Mary Helen blinked. If she didn't know better she'd have sworn it was Barry Fitzgerald with a cigarette clamped between his lips.

"What can I get you ladies?" the publican asked, cheerfully. He slapped down two napkins on the bar quite close to the old man who looked up guardedly.

"Ladies." The old man studied them for a long minute as though he doubted it. "Ye must be Yanks," he said finally, closing one eye against the cigarette smoke.

"Yes, we are," Eileen answered sweetly.

"Where are your husbands?" His voice was unexpectedly strong.

"We haven't husbands."

"Ah, widows, then?"

"No, not widows," Eileen answered.

Mary Helen wondered uneasily where this was going. By now even the publican was getting curious.

The old man looked at them with new interest. "Divorced, then?" he asked brightly.

"No," Eileen said, tightening her lips.

The old man, a long gray ash hanging precariously from the end of his cigarette, stared in honest bewilderment. "What the hell are ye, then?"

Paul came up behind them. "They are nuns, Mick," he announced, a twinkle in his eye.

Mick's face fell. "I've forty cousins nuns," he muttered, turning his back to them, "and if you ask me, they're a bitchy bunch."

Amid howls of laughter from the lads on the stools, Paul led the two Sisters into the back of the tavern.

"Don't mind old Mick Moran," Paul soothed. "He's quite a character."

"Quite," Eileen said primly.

In the back of Moran's was a warren of small rooms that smelled of tobacco, beer, and a peat fire. Paul escorted the two nuns to a table by the open fireplace.

"Go on now, Paul," Eileen said. "Join the lads. We'll be fine."

"You led the old man right into that, on purpose," Mary Helen said once Eileen and she were alone.

"Life isn't worth the effort, if you can't have a bit of fun," Eileen said in her own defense. "Besides, we can dine out on that story for years."

The two old friends were still laughing when Mary Helen noticed a familiar Donegal tweed cap a few tables away. Willie Ward with his notebook open was deep in conversation with Owen Lynch, the chairman of the festival. *Maybe it's an interview,* Mary Helen thought, although she didn't see the reporter writing anything down.

Owen's face was pale, and behind his horn-rimmed

glasses his eyes were red-rimmed and bloodshot. He must be exhausted, Mary Helen thought, and she wondered what time last night's wine tasting actually broke up. With this big an event, there is so much planning, and so much that can go wrong. He didn't look too happy being buttonholed by Willie Ward.

But she didn't need to worry about Lynch. All at once he stood up, and over the noise floating in from the now packed bar, she heard him say, "I don't have time for this right now, Willie."

"Later then, Owen?"

"I might never have time for it." The chairman's face turned dangerously dark.

"I'd be surprised to hear that," Willie said. "I think it would be in your best interest."

Slamming his glass on the tabletop, Owen Lynch clenched his fists. For a moment it looked as if he might take a swing at the reporter. Ward must have thought so too, for without another word he got up and headed back to the bar.

Mary Helen tipped her head toward the table where Lynch now stood alone. "I wonder what all that was about."

Eileen's eyebrows shot up, and she shrugged.

"It sounded almost as though Mr. Ward were threatening him, didn't it?" Mary Helen said.

Before Eileen could answer, Patsy Lynch entered the room.

"Oh, there you are," she said, spotting her husband. She frowned. "What on earth is wrong? You look like a thunder cloud."

"It's that bastard, Willie Ward." Lynch spat out the name. "He wants a comment for his damn rag."

"A comment on what?" Patsy's long face grew even longer with concern.

"Seems he's heard a rumor that the queen competition wasn't on the up-and-up."

Patsy's high-pitched laughter mingled with the bar noises. "Now we know for certain that the man's an *ee-jit*," she said. "Not to worry, love. He has nothing to go on, nor will he find anything. How about a jar before the boats come in?"

"Sisters." The publican's voice startled Mary Helen. She hadn't heard him come into the room. "The winner should be rounding the bend soon," he said. "There's just time enough for a pint before he does. Can I get you one? Or a coffee? Or maybe a cup of tea?"

The two nuns opted for the tea.

"On the house," he said apologetically. "Pay no mind to old Mick. He's a shirttail cousin. Came with the pub."

Mary Helen was glad to see the raisin scone that accompanied the tea. Despite the enormous breakfast they had eaten, she was beginning to get a little hungry. *Why not?* she thought, checking her wristwatch. It was nearly four o'clock.

"They're coming," someone shouted.

Without another word, Moran's emptied. The nuns, infected by the crowd's enthusiasm, finished up their tea and hurried outside, too.

The cheering crowd filled the ridge overlooking the water. "Over here, Sisters," Paul called, leading them to a spot where they had a view.

Thin dark clouds had formed and were fast-forwarding across the late afternoon sky, changing the water to steely gray on their way. One white mast was seen, and the crowd roared and waved and pushed forward. Ward's Donegal tweed cap waved above the rest. The noise was deafening.

"That Willie Ward really gets around," Mary Helen said, although she was sure no one could hear her.

"Insufferable man!" someone answered.

Paul Glynn laughed. "Sister," he shouted, "have you met Oonagh Cox?"

They were suddenly pushed together. Although they had not met formally, Mary Helen recognized her as the woman who had claimed her daughter's prize for the best Irish soda bread at last night's wine and cheese tasting.

"How do?" Mary Helen said.

Enormous drops of rain began to fall. Squealing, Eileen dashed into Moran's with Mary Helen close on her heels. Oonagh Cox followed them. The rest of the spectators, seemingly oblivious to the storm, stood on the ridge and shouted.

Only old Mick Moran remained at his bar stool. "Ah, the widow Cox and the nuns," he mumbled, releasing a narrow stream of smoke from his mouth.

"Mind your manners, Mick," Oonagh cautioned.

He looked puzzled. "How's that, Oonagh?"

"Shut your gob!" she said, which to Mary Helen seemed quite clear.

The three women huddled near the roaring fireplace. "Fools don't know enough to come in out of the rain," Oonagh said, shaking her short gray hair. Flicks of water shot around and hissed when they hit the flames. "And that old fool out there doesn't know when enough is enough."

The wind caught the front door when it opened and flung it back. Willie Ward stood there bareheaded, a condescending smile on his face. "Aha," he said, "if it isn't Mrs. Cox."

Sister Mary Helen saw the woman stiffen. "Mr. Ward," she acknowledged with a cursory nod. "What mischief will you be up to today?"

Willie's face darkened but his smile never faded.

"Just doing my job," he said lightly. "As always, just doing my job."

"And what is that, Mr. Ward?" Oonagh's blue eyes flashed. "Making other people's lives miserable?"

Willie put his hand to his heart. "That hurts, Oonagh, dear, that you think such a thing."

Oonagh held her tongue, but her eyes shot fire. If the woman had her way, Mary Helen thought, there would be a mere cinder where Willie Ward now stood.

The tavern door opened again, and Mary Helen was relieved to see their driver come in. "Morrissey won," he shouted.

"Were you rooting for him?" Mary Helen asked.

"Any thinking man was," Paul said with a smile. "Morrissey wins every year."

Sensing the tension he'd stumbled into, Paul hesitated. "Are you ready to go home, Sisters?" he asked, draining his pint. "You don't want to miss the I Believe Team from Guinness. They should be arriving in Ballyclarin soon."

Mary Helen had no idea what the I Believe Team was, but at the moment she was ready to leave Moran's Tavern.

As they made their way out, the jubilant crowd was, once again, spilling into the bar. Mick Moran sat on his stool, eyes half closed, drawing on his cigarette.

"Good day, Mr. Moran," Eileen said pleasantly as she passed him.

"Bitchy bunch," he muttered, tipping his cap.

Rain beat down on the hackney while the windshield wipers worked furiously to clear the view.

Paul followed a line of cars on the way back to Ballyclarin. "Did you enjoy yourselves?" he asked, happily. Obviously, he had.

Shouting over the noise of the storm, Mary Helen said, "It was interesting."

Paul turned toward her. It was all she could do not to tell him to keep his eyes on the narrow rain-drenched road.

The line of cars stopped suddenly. Brakes screeched, but Paul seemed not to notice. "How so?" he asked.

"How so, what?" Mary Helen's fingernails were biting into the palms of her hands. She unclenched her fists.

"How so was it interesting? I was afraid you'd hardly seen the race at all. You spent most of your day in the tavern."

"That is what I found most interesting. The people in Moran's."

"My friend is a student of human nature," Eileen piped up from the backseat. "And there was plenty of that to study in there today, starting with Mick Moran."

"Right ye are." Paul nodded, warming to the topic. "And you'd need to be blind," he said, "not to notice the bad blood between Oonagh Cox and Willie Ward."

"I was wondering about that," Mary Helen said. "Oonagh didn't try to hide her animosity toward him at all."

"Hide it?" Paul's laughter filled the cab. "She flaunts it every chance she gets. Despises the man."

"Does anyone know why?" Mary Helen asked, hoping her question didn't sound too intrusive.

"Everyone knows why," Paul said. "It is no secret that when her husband was dying of cancer she managed to get a little cannabis to relieve his pain. Sure, if old Willie didn't hint at it in his column. No names, mind you, but everyone in the village knew he was talking about the Coxes. If the garda from Galway City had got wind, Oonagh would have been in serious trouble. As it was, her husband insisted she get rid of it. Poor man would rather suffer the torments of the damned than put his wife in that position."

"Why would Willie do such a thing?" Mary Helen asked, genuinely puzzled.

"He said he was just doing his job. But we all know that at one time he had a soft spot for Oonagh Cox. Bright woman that she is, she would have nothing to do with him."

As they neared Ballyclarin the rain began to let up. Mary Helen closed her eyes. They burned as she listened to the windshield wipers beat their steady, soothing rhythm. *Swish, swish. Swish, swish.* Willie Ward. Willie Ward.

The list of those who disliked him seemed to be growing with each passing day. Oonagh Cox, Jake the tinker, Owen Lynch, Zoë O'Dea. And from the little she had seen, Mary Helen didn't care much for the man either.

Swish, swish. Back and forth. Mary Helen wondered crazily how it must feel to be a man so easy for others to dislike.

The rain had completely let up when Paul dropped the two nuns in Ballyclarin. "Will you be needing me for anything else?" he asked, sneaking a peek at his wristwatch.

"No, thank you." Sister Eileen closed the hackney door behind her. "You get on home to your wife. She must be waiting for you to take her to tonight's doings."

"Enjoy yourselves," Mary Helen said, watching a relieved-looking Paul speed away. For her part, she wanted nothing more than to put her feet up. This napping could get to be a habit.

The main street of the village, still slick from the rain, was crowded with people—some in formal dress, some dressed a little more casually, but all obviously in a party frame of mind. Couples greeted one another loudly and friends waved and called to friends. Pub patrons spilled out into the street and cars slowed to a crawl, ready to drop off revelers.

Magically, the mood was infectious. Tired as she thought she was, Mary Helen felt her spirits lift.

"What fun!" said Eileen, whose spirits had never drooped.

After a brief stop at the mews to freshen up and grab their raincoats, just in case, the two nuns joined the growing crowd. To Mary Helen's surprise, an enormous tent had risen like a gigantic mushroom on the grassed area next to the Monks' Table.

"Hello, Sisters." Startled, Mary Helen turned quickly to discover the pastor, Father Keane, behind them. "Are you two lost?" he asked, putting a large hand on each shoulder.

"Somewhat," Eileen answered. "We were just wondering about tonight's doings."

"Tonight, you won't want to miss," he said. "It's the Oyster Gala. That is what this tent is for." He pointed to the huge white canvas structure on the lawn. "It rose like a miracle this afternoon," Father Keane said, rolling his eyes heavenward as though to remind them of where miracles come from. "I'm sure that by now, the band has arrived and that for the last couple of hours people have been rushing in and out with dishes and glasses and seafood and, of course, great barrels of Guinness. The I Believe Team should be here any minute. They'd make a believer out of me, for sure."

As if on cue, the slow, somber beat of drums filled the street. The crowd quieted somewhat, and then it parted as four men dressed in the rough brown woolen robes of friars moved unhurriedly toward the tent.

Their drums, which Mary Helen noted were empty metal Guinness barrels, continued the hollow baleful thuds as the friars chanted in loud ominous voices, "Repent! Repent and believe."

Right behind them a white shrouded figure with a black skeleton mask, obviously portraying Death, walked on stilts. He peered down at the partygoers. Like the Grim Reaper, which he undoubtedly was supposed to be, he carried a long scythe. With a shrill wicked laugh, he twirled his scythe over the heads of the crowd, barely missing some of the taller fellows. The *swish* of the sharp blade made the hair on Mary Helen's arms stand up.

"Believe! Repent and believe!" the friars chanted soulfully and beat their drums as they led Death toward the entrance to the tent.

"Isn't that a little dangerous?" Mary Helen whispered, watching Death make his way down the street.

"Just good fun," Father Keane answered, squeezing her shoulder. "We've never lost a head yet."

"Which is a miracle in itself, if you ask me," Mary Helen mumbled, watching the priest disappear into the crowd. "What does it mean anyway?"

Eileen shrugged. "It's a promotion for Guinness," she said, and then she winked. "Although, if you ask me, from the looks of things Guinness doesn't need too much promoting."

"Sisters, are you ready for the Oyster Gala?" Mary Helen was surprised to see Owen Lynch, who must have left Moran's early or else knew a shortcut back to the village. Lynch wore the stiff smile and spoke with the forced cheerfulness of an event chairman who can hardly wait until the whole thing is over.

"You've tickets, I assume?" He fumbled with several still in his hand.

"Yes, indeed," Eileen answered. "My nephews saw to

that." She dug into her pocketbook and with a look of triumph produced two tickets.

Death and the brown-robed friars huddled around the tent entrance, urging all who entered to "Repent," boom-boom. "Repent," boom-boom, "and believe."

Quickly Eileen handed Mary Helen her ticket. She wondered at the price. Fifteen euros seemed inexpensive for food and a band.

Once inside, Mary Helen realized that what the gala lost in ticket price, it more than made up for in quantity of attendees. There were easily three hundred people already in the tent and more waiting to get in. The lines for food and drink were long but seemed to move quickly. The crowd was a happy one, and the band was already in full swing. Couples of all ages circled the dance floor in perfect rhythm. . . . *Like figurines on the top of a music box,* Mary Helen thought, watching several of the older couples. As a matter of fact, it seemed to her that the older the couple, the better dancers they were.

The band played one number after another, varying a waltz with a fox trot and throwing in a little jitterbug. Mary Helen thought she recognized a jazzed-up version of "The Fields of Athenry." *Can that be?* she wondered. Wasn't there some unwritten law against defaming traditional tunes? If there wasn't one, there ought to be.

But by now, regardless of what the band was playing, everyone in the tent seemed to be dancing—men and women, women with women, children with one another and with adults, even one of the brown-robed friars.

Sisters Eileen and Mary Helen found two vacant chairs along the wall of the tent and hung a folded raincoat on the back of each. A universal "reserved" sign, Mary Helen thought as they went to join the food line. Returning to their chairs with full plates, they were content to sit, eat, and people-watch. Mary Helen realized with a sense of accomplishment that she was beginning to recognize some of the villagers.

It was nearly eleven o'clock when the band took a well-deserved break.

"Did you get something to eat?"

Mary Helen turned to find Patsy Lynch, the chairman's wife, grinning down at them. Patsy had dolled up for the evening, Mary Helen noticed, even put on some makeup and a drop of a flowery perfume.

"It seems as if we've done nothing else except eat," Eileen said, "but thank you."

"Well, don't hesitate. There's plenty," Patsy said, then looked away, frowning. Obviously, someone or something else had caught her attention. "If you'll excuse me," she said. Mary Helen watched Patsy's gray head disappear as the woman elbowed her way toward the front door.

The nun stretched to see what was going on, but the crowd was too dense. Besides, Eileen and she had deliberately sat far enough away from the entrance so that they couldn't hear the drums. Both of them had had enough of the I Believe Team to last a lifetime.

"We meet again."

Mary Helen looked up. It was Oonagh Cox. She wore a lovely sky-blue silk dress that highlighted her eyes and a large diamond lavaliere with matching earrings.

At first glance, it would have been difficult to recognize the wet, angry woman of this afternoon. It was as if she had been transformed.

Oonagh smiled apologetically. "I'm glad I ran into you," she said. "I hope my little fit at Moran's didn't drive you away." Her cheeks reddened. "It is just that I see Willie Ward and I rear up. I should know better than to let him bother me."

"Not at all," Eileen said, patting an empty chair next to her. "Do you want to join us?"

Oonagh appeared as if she might, but the band started up again and a tall, handsome, young man tapped her on the shoulder. "May I have this dance, Mam?" he said.

"My son, Dermot," Oonagh introduced him, then linked her arm through his. "If you'll excuse us."

"Sweet," Eileen said, watching the pair waltz away in a swirl of sky blue.

A sudden roar from the bar area caught Mary Helen's attention. She thought it had come from a tall sinewy man with straight black hair slicked back to reach his collar. He was nose to nose with Owen Lynch, and neither man appeared to be giving an inch.

"Enough, me arse!" she heard the tall man shout. She was about to ask Eileen if she knew who he was, when Paul Glynn and his redheaded wife danced over to them.

"How're ye keeping?" Paul asked cheerfully.

"Grand!" Eileen answered for the two of them.

Paul looked around. "It's a beautiful party now, isn't it?" he said.

Mary Helen nodded, waiting for her opportunity to ask about the man with the slicked-back hair, but when she looked up, he was gone, and Owen Lynch was making his way to the bandstand.

Tapping the microphone, Owen called for attention. Amazingly, the crowd quieted down as the chairman once again introduced the Oyster Queen, Tara O'Dea, in her green taffeta dress and rhinestone tiara.

Tara smiled shyly as Owen handed her a bouquet of deep red roses. The applause rose to a roar, and the friars picked up their barrels for one final metallic drum roll. Zoë O'Dea stood below the stage, unself-consciously wiping tears from her cheeks.

Sister Mary Helen looked around the crowded tent. Where was Willie Ward? she wondered. Shouldn't he be here to interview people for his column? It looked as if everyone in the village was present except Willie and the shrouded figure of Mr. Death. Maybe that was where Willie had gone, to interview Mr. Death.

Sister Mary Helen was glad to see her friend yawn, at last. "Tired?" she asked, trying not to sound too hopeful. Party or no party, she could barely keep her own eyes open, although she was making a brave try at it, not wanting to spoil Eileen's fun.

"Exhausted," Eileen admitted. "All that fresh air." She studied Mary Helen's face. "Oh, my!" she said. "You're the color of death warmed over. I forgot about jet lag. We ought to both be in bed. Tomorrow is another day."

"What's the event tomorrow?" Mary Helen asked, hoping it started late.

Eileen rummaged in her pocketbook and dug out a bright yellow brochure. "An art and photo exhibit at the school hall," she read, "from noon to five. And then, in the evening, a game of whist at Rafferty's Rest in Kilcalgan. That's the next village," Eileen explained. "With generous prizes, it says here."

Quickly, the two nuns picked up their raincoats and slipped through a side exit of the tent. Mary Helen hoped no one spotted them. She doubted if she had enough energy left to smile and say, "Good night."

Mary Helen hadn't realized how warm the tent was until a blast of cold air hit them as they stepped outdoors. It felt as if it had come right off the Atlantic. Beside her, Eileen shivered. Although the rain had stopped, the grass under their feet was still damp and smelled of wet earth.

Head back, Mary Helen stared up at the night sky, a welter of bright stars. Away from the city lights, the stars always appeared closer. But here in Ireland, they seemed even clearer and nearer still. Almost as if she could reach above her head and touch them. She drew in a deep breath. Ireland! She still could not get used to the idea that she was actually here.

"Isn't it beautiful, Eileen?" she whispered, still fixed on the heavens.

But Eileen was digging in her pocketbook again.

"What in the world are you looking for?" Mary Helen asked.

"This." Eileen pulled out a small flashlight. "Without our torch, God knows where we'll end up. At night, it gets as dark as pitch around here." Eileen offered her arm. "Hang on to me," she said.

They had moved only a few yards away from the lighted tent when Eileen proved to be right. Carefully, they followed the torch's beam, trying to avoid the bumps and dips in the lawn. Mary Helen's damp feet were beginning to feel frozen.

"Careful of the sprinklers," Eileen cautioned, her flashlight picking out the round disc.

"Maybe we should have used the front door," Mary Helen whispered, beginning to feel a little panicky. The road had seemed much closer in the daylight. And it was so still. Even the band music was beginning to sound far, far away.

She stumbled forward, still holding tight to Eileen's arm. Wasn't there a large drainage ditch bordering the other side of the Monks' Table? Who would find them if they stumbled into it? She was just about to ask if Eileen was sure they were going in the right direction when she heard a low muffled growl. Goose bumps ran up both her arms. That's all we need, she thought, wild animals.

"What is that?" she whispered.

"What is what?" Eileen stopped abruptly.

"That sound. Listen. Can't you hear it?"

Eileen shook her head, but she arched the beam of her flashlight to the right and then to the left, just in case. All they saw was wet grass. "Maybe it's a bird," Eileen said. "We may have disturbed a sleeping bird."

"Maybe," Mary Helen conceded, although she hadn't noticed any trees. Don't birds usually sleep in trees? she wondered, and she hung tighter to Eileen's arm.

They moved forward several yards. The stifled noise sounded again. Louder, this time. Far too loud to be a bird.

Much to Mary Helen's relief, Eileen heard it, too. She swung around. "It seems to be coming from over there," she whispered.

Her light fell on a clump of red fuchsias that seemed quite out of place on the lawn. Cautiously, they crept toward the noise.

"What kind of animals roam around here at night?" Mary Helen asked, wondering if approaching the noise was such a wise idea. Maybe they should go back to the tent and get Mr. Lynch.

"Not bears or tigers, if that's what you're worrying about," Eileen said, as her flashlight beam fell on two stockinged feet sticking out from behind the fuchsia bush. "Whatever it is, it looks pretty human."

The muffled noise grew louder.

"And it sounds human, too."

Slowly she let the light travel up the hairy legs until the two nuns were staring down into the frightened blue eyes of a young man who seemed to be wearing only his undershorts. He was bound hand and foot with what looked like an old piece of clothesline, and a large white handkerchief had been shoved into his mouth.

His eyes filled with quick tears of relief when he saw the two nuns. Obviously he recognized them, although

Mary Helen had no idea who he was. Eileen held the flashlight steady while Mary Helen untied the hankie and deftly removed it from his mouth.

"Thanks be to God," he said hoarsely, then, shivering, squirmed around so that she could untie his hands. "I thought I'd bloody well freeze to death before anyone found me."

"What happened?" Eileen asked while Mary Helen and the young man worked on the ropes binding his feet.

"Damned if I know," he said, his teeth now chattering uncontrollably. "I just stepped outside of the tent to have a fag and someone hit . . . hit me from behind." He rubbed the back of his head. "I must have gone . . . gone out for a few minutes. When I woke my head was throb . . . throbbing and I had that gag in my mouth. I tried to move but I was bound like a pig . . . pig for market and my clothes were g-gone." He squirmed self-consciously and looked grateful when Mary Helen threw her raincoat around his shoulder.

For her part, she was happy that she had decided to wear a sweater underneath it. They all needed to get inside out of this cold.

"You didn't see anybody then?" Eileen asked.

"Not a soul." He rubbed his wrists, which were red and swollen. "But I swear, if I ever find out who did this, the bastard will wish he'd died as an infant."

He stood and pulled himself up to his full height. He might have looked ferocious, if he hadn't been dressed in white cotton work socks, jockey shorts, and a woman's raincoat that only half covered his body.

"Why do you suppose someone took your clothes?" Eileen asked, handing him her raincoat as well. She moved the flashlight away to give him a bit of privacy.

"All I can figure out is that someone wanted the Death outfit pretty bad."

Mary Helen's heart raced. "You are Mr. Death?" she asked.

"Actually, I'm Tommy Burns with a raging headache," he said weakly. "I only wish I was dead."

Eileen shone the flashlight in his face. The color was gone, and he looked as though any minute he might collapse back onto the wet grass.

Mary Helen grabbed his arm, not that she'd be much help if he actually did fall. "You sit back down, Tommy," Eileen said as she helped steady him. "We'll go back to the tent as quickly as we can and find Owen Lynch and a blanket," she said softly. "Sit yourself down, now."

With a moan, Tommy Burns lowered himself to the ground and drew the raincoats around him. "What kind of an arse would take me costume?" he called out after them.

Let's hope it's not one who intends to put it to good use, Mary Helen thought, following Eileen's flashlight beam back across the damp lawn toward the tent.

"Who's there?" a deep voice boomed out of the darkness.

Both nuns froze. Mary Helen's heart was thudding. Quickly Eileen switched off the flashlight and grabbed her arm. Except for the dim lights of the tent, still several hundred yards ahead of them, they were in total darkness.

Mary Helen was sure that she'd heard that voice before, but who was it? Her mind raced, but for the moment fear had short-circuited all its connections. For the life of her, she couldn't place it.

She felt Eileen's grip on her relax. She must be having better luck. Or, at least, Mary Helen hoped so.

"Is that you, Father Keane?" Eileen asked with obvious relief. Her flashlight beam came back on and hit the parish priest full in the face. For some reason, he loomed even taller than Mary Helen remembered, and the dampness of the night air had made his gray hair curlier.

Blinking, Father Keane's hand shot up to protect his eyes from the glare. "Turn that blasted torch away," he said, still trying to determine who they were. "Who is it?" He squinted against the light. "Are ye the nuns from America?" he asked in disbelief.

"We are." Eileen beamed the flashlight on the ground between them.

"Why in God's name are you two out here in this field? Don't you know there are all kinds of potholes? You could easily stumble in the dark and hurt yourselves."

"We are fine," Eileen said quickly, then skipping over the whys of their being outside, she told the priest what they actually had stumbled upon.

"We have come to find Owen Lynch," she said, her words coming out in small icy puffs.

By now both the nuns and the priest were shivering with the cold. "You must be nearly frozen," he said. "I know I am. Let me go and find Owen myself and tell him what you've told me. You needn't trouble your heads." He thought for a moment. "Why don't you two go around the outside of the tent to the Monks' Table? Have a cup of hot tea. I'll join you there as soon as I can."

Without another word, Father Keane started back toward the tent. Silently the nuns stared after him.

"A cup of hot tea sounds good," Eileen said, making a path with her flashlight.

The combination of fear, cold, and weariness made Mary Helen feel almost drugged as she followed her friend toward the Monks' Table. It didn't occur to her until they had almost reached the pub that they hadn't asked Father Keane what in God's name—if it was in

God's name—he was doing out in the cold, dark, dangerous field himself.

Sister Mary Helen drew back the heavy wooden door of the Monks' Table and stepped aside to let Eileen go in first. The sudden blast of warm air fogged up her bifocals, momentarily blinding her.

"Welcome," she heard the publican call.

Finding a clean tissue in her sweater pocket, she wiped her glasses. Once she did, she saw that only three men were at the long bar. One sat at each end and one squarely in the middle. *Making sure the publican gets his exercise,* Mary Helen thought—*that is, if they ever actually drink from their glasses.* From where she stood, all three seemed to be doing more staring at the rich dark liquid than actual sipping.

"Mind your step," the publican reminded them as they made their way toward the dining area in the back of the pub.

"Let's get a table close to a fireplace," Mary Helen suggested. Her feet and hands felt like ice sculptures. She wondered, as the warmth began to make them tingle and burn, just how long it would take for them to feel normal again.

"Any place at all," a middle-aged waitress said. "What with the gala tonight, the place is nearly empty."

Eileen chose an alcove with a table that was next to an open fireplace. "How's this?" she asked.

"Great." Mary Helen slid into the high-backed bench. The two of them put their feet as close to the fire screen as seemed safe.

"Hot tea?" the waitress asked in a weary voice.

"And two scones, please," Eileen added.

"Sorry, dearie. No scones at this time of night." The

waitress tapped her pad with the tip of her pencil. "But the rhubarb pie is grand tonight."

"Rhubarb pie it is, then," Eileen said, smiling over at Mary Helen. "You have never tasted anything like this rhubarb pie."

"Will you be having that with the whipped cream?" the waitress asked.

"Please," Eileen said.

Mary Helen groaned. "Just thinking of the calories."

"We need it for energy," Eileen rationalized, as if they needed a reason.

"The place really is deserted," Mary Helen said when the waitress had gone for their order. The high-backed benches made it impossible to tell if any other diners were in the alcove. If there were, they were awfully quiet. In fact, the entire pub was eerily quiet.

"Everyone must still be in the tent." Eileen rubbed her hands together in an effort to warm them. "I wonder how long it will take Father Keane to find Owen Lynch in that crowd?" she whispered, in case there was anyone to overhear. "And after he does, they'll have to take care of Tommy Burns, poor lad. I hope he's not frozen to death."

"Surely they'll call the police, too," Mary Helen said.

"Who'll have to come from Oranmore," Eileen speculated. "At this time of night, it shouldn't take more than fifteen or twenty minutes."

"Maybe you are right about our needing energy," Mary Helen said as the waitress set down two large triangles of rhubarb pie topped with a mound of whipped cream. "It looks as if it is going to be a very long night."

She was amazed at how quickly the pie disappeared. And Eileen was right, Mary Helen thought, as she resisted the temptation to order another piece: she had never tasted rhubarb pie quite so delicious.

The sweet aroma of hot tea filled the alcove. Cradling the cup in her hands, Mary Helen felt its warmth slip down her throat and settle in her bones. A medley of traditional Irish tunes played softly in the background. She was afraid to close her eyes. Surely she would fall asleep. Or maybe she was asleep. Maybe this was all a dream.

"Just what the doctor ordered!" Eileen sighed and settled back against the high bench.

Voices floated in from the bar. "Did you hear the one about the fellow who had a little too much to drink?" someone asked the publican, who said he hadn't.

"Driving home from the pub he's weaving and the garda stops him.

" 'It looks as if you've had quite a few,' the garda says.

" 'I did, all right,' says the fella.

" 'Did you know that a few miles back your wife fell out of the car?'

" 'Oh, thanks be to God,' says the fella, 'for a minute there I thought I'd gone deaf.' "

"That's a good one," the publican said, laughing.

"Unless you're *herself*," the waitress said to the nuns as she cleared off the pie plates. She stifled a yawn. "That's old Terry Eagan," she said. "He thinks he's quite the card. I say ignore him. Is there anything else I can get for you?"

"No, thank you," Eileen said. "We are waiting for—"

"No matter," the waitress interrupted, untying her apron strings. "Wait as long as you like. You can settle up with the publican when you're ready. I have got to get off my feet."

With the waitress gone, the Monks' Table grew even more deserted. Mary Helen stared dreamily into the crackling fire. Without warning, a log crashed to the hearth. Sparks exploded, hitting the screen.

Eileen jumped and her hand flew to her chest. "If I had a heart, I'd be dead," she said, standing up to make sure no embers had fallen on the rug.

"Over there." Mary Helen pointed to a small glowing spot on the other side of the alcove. "While you're doing that, I think I'll make a little visit." She moved toward a hallway with a large sign that read, "Toilets." *No confusion there,* she thought, stopping at the narrow door marked "Ladies."

Pushing open the door, she was greeted by a faint flowery smell that seemed to be fighting with a sharp acrid odor. Although the small room appeared unoccupied, the stall door was shut. Quickly Mary Helen stepped outside. Everyone appreciates a little privacy.

For several minutes she studied the framed photographs that hung on the wall across from the ladies'. They were candid shots of some of the pub's more illustrious visitors with a man she presumed must be the owner. She was fascinated to find such celebrities as Noël Coward, Princess Grace, Bing Crosby, John Steinbeck, and Joan Baez. There was even a photograph of Princess Margaret and Lord Snowdon!

Eileen will be wondering what happened to me, Mary Helen thought, staring into the blue eyes of a smiling Paul Newman. She listened for the sound of water running. There was no sound at all. Perhaps no one was in there after all. Perhaps the stall door is always shut. *I really didn't look,* she thought, again pushing open the door to the "Ladies."

Once inside, Mary Helen bent over to check the stall for feet. Sure enough! There were two feet firmly planted on the floor. Big feet, actually. Muddy feet and long pants. But still no sound.

"You-hoo," she called softly. "Are you all right in there?"

No one answered. Odd, she thought, as a shiver of fear shot down her spine.

"You-hoo," she called again, her hand on the top of the stall door. At her touch, it swung open. Mary Helen froze. A large, beefy man sat on the closed toilet seat. He might have been expecting visitors except that he was slumped sideways, his head resting against the tank. The old-fashioned pull chain dangled past his sightless eyes. The handle of a small kitchen knife protruded from his chest. A bright red halo of blood soaked the front of his shirt, right where his heart ought to be.

"Are you all right?" Eileen pushed open the door. "I was beginning to worry," she said, and then she stopped. "What is it?"

Mary Helen pointed. "It's . . . it's Willie Ward," she whispered, scarcely able to catch her breath. "He's dead." Afraid her knees might buckle, she leaned against the stall wall.

Eileen was saying something, but all Mary Helen could hear was the sound of her own blood pounding in her ears.

The poor man, she thought crazily, *should not have had to die sitting on a toilet seat with that silly old Donegal tweed cap perched on his head, even if no one seemed to like him very much.* Everyone deserved more dignity than that!

Sister Mary Helen wasn't sure what happened next. Suddenly, Father Keane was there and the publican whose name was Hugh Ryan and Tommy Burns, Mr. Death, with clothes on. Although from the fit it was easy to see they weren't his. Not that it mattered, Mary Helen thought; this surely was not a fashion show. And Owen Lynch, the chairman of the Oyster Festival, was there with them.

The priest's first order of business was to give the poor man the Last Rites. "I'll just pop over to the rectory for the oils," he said and was back in no time.

The group lined the hallway in solemn silence while Father Keane pronounced the sacred words over Willie Ward's dead body. "By this holy anointing," he intoned, "and His loving mercy, may the Lord forgive you whatever wrong you have done. . . ."

When he finished, Father Keane insisted that they all sit down at the bar and have a hot whiskey to steady their nerves while they waited for the gardai to arrive. Tommy Burns didn't need to be asked twice. Hugh Ryan, who had locked the front door of the Monks' Table, seemed pleased to have something to do. And poor Owen Lynch looked as though he could use a double.

"Ah, Hugh, just a bit of it," Father Keane said, watching the publican fill his glass.

"Nothing like this has ever happened before in the entire history of the Oyster Festival," Owen whined.

"I hope the gardai get here before the tent empties," Hugh Ryan said. His dark eyes shifted from the hallway to the front door of the pub. "Sure, some of the lads will want to stop in for a quick one before they go home. What am I going to tell them?"

His question hung in the air unanswered. Owen Lynch nervously checked his wristwatch. "The gardai should be here any minute," he said, his lips quivering slightly. "Only they think we called about someone assaulting Tommy. They were on their way before . . ." He hesitated, giving the two nuns what could only be called an accusatory look. "Before," he repeated, "this happened."

Mary Helen felt her spine stiffen. *This,* as Mr. Lynch put it, was not their fault. For heaven's sake, they had simply discovered the man. A few more sips of hot whiskey and she might be tempted to tell him so!

"Poor Willie," Father Keane lamented, twirling his glass. "The scoop of his life—mayhem and murder at the Oyster Festival—and he missed it."

"I'd hardly say he missed it, Father." Ryan polished the already clean bar. "He was the main attraction, save for Tommy here. I don't mean to make light of your bump," he said, refilling the young fellow's whiskey glass. "Need some ice for the head?"

"No, thank ye." Tommy raised both his hands. "I've had enough cold for one night," he said, shivering.

"A bit more, Father?" Hugh reached for the priest's glass.

"Might as well be drunk as the way we are," the priest said, pushing his glass forward. Mary Helen hadn't heard that old saw in years.

The publican had just topped off the priest's drink when the tires of a car crunched in the gravel outside the pub.

"Thanks be to God, they're here." Owen Lynch left his stool and bolted for the front door. Swearing softly, he fumbled with the lock until finally the heavy door swung open.

Two young men in blue stood in the doorway. If Mary Helen had to guess, she wouldn't put either of them over twenty-five. One still had pimples, for heaven's sake.

"We received a call from—" the one with the pimples began.

"From me, Liam," Owen Lynch interrupted. He seemed to know the young garda. "I called about an attack on Tommy Burns." He pointed to Tommy, who smiled self-consciously at the two gardai. "But in the meanwhile, something much worse has happened." At the very mention of it, all the color drained from Owen's face. "Follow me. I'll show you," he said. And the two gardai did as he asked.

Almost immediately, a retching sound came from the toilet area.

"It's, no doubt, their first death by misadventure," the publican said, then shrugged. "Mine, too, for that matter."

Neither Mary Helen nor Eileen said a word. In fact, as if by plan, they avoided one another's eyes. It would never do to mention how many "misadventures" they had stumbled upon in San Francisco.

Sister Mary Helen said a quick prayer that no one here would have any reason to contact Inspectors Kate Murphy or Dennis Gallagher, both San Francisco homicide detectives, whom the Sisters had worked with on numerous occasions. While the Sisters were delighted to assist where they could, the inspectors, in most cases, were far less delighted to receive their assistance. From where she stood, however, these young gardai looked as if they could use all the help they could get.

One of them emerged from the hallway. Freckles stood out on his ashen face. "I'll put up the tape," he said to no one in particular, then made quickly for the front door.

"You look as though you could use some air," Sister Eileen said kindly, pretending not to hear him gag.

The pimple-faced garda whom Lynch had called Liam reappeared briefly, then ducked into an alcove, his cell phone on his ear.

"He must be giving the Serious Crimes Unit in Galway City a call," Father Keane said softly.

Fat drops of rain had begun to fall again. They hit the roof of the Monks' Table with an uneven rhythm. The young garda cleared his throat. "I have just talked to the Central Station in Galway," he said a little breathlessly. "Two inspectors are on their way here now. So, if you'd all just stay seated until—"

Owen Lynch jumped off the barstool. "I am the chair-man of the event," he said, painfully clearing his throat. "I have got to get back to the tent. They are probably looking for me right now to say some closing remarks. My wife must be frantic wondering where I'm off to."

The pimple-faced garda looked sympathetic but un-moved.

"Owen is right," Father Keane said. "You'll have the entire crowd of them up in arms. Perhaps you could let Owen go and try to pretend as if nothing happened. . . ."

"Won't they guess when they see the blue and white tape?" Tommy Burns asked. It was the first sensible thing he'd said since the nuns discovered Willie Ward's dead body.

All eyes shifted to the young garda. Without warning, his cheeks flushed a brilliant red. "I'm in charge here," he said in a voice that startled everyone. "Please, sit down!" he commanded. "We will wait for the inspectors."

Without another word, they all sat.

Fortunately, they did not have to wait long. The screech of brakes and the slamming of doors announced the ar-rival of the inspectors.

"In here, sir," they heard the young garda say as he pushed open the pub door. Standing back, he let a short, squat man enter.

Mary Helen didn't know what she expected at this hour, but all she could think of was an unmade bed. He looked as if he had just rolled out of one. His brown eyes were bloodshot and his dark hair, wet from the rain, stood on end, as though he had made some effort to comb it with his fingertips. The collar of his suit jacket was caught at the neck and, unless Mary Helen was mis-taken, it didn't really match his pants.

The inspector stood by the front door for a few seconds, rubbing the stubble on his chin. It was as if he was trying to get his bearings.

"Ah, Hugh," he said, obviously recognizing the publican, "have ye a cup of hot coffee?"

Who did he remind her of? Columbo, of course, minus the trench coat, half smoked cigar, and wandering eye. Columbo with an Irish brogue!

While Hugh was serving up the coffee, Mary Helen noticed a second inspector slip into the Monks' Table. He appeared to be several decades younger than his partner. *Talk about daylight and darkness,* she thought, studying the second man, who was tall and muscular with a full head of red hair cut short.

White shirt cuffs with gold cuff links showed below the sleeves of his tan Burberry raincoat. And Mary Helen was sure that she could smell his aftershave lotion from where she sat.

"I'm Detective Inspector Brian Reedy," he said in a deep no-nonsense voice. "And for anyone who might not know him, this is my partner, Detective Inspector Ernie White." He nodded toward the man sipping the coffee. "If you would all remain where you are, please, until we've examined the body."

"It's Willie Ward," the publican blurted out.

Inspector White raised his eyebrows. "*The* Willie Ward?" he asked, putting his coffee cup on the bar.

"None other," Hugh said.

"Holy Mother of God," White swore softly, "just our luck, Brian, to get a high-profile case when I'm hoping to go on holiday."

Without further comment, he followed Reedy into the ladies'.

The others sat in a small silent circle. Like six wary suspects, Mary Helen thought, guarded by two of Ireland's finest, standing at ease. Although highly unlikely, she couldn't stop herself from wondering wildly if one of them was guilty. And if so, who?

Owen Lynch's face was so pale that he looked as though he were about to join the poor man on the toilet. He must have felt her eyes on him, for he looked up suddenly, frowning. Their eyes met and he became paler still. *If he ever tried to kill anyone,* Mary Helen thought, *the poor devil would probably keel over, right on top of his victim.*

Next to him sat Tommy Burns, Mr. Death. A bruise near his left eye was beginning to darken. It must be where he'd fallen in the field. *It couldn't be he,* she thought. He was all tied up. She fought down the nervous urge to laugh at her own unexpected pun.

Beside Tommy was the parish priest, Father Keane. His gray curly hair was still damp from the rain, which seemed to have stopped as suddenly as it began. At least, Mary Helen could no longer hear it battering the roof.

Surely it couldn't be Father Keane, she thought. He seemed such a good-natured fellow. Besides, he had gone to find Owen Lynch and then Tommy Burns after he'd met Eileen and herself in the field.

Nor could it be Hugh Ryan, the publican. He was behind the bar all evening, wasn't he? Drawing pints, chatting up the patrons.

"And who found the poor blighter?" Inspector White's question startled Mary Helen. She hadn't heard him come down the hall. It took her a moment to catch her breath and respond. "I did, Inspector," she admitted.

"And who might you be?" White's brown eyes were not unkind.

"This is one of the nuns on holiday from America," Father Keane spoke up.

"And she looks well able to speak for herself, Father," White said without taking his eyes off her.

Sister Mary Helen thought she was going to like this
man. "Indeed, I am," she said, adjusting her bifocals,
which had the annoying tendency to slip down the
bridge of her nose. She swore she would get contact
lenses one of these days. "I found Mr. Ward when I went
to use the . . ." She hesitated. *Toilet* sounded a bit in-
decorous and *restroom* surely did not fill the bill. She
pointed down the hallway.

"Didn't you think it odd to find him in the ladies'?"

"I thought it odd to find him dead at all, Inspector,"
she said. "After that, I never gave much thought to
where I found him."

Inspector White grinned.

"Ernie," Detective Inspector Reedy called, emerging
from the hallway. "I've notified the lads from forensics,"
he said. "They're on their way."

"Hugh," a voice called from outside. "Are ye open?"
The question was followed by two heavy bangs on the
door.

"The gala must be breaking up." Lynch stood and ran
a finger around his shirt collar, as if he were choking.
"Patsy will be wild with worry. The streets will be
mobbed and the lot of them will be wondering what
happened. . . ." His voice trailed off.

"Not a'tall." Detective Inspector Reedy nodded to the
two gardai, who immediately left the pub.

It seemed implausible to Mary Helen that he expected these two youngsters to control hundreds of revelers. She must have looked uneasy.

"The locals are a friendly lot," Inspector White said.
"Just curious, is all. After a few minutes they'll all totter
on home."

Despite the shouting and catcalling, after a few minutes Mary Helen heard car engines begin to rev and tires
hiss on the wet macadam. Conversation and laughter

grew fainter and fainter, and two tenors singing "Danny Boy" faded into the distance.

"Did any one of you touch anything before we arrived?" Detective Inspector Reedy asked, slipping his cell phone into his raincoat pocket.

"I gave the poor man the Last Rites," Father Keane said. "I touched the holy oils to his eyes, lips, and ears."

"What about his hands and feet? Aren't you supposed to anoint those, too?" Reedy asked.

The priest's face flushed. "Technically," he said, "but Willie and I were having a hard enough time both fitting in the stall without me crawling around him to touch his hands and feet."

"You've a good point, Father," Detective Inspector White said, then turned to his partner. "The lads better get here before rigor mortis sets in or they'll have a devil of a time moving him out of that stall."

Behind her, Mary Helen heard Hugh Ryan's breath whoosh out as if he had been punched in the stomach. Her own stomach felt a little queasy, and she tried not to visualize the scene.

"While we're waiting for the lads, why don't we ask you folks a few questions?" White checked his wristwatch. "It's half one," he said. "You must be ready for bed."

Only 1:30! Mary Helen had thought it surely must be nearly dawn. She found it hard to believe that it wasn't later. Then the thought hit her like a bolt. Rigor mortis usually sets in within a couple of hours. So Willie must have been murdered at about 11:30. Were Eileen and she still in the field when it happened? Was he already dead when they were eating their rhubarb pie and whipped cream? It couldn't have happened when they were in the Monks' Table. They would have heard something, wouldn't they?

Numbly, she watched Detective Inspector Reedy duck into one of the alcoves off the bar. "We can use this room to talk," he called to his partner.

"Where shall we begin?" Inspector White surveyed the group. "Why not start with the blow-ins?"

"Who?" Mary Helen asked.

"Us," Eileen whispered. "He means the nonnatives." Sure enough, Eileen was correct.

Sister Mary Helen sat across from the two detectives, who asked her for some personal information such as why she was in Ireland, how long she planned to stay, and where she lived in America. Her eyes felt gritty with fatigue as she told them as quickly and thoroughly as she possibly could about Eileen, and her finding Mr. Death in the field, telling Father Keane about their discovery, going to the pub to wait for him and Owen Lynch, and finally about finding Willie Ward in the ladies'.

Detective Inspector Reedy said very little; his partner less. Mary Helen had the distinct impression that neither man was missing much.

"That seems to be it, Sister," Detective Inspector White said finally. "We'll talk to your friend. We shouldn't be long. Then the two of you can go. You're just down the road, so we know where to find you, if needs be."

As he had promised, Eileen's interview was short, a little too short for Mary Helen's liking. Somehow its brevity made her feel like the chief suspect. *Nonsense,* she chided herself as they bundled into their raincoats. Her rendition had been so complete that the two men may have seen no need to have Eileen go through it all again, especially at this time of the morning.

"Good night, Sisters," the pimple-faced garda at the door said, letting them out. The moon shone brightly between the racing clouds. "Sleep well," the second garda called, tipping his cap.

"Fat chance," Mary Helen grumbled as the two of them hurried along the wet, deserted street to their mews.

Monday, September 1

May you live to be a hundred years,
With one extra to repent!
—Irish blessing

Sister Mary Helen awoke feeling groggy. Eyes closed, she patted the nightstand, feeling for her glasses. It took her a few minutes to work up the courage to put them on and check the time.

She groaned. Eight o'clock! She'd had six hours of sleep, if one could call that fitful catnapping that she'd done sleep. Actually, she was more tired now than when she'd gone to bed.

In the distance she heard the rumble of a lorry and the slamming of car doors. The doleful caw of a crow in the yard seemed to signal the beginning of another day in Ballyclarin. Yet the mews itself was silent. Eileen must still be in bed, she thought. Thanks be to God! It was far too early to begin the day.

Let the lorries roll and the crows cackle. She'd just stay put and hope to drift off again. She pulled the down comforter up under her chin and tried to focus on the gently sloping green fields and the soft textured clouds of blue and gray that she had enjoyed during her few days in Ireland. She took a deep breath and let it out slowly.

Despite her best efforts, all the patterned fields, shifting clouds, and deep breaths were not able to push aside the sight of Willie Ward in his tweed cap enthroned in the ladies'. She cringed and tried to blot out the terrible scene. Surely no one in this peaceful idyllic village could have done such a thing. Yet the man was dead. That was a fact. Unless last night was nothing more than a nightmare. Wouldn't it be grand to wake up and discover it was all a bad dream?

If it was not, then a stranger must have stolen into the Monks' Table and committed the murder, a very strong stranger. One had to have strength to stick that small knife into a man's heart.

Enough of this, Mary Helen thought. She shut her eyes tight to keep out the daylight that was struggling to get around the closed drapes and into the darkened room. But sleep refused to come.

Instead, again and again, Willie Ward flashed before her, a knife protruding from his blood-soaked shirt, a plain old kitchen knife that could be found in anyone's drawer. Where had she seen one like it recently?

The answer played on the edge of her memory, just out of reach. Like names and places and faces often do when you are trying to pin them down. *Just relax,* she assured herself, *and it will come.* It had to have been within the last few days.

Of course, market day on the village green! Hadn't Eileen and she watched the farrier at work? She was almost positive that at his booth was a display of handmade kitchen knives.

Surely Detective Inspector White and his partner were aware of that. But just in case, she'd mention it, if she had the chance. She tossed uneasily. Did the farrier have any reason to murder Mr. Ward? None she knew of, anyway.

She remembered thinking at the time that he looked like a pleasant sort of fellow—peaceful, really, as he pounded the hot metal. Not that looks had anything to do with murder. In the few days since she arrived in Ballyclarin she'd met up with several locals who seemed to thoroughly dislike Mr. Ward. Maybe one of them had snatched a knife up from the farrier's booth when the man's attention was on shoeing the horse.

Mary Helen caught herself. This was police business, not hers. She was in Ireland on holiday, as they say. It would never do to get involved in what was certainly no concern of hers. She must remember that!

A sudden loud knock on the kitchen door of the mews startled her awake.

"Are ye up?" She recognized the cheerful voice of Paul Glynn, their hackney driver. "It's half twelve," he called. "I was afraid there was another dead body or two."

Twelve thirty! Mary Helen's eyes shot open. How had she missed the tolling of the mass bell?

"We've had a very long night," she heard Eileen whisper.

"So I hear." Paul warmed to the topic.

"Can I fix you a cup of tea?" Eileen asked softly.

"Beautiful," Paul said, and Mary Helen heard the door bang as he settled at the small kitchen table.

Many a day we shall rest in the clay, she thought, forcing herself out of the bed.

"Well, if it isn't herself!" Paul exclaimed when a few minutes later Mary Helen joined them. She had dressed so quickly that she stole a glance at her feet to make sure her shoes were a pair.

"How's the celebrity this morning?" Paul asked, obviously in high spirits.

"Celebrity?" Mary Helen was taken aback. "What celebrity?" she asked halfheartedly. She was really too tired for guessing games.

"It's all over the village. Yes, indeed!" Paul grinned. "Yank nuns found Willie Ward's body, God rest him, in the ladies'." The driver's hazel eyes danced behind his rimless glasses. He was having great fun.

Mary Helen felt her face grow warm. "The man was murdered, Paul," she said.

"Ah." Paul paused. Looking penitent, he ran his fingers through his straight dark hair. "None deserved it more," he said piously.

Another knock came on the kitchen door. This was going to be a busy day. Before either of them could answer, the door was pulled open. Mary Helen was not surprised to see Detective Inspector Ernie White, still in his rumpled suit jacket.

His face was puffy, and the small dark moons that had formed under his eyes left no doubt that he'd been up all night, or at least a good part of it. His thick dark hair looked more than ever like a haystack. Mary Helen wondered if White had a wife or perhaps a lady friend who would tell him he needed a haircut. Badly!

"Can I fix you a cup of tea?" Mary Helen asked, trying not to stare.

"Ta," the inspector nodded wearily and crumpled into the last chair at the table.

"Good morning, Sisters." Detective Inspector Brian Reedy stood in the doorway.

"Tea, Detective Inspector?" Mary Helen asked, surprised that the man looked as fresh as he did. *Ah, youth!* she thought, going into the living room to pull in another chair.

"You needn't go to any bother," Reedy said. "I'm on my way to headquarters. I just wanted to let Ernie here know."

"Good luck, then," White said, leaving Mary Helen wondering what all that was about.

For several minutes the only sound in the small kitchen was the sound of sipping.

Finally White cleared his throat. "Did you get any rest last night?" he asked.

"Some," Eileen said, "but it was quite unnerving. Finding that poor man . . ." Her voice trailed off.

"Indeed." White tilted back in his chair to study something on the ceiling. Then, bringing his chair forward, he seemed for the first time to notice the hackney driver. "And you, Paul?" he asked. "How did you sleep?"

"Fine, indeed, sir." Paul looked surprised to be asked. "My wife and I had no idea what happened until this morning."

"You didn't wonder a'tall when you left the tent and saw the tape and the garda at the Monks' Table?"

Paul shook his head. Not too vigorously, Mary Helen noted. "According to my wife, I was feeling no pain. She drove us both home," he added quickly, in case the inspector had any question about his driving under the influence.

Dumbfounded, Mary Helen watched the exchange. Surely Detective Inspector White didn't think Paul had anything to do with the murder, did he? Unfortunately, his face gave nothing away.

"May I ask why you are here now?" His tone was friendly, almost chatty. At least, Mary Helen thought it was.

"I just came by to ask the nuns if they needed me today. I didn't know a thing about any murder till I came into the village. The whole place is full of nothing else."

Paul's explanation seemed to satisfy White, who rose abruptly. "And you do understand," he said, without taking his eyes off the driver, "that what you hear in this room, especially from the nuns, remains in here?"

"Yes, indeed, sir," Paul answered, his tone all business, but his face barely masking his disappointment. Mary Helen thought she understood why. Recounting any fresh news to the enjoyment of the lads in the pub surely would earn him at least one free round.

"When you've finished your tea, Sisters," White said, as if he'd just remembered that they were there, "may I have a word with you both at the Monks' Table?" He drained his cup. "I have a few questions. It shouldn't be long."

When he left the room, an uncomfortable silence filled the cozy kitchen, but only for a few seconds.

"The nerve of that man," Paul snarled, his cheeks reddening, "practically accusing me of doing in the old get."

That word again! From his tone Mary Helen was pretty sure she shouldn't ask what precisely *get* meant.

"He did no such thing!" Eileen said, clearing the teacups. "He was simply asking you a few questions."

"It came off as if he had me in mind," Paul complained, sounding reluctant to let go of the affront. "The man is an odd duck, if you ask me."

"He's probably just exhausted," Eileen said.

"A lot you know about the gardai," Paul snapped testily.

A lot more than I want you to know, Mary Helen thought, catching Eileen's eye.

"Do you think we will have time to go to the art show this afternoon?" Mary Helen asked, eager to change the subject.

"It will depend on how long they keep you, won't it?" Paul said, beginning to get back his good humor. "I'll check in at half two, if that's to your liking."

"Why don't we meet with the detective inspector right now?" Eileen suggested, after assuring Paul that a 2:30 pickup was to their liking, indeed. "The sooner, the quicker," Eileen, ever practical, remarked.

Outside the sky was a brilliant blue with startling white clouds all in a line. Cottage doors and windows were flung wide open, and wash hung out to dry. It was going to be a grand day. Everyone seemed to be counting on it. At least, Mary Helen hoped it would be a grand day. For Eileen and herself, it all depended on Detective Inspector White.

Sister Mary Helen recognized the pimple-faced garda from last night standing at attention in front of the door of the Monks' Table. Liam, Mr. Lynch had called him. *He has to have a last name,* she thought, smiling at the young man. *I can't keep referring to him, even in my own mind, as Liam with the acne.*

The garda tipped his hat when the two nuns passed, revealing a head of thick sandy-colored hair. "Morning, Sisters," he said, his cheeks glowing red.

"Good morning, Garda . . ." Mary Helen searched his chest for a name tag or some sort of identification, but a large yellow rain slicker covered any place she could expect to find one. She might as well come right out and ask.

"Garda Liam O'Dea," he answered smartly.

Wasn't O'Dea the Oyster Queen's name? Something-very-Irish O'Dea? "Are you by any chance related to that lovely young women who is the queen?"

"If it's Tara you mean," Liam O'Dea offered.

Mary Helen nodded. That was it. Tara O'Dea.

His face lit up. "In the West of Ireland we all seem to

be related somehow," he said. "But, yes, I am. Tara O'Dea is my first cousin. Her da and my da are brothers."

The acne skin must be from his mother's side, Mary Helen thought, not unkindly, smiling up at the young man.

"But enough of my relatives," Liam said, suddenly all business. "Detective Inspector White is expecting you. I have strict orders to show you in as soon as you get here."

Straightening his shoulders, Liam O'Dea pulled back the door of the Monks' Table and watched the two nuns walk inside. When he was sure the heavy door was completely closed, he moved closer to it, hoping he could overhear some of the goings-on. Hard as he tried, he heard not a sound. He glanced around nervously. It would never do for someone to catch him eavesdropping. No indeed, he thought, deliberately taking up his position closer to the curb.

Although Liam O'Dea had only been a *Garda Siochana,* a Guardian of the Peace, for a little over six months now, he could not remember a time when he hadn't wanted to be one.

Maybe for a week or two after his First Holy Communion he had thought he might like to be a priest, saying Mass and passing out the hosts at Communion time and hearing everyone's sins, even his da's.

But then one of the lads in his class told him that priests weren't allowed to kiss girls, and he had abandoned the idea immediately. Especially when he thought of never being able to kiss Carmel Cox, the doctor's blue-eyed daughter. When they were youngsters, Carmel with the long auburn curls had lived down the road with her parents and her three brothers.

Liam felt his face grow warm. Now it was not the

priesthood that kept him from trying to kiss the beautiful Carmel. It was her brothers. Somehow after their father had passed on, they felt it was their duty to keep
everyone away from their sister. The way they were going at it, poor Carmel might as well be a nun.

"What is going on in there?" a sharp voice cut into
his thought. Liam froze. That voice could only belong to
one person, his Auntie Zoë. He had been so preoccupied
he hadn't heard her coming in time to make his escape.

"The woman has a tongue so sharp," his da had said
many times, "it could clip a hedge."

Liam pressed his lips together to keep from grinning
at the thought of two sharp clipper blades protruding
from Zoë's thin lips and snipping away.

"I can't say, Auntie," he replied, avoiding her piercing eyes.

"Can't say! Humph! Won't say is more like it. Ever
since you went to that garda school, you've been acting
like a perfect *eejit*. If you had any brains at all, you'd
have gone into the funeral business, like the rest of the
O'Dea clan. And you wouldn't be standing on your feet
all day guarding a door!" She stared up at him.

Liam clenched his teeth, trying to keep his face from
showing any emotion. The old cow! Dumb as dirt, she
was. He had no intention of guarding doors all his life.
No, indeed! He was set on being a detective inspector.
As a lad he had watched hundreds of hours of detectives
on the telly—Inspector Morse and that nice chap, Inspector Barnaby from Midsummer. Although they did
seem to have an excessive amount of murders in Oxford
and that little village, but that was England for you.

Then there was the American telly with the detectives
shooting and jumping and chasing. *The Streets of San
Francisco* had been one of his favorites. He remembered

as a lad bragging at school that he had a second cousin who had actually visited that dangerous, hilly city.

He could feel his aunt's eyes still on him. "Well, Liam?" she said. "Are you going to tell me or not?"

"Not," he said, feeling his cheeks burn. Hands clasped behind his back, he stared straight ahead, wishing that she would go away.

"That's beautiful," she said sarcastically, "a young man who wouldn't even give his auntie the time of day. After all I've done for you!" She took a breath, ready, he knew from past experience, to start a long harangue on the ingratitude of modern youth with a number of pointed references to himself.

Feeling like one of the martyrs Father Keane often talked about at Mass, Liam was determined not to hear a word. *The woman is mad,* he kept repeating to himself, *plain mad.*

He was concentrating so hard that he almost missed the slamming of the car door that saved his day.

"Morning, Liam," Detective Inspector Brian Reedy called in a cheerful voice, despite the fact that he'd only a few hours of sleep. The man was remarkable!

Checking the sky, Reedy slipped into his raincoat. Although a watery sun still shone, dark clouds were tumbling into view. You didn't have to be much of a detective to realize that rain was on its way.

"And what can we do for you today, Mrs. O'Dea?" Reedy asked, not bothering to lock his car door.

"Not a thing, Brian," his auntie said, her thin face burning. Then, muttering something that Liam was just as glad he could not make out, she hurried away.

"She's quite a woman." Reedy shook his head. "But what a beautiful daughter."

"Yes, indeed, sir," Liam answered, aware that Reedy

had that look on his face again, the one that he always had when Tara was mentioned. It reminded Liam of the look of a sick cow.

Brian Reedy was one of the nicest fellows you could ever meet on a day's walk, yet Liam was not sure how he'd feel about having Reedy as a cousin-in-law, if that was Reedy's intention. Would Liam still call him sir?

"Ernie here?" Reedy interrupted his thoughts.

"Yes, sir," Liam answered smartly. "He's here and he sent for the two nuns from America."

Reedy looked at him quizzically.

"They are in there with him now," Liam said. "They've been inside for about twenty minutes."

"Poor old dears must need a cuppa by now," Reedy said. "I could use one myself." He checked his watch. "How about you, Liam?"

Liam tried not to answer too quickly. If the truth be told, he would do just about anything to get inside and watch Detective Inspector White at work. Although Reedy was a grand fellow and full of chat, White was a regular genius when it came to solving crime.

Garda Liam O'Dea was determined to learn as much from him as he possibly could.

Inside, the Monks' Table was dark. Only a few lights were on, and the whole place reeked of spilled beer and stale smoke.

What this pub needs, Mary Helen thought, wondering if her clothes would retain the odor, *is a good airing out.*

Obviously the smell was the farthest thing from Detective Inspector White's mind. Sister Eileen and she had told him and retold him their every move from leaving the tent to finding the fully clothed body propped on the toilet seat. So much so, that Mary Helen was beginning to wonder if the man was a little thick.

"Is everybody ready for a cuppa?" Brian Reedy

called out as the heavy front door of the pub closed behind him.

Strangely, Mary Helen felt saved.

Without waiting for an answer, Reedy, with the assistance of Garda O'Dea, poured and passed the teacups. He helped himself to a couple of bags of crisps, which he tore open and passed around.

Potato chips and tea were an unusual combination, but under the circumstances, Mary Helen found they hit the spot.

Teatime was over too soon.

"A word, Brian," Detective Inspector White said, motioning his partner into a side alcove. The two nuns were left with Garda O'Dea, who shifted self-consciously from foot to foot.

Sister Mary Helen watched the color spread like melting butter from his jaw to his hairline as he struggled to look official. She was wondering what she could say to put him at his ease when both of the inspectors returned. *It must have been really just "a word,"* she thought.

"Now, then, Sisters," White began, clearing his throat. He tilted back as though he were studying a spot in the ceiling. The way he had in the kitchen.

Mary Helen wondered if that helped him think or if it was a technique he used to make those he was questioning nervous. It was impossible to tell.

Without warning, his head snapped forward and his brown bloodshot eyes fastened on her.

"I don't suppose you ever get used to finding dead bodies," he said out of the blue.

Mary Helen frowned. Had she heard him correctly? "Pardon me?" she said.

"Last night when you told me your name and that you were from San Francisco, I wondered."

"Wondered what?"

Detective Inspector White blinked several times before he continued. "I wondered if you were the same nun that my wife's cousin sent us a clipping about," he said finally.

"A clipping?" Mary Helen's mouth went dry.

White nodded. "My wife's cousin Maura lives in San Francisco. She sent us a clipping from the newspaper there about an older nun who was involved in solving a homicide. She thought that because I deal with death under suspicious circumstances myself, I might be interested, which, indeed, I was.

"So when I went home last night, I found it on the mantelpiece where my wife had left it, and sure enough, it was you!" He paused to let that much sink in. "Brian, here, confirmed it this morning with a quick call to San Francisco and to an Inspector Gallagher, whose name was also mentioned in the article."

Uh-oh, here it comes, Mary Helen thought, feeling something inside turn over and sink.

"He was helpful, indeed," Reedy said with a wicked little grin on his handsome face. "A bit gruff, but who can blame him? Poor *divil* had his horn ringing at half four in the morning, his time. I did get an earful about you and your friend here." He nodded toward Eileen.

Detective Inspector White leveled his eyes at the two of them. "Now, you may get away with these shenanigans in America, but this is Ireland," he said sternly. "We do things a little differently here. We do not have our nuns, or anyone else for that matter, poking into our homicide cases, putting themselves into danger. Is that clear?"

Sister Mary Helen felt her cheeks burn. "Detective Inspector, we had no intention of—"

"Sister," he interrupted, a pleasant smile returning to his face, "surely you must know that the road to hell is paved with good intentions. As I said, we will tolerate none of it. Am I clear?"

"Very," Eileen answered for the both of them.

But that didn't seem to satisfy White. "Sister?" He was talking to her.

"Very clear," Mary Helen replied stiffly, resisting the childish urge to stick out her tongue.

Seemingly convinced, he checked his wristwatch. "You are free to go now. You'll be right in time for the art show. Paul Glynn is waiting for you, no doubt. Enjoy yourselves, and remember." He paused. "Stay as far away as possible from anything remotely connected with Willie Ward's untimely death."

The door of the Monks' Table shut behind them.

"Men," Mary Helen fumed. "They are all alike!"

Sister Eileen started to giggle.

"What is so funny?"

"Can you imagine what Inspector Gallagher said? The phone lines must have been burning blue."

Eileen's laugh was infectious. "And did you see the expression on that young garda's face?" Mary Helen asked. "I wonder what the poor kid is thinking."

Actually, Liam O'Dea wasn't thinking anything very profound, thank you very much indeed. If anything, he was in shock. How was it two elderly nuns weren't frightened to get involved with death under suspicious circumstances? They seemed rather frail, but according to what he had overheard Detective Inspector White say, they had solved murders on the streets of San Francisco.

Liam's heart began to thud as he envisioned the hilly

chase and the final shoot-out. Perhaps he should be watching *them* for techniques, as well as Ernie White.

"Find Owen Lynch, will you please, garda. And tell him I have a few more questions."

Liam almost missed White's order.

"Yes, sir," he said.

"If he's not at home, he's most likely at the art show," Reedy added.

"Yes, sir," Liam answered again, and he hurried down the road.

Owen Lynch was at home, just finishing up his dinner, when Liam knocked on his front door.

"Should I go with you, love?' Patsy Lynch asked. Her usual cheerful expression seemed to have been replaced with a worried frown.

"No, pet. I'll be fine," Owen answered too quickly.

"But you haven't had dessert," Patsy said.

"When I come home." He patted her hand.

Liam thought he smelled fear on the man, but perhaps it was just the turnips still on his plate. "The detective inspector only wants to see Owen," Liam said, hoping he sounded like a man in charge.

"You tell Ernie White—" Patsy began, but her husband hushed her.

"Never mind, pet," he said, taking off his horn-rimmed glasses and polishing them. "It is only routine. I'll be home shortly."

"The twins have their artwork on display." Patsy's voice was small. "They are so proud of it."

"I wouldn't miss it for the world," Owen assured her, and he bent to peck her on the cheek.

"They have no talent, you know, our twins," Owen said once he and Liam had stepped out into the street. "But the missus won't be convinced. We've spent a king's ransom on art lessons and dance lessons."

Odd thing to say about your own children, Liam thought as the pair walked briskly toward the Monks' Table.

Liam stood tall and threw his shoulders back on the off chance that Carmel Cox might see him escorting a suspect to be interrogated. But no such luck. The village was all but deserted. Liam guessed that the townsfolk were either at the art show or at home recovering from last night's gala.

"In here, Owen," he heard Detective Inspector White call as they entered the pub. "Have a seat. When was it, now, you said you last saw Willie Ward alive?"

"Should I come back for you in an hour's time?" Paul Glynn asked when he dropped the two nuns at the old convent school.

"Aren't you going to view the artwork?" Eileen asked, a hint of *divilment* in her voice.

Paul's groan was answer enough.

The convent school auditorium was crowded, although the art on the walls seemed to be the last thing on anyone's mind. Small tight groups had formed all around the room. They seemed more interested in what their neighbors had to say than they were in viewing the displays.

Sisters Eileen and Mary Helen squeezed past, trying to enjoy the art. Was it her imagination, Mary Helen wondered, or did several conversations stop as they neared? She was sure she'd heard Willie Ward's name mentioned and the Monks' Table. "How do?" she said cheerfully to a woman who seemed to be staring, but the woman quickly turned away.

"All I did was find the body," Mary Helen whispered to Eileen. "Why do I feel so guilty?"

"It's the Irish way," Eileen quipped, narrowing her eyes to study a watercolor.

"These must be local artists," she whispered, staring up at a garden that clearly lacked both perspective and technique. Next to it was a pencil sketch of a horse behind a fence. The fence appeared to have been flattened by a strong wind.

"Pretty awful, aren't they?" a woman's soft voice remarked. "The art, I mean."

Mary Helen turned quickly and was surprised to see Oonagh Cox holding a glass of white wine.

"May I get you some?" she offered, her blue eyes sparkling. "You look as if you could use a glass. Besides, these works of art tend to improve after a glass or two."

Eileen and she followed the small woman to the refreshment table. "I suppose you are wondering why we have an art show at all," she said, handing them each a glass and a napkin.

Knowing there was no tactful answer, Mary Helen took a sip of her wine. She noticed Eileen did the same.

"It's a tradition," Oonagh said, "started by my dear, late husband, Kevin. And everyone seems to think that they will offend his memory if they stop it." Oonagh rolled her eyes. "Frankly, Kevin is most likely turning over in his grave if he can see what is being hung on these walls and called art." She sighed. "Truly, the only one in the village who has any talent at all is Jake."

"Jake?" Mary Helen asked.

"Jake, the tinker," Oonagh explained. "Although some would not acknowledge it. It is as if admitting that a tinker has any talent is more than they can bear."

"Was he the same fellow who had words with Willie Ward at the wine tasting?" Eileen asked.

"Everyone's had words, as you put it, with Willie," Oonagh said, refilling her glass. "To know Willie is to despise him. Come," she said, "let me show you Jake's work."

They followed Oonagh's curly head through the crowd—which did seem friendlier after a little wine—to a small display of photographs fastened to a wooden divider. Mary Helen caught her breath. Oonagh was right. Jake was extremely talented. His photographs had captured in black and white the wild beauty of the Irish landscape. There was a clarity and simplicity to his work, almost a spiritual quality about it.

As the three women stood in silence, taking in the richness of his photography, Mary Helen wondered if he might sell one, and if so, how much he would charge. It would be a lovely gift to bring home to the convent in San Francisco.

"He'll win the prize again this year, no doubt," someone behind them said in a low whiney voice.

Turning, Mary Helen recognized Zoë O'Dea, Tara's mother.

"Look who's here," Eileen said under her breath, "the Queen Mum."

"And why shouldn't he? He's the best," Oonagh answered without even turning around. "The O'Deas can't win everything, Zoë. Your daughter is queen," she snapped. "What more do you want?"

"And these must be the nuns from America who found poor Willie in the loo," Zoë said smiling.

Mary Helen wondered if the woman had heard Oonagh.

"You know very well they are." Oonagh clearly had little patience with Zoë O'Dea.

"A little testy this afternoon, are we?" Zoë's voice dripped with concern. "Maybe next year your Carmel will be the queen. Lovely girl she is, too, so like her dear father, may he rest in peace."

Oonagh's face darkened and her eyes blazed. Mary Helen wondered uneasily where this was going.

"Oh, Patsy," Zoë O'Dea called across the room. "May I have a word?"

Sister Mary Helen watched Zoë O'Dea turn on her flat heel, cross the auditorium, and corner Patsy Lynch, the chairman's wife.

"That thick cow!" Oonagh said hotly. "If there's another murder in this village, it is sure to be hers! It's a bloody miracle somebody hasn't murdered her already."

Despite the heat in the crowded room, Mary Helen shivered. Where had she heard those words before? It took her a moment to remember—at the Monks' Table the day she arrived. Zoë was saying them to Willie Ward: *I'm surprised someone hasn't killed you already.*

"What is it, Mam?" The voice startled Mary Helen. She hadn't heard anyone coming up behind them. She turned to find a smiling Carmel Cox.

The girl put an arm around her mother's shoulders. "You're not letting Mrs. O'Dea rile you up, are you?" she asked.

"Of course not, love." Oonagh smiled up at her daughter and pushed a stray curl from Carmel's forehead.

"These are the nuns from America." Oonagh seemed anxious to be done with Zoë O'Dea.

"The ones everyone is talking about?" Carmel grinned. "Your ears must surely be ringing. Guess who is guarding the door at the murder scene, Mam?" Carmel's blue eyes twinkled. "Liam O'Dea! Can you believe it? Liam is a garda!" The girl shook her head and her auburn curls bounced. "Should I go chat him up?"

"If he's on duty, love, he won't be able to chat," Oonagh said, but Carmel was already on her way out of the auditorium.

Oonagh watched her go. "She's a mind of her own, that child," she said fondly. "Her brothers say I spoil her and that she is going to be a handful. But she's my only daughter."

Both Mary Helen and Eileen knew better than to comment.

"At last! Here comes our chairman." Oonagh pointed toward the entrance to the auditorium. "This dreadful event should be over soon."

Sure enough! Owen Lynch stood by the door, his face flushed. Looking distracted, he shook hands and greeted people on his way across the room toward the refreshment table where the three women stood. "I need something a bit stronger than this," he said, taking the glass that Oonagh held out to him.

"Where have you been?" she asked quietly.

"With the garda, answering a hundred thousand questions." Noticing the nuns were listening, he stopped abruptly.

"They can't think you had anything to do with it, can they?" Oonagh sounded concerned.

Owen shook his head, then dug in his trousers' pocket for a handkerchief and wiped the sweat from his forehead.

"Let me get your glasses," Oonagh said. "They are full of fingerprints."

Sister Mary Helen was surprised that he let her take off his horn-rimmed glasses and disappear with them.

"I'm blind as a bloody bat without them," he said, smiling sheepishly. "She'll be right back."

And she was.

"Ah," he said, putting the glasses back on, "that is much better. Ta.

"Sweet Jesus!" he said suddenly. "Look! Patsy's been cornered by Zoë O'Dea. Sorry, I need to rescue my wife."

"The gardai must have been rough on him," Oonagh said to no one in particular.

"Or maybe they are just being thorough." Eileen sighed. "We were in with them ourselves. Detective Inspector White seems quite competent."

"Oh, indeed," Oonagh said, a smile playing on her lips. "Ernie White always gets his man. Or in this case, maybe it will be his woman," she said, turning away.

Studying the woman's profile, Mary Helen couldn't help wondering if Oonagh Cox knew something she wasn't telling. It was difficult—no, impossible—to know.

A flurry of activity at the entrance caught their attention.

"Look who it is." Eileen pulled on Mary Helen's sleeve.

It was Tara O'Dea, and she was on the arm of Tommy Burns, Mr. Death. Tommy looked quite dapper in his suit, Mary Helen noticed. The gardai must have let him go home last night. Except for the bruise under his left eye, he looked none the worse for wear.

Owen Lynch clapped for attention, and the room quieted. All eyes focused expectantly on Tara and Tommy.

Tara fidgeted self-consciously with her green taffeta dress that by now, Mary Helen thought, must smell a little ripe.

With one hand Tara held up her long skirt and with the other held on to her tiara as she stepped onto a raised platform. Microphone in hand, Owen stood below her.

"Let's give our Oyster Queen a round of applause," he urged, and the crowd obliged. "In a few minutes, our committee will count the votes, then Queen Tara will announce the winner of this year's Ballyclarin Oyster

Festival Art Contest. So, please, those of you who still have to vote, please do so. The ballot box is over by the door." He pointed to a wooden box, which looked quite official. "Our pastor and committee chairman, Father Keane, will start to count in ten minutes."

The noise in the room began to swell as people stepped up to the table to refill their wine glasses and view the displays.

Sisters Eileen and Mary Helen quickly circled the room to see if they'd missed anything. They hadn't. Jake's black and white photographs were clearly superior to any other work in the auditorium.

"Good afternoon, Sisters," Father Keane greeted them. Mary Helen hadn't noticed him come in. In fact, she was rather surprised that he was the committee chairman. He didn't look the type that would know that much about art. Although, if pushed, she'd have been hard-pressed to say what "the type" looked like.

"I'm the committee chairman," he whispered as if he could read her mind, "because they insist. Somehow, they think a priest will keep the vote honest."

"I should hope so," Eileen said, watching Father Keane hurry toward the ballot box where the other members of the committee were assembling.

After what seemed like a long time, Owen Lynch, his face unusually pale, once again took up the microphone and called for attention. The wine had lifted everyone's spirits, and it took him three tries to finally get the crowd quieted down.

Once he had, he handed the mike to Tara, who had a bit of difficulty getting it to stop screeching. When at last she did, Tara gave a short, hiccupy cough, then announced, "We have two winners this year."

Tara paused, and the crowd became very still. The mike squealed. Again, she cleared her throat. "Jake's

black and white photo of sheep on a hillside," she said
clearly.

Good choice, Mary Helen thought, remembering the
photo. Sun filtered in and out of high clouds, creating
light and shadow on a steep hillside to which black-
faced sheep seemed to be attached, as some wag had put
it, by Velcro.

"And." Tara paused. "The Lynch twins' pencil sketch
of the horse in the pasture."

"The one with the collapsed fence?" Eileen whispered.

"You have to be joking," a loud voice cried, and the
crowd burst like a sudden storm into an angry roar.

Mary Helen checked her wristwatch. Thank God, she
thought, Paul should be here at the old convent school
any minute to collect them.

Garda Liam O'Dea would rather have been hanged than
admit to anyone that his legs ached and his feet hurt. Actually, the soles of his feet felt as if they were on fire. It
must be the socks he'd bought on sale at Penny's De-
partment Store in Galway City.

"No sale is a good sale if you can't use what you
buy," his old granny used to say. At this moment he
knew she was right. He wiggled his toes for relief and
looked toward the sky, which was beginning to cloud
up. A sharp wind blew in off the Atlantic, snapping the
blue and white tape cordoning off the door to the pub,
the same one that he was guarding.

Liam had been guarding the front door of the Monks'
Table for hours. At least, it seemed like hours, and he
wasn't sure why he was needed. Not a single living soul
had tried to get in, except, of course, Owen Lynch,
whom the detectives had summoned.

But Lynch had left several minutes ago and hurried toward the old convent school, which made sense.

Liam rolled his shoulders back, then forward. He could use a bit of a break.

"Hello, Liam!"

Without looking, he recognized the voice. Carmel Cox. He felt the heat start at the collar of his uniform shirt and rise to the brim of his hat. Oh, how he wished he could control his blushing. He must look the fool. He cleared his throat. Maybe she wouldn't notice.

"Good afternoon, Carmel." He put his hand to his hat brim and tried to sound very official. "Sorry, but no one is allowed in the pub. Police business, you know." He pressed his lips into a straight, no-nonsense line.

Carmel giggled. "Of course I know. Everyone in the entire village knows that Willie Ward was murdered here last night, silly. It's all the talk at the art contest. I just came by to see you."

Liam's cheeks burned. Next his acne would start to itch. "You did?" He paused, not knowing exactly what to say next—afraid that he might stutter. Sometimes when he was very nervous, he stuttered.

Although there was nothing really to be nervous about. Carmel and he had known each other since they were wee tots. They had played together for hours in the vacant fields behind her father's surgery.

Sometimes they played tag; sometimes hide and seek; sometimes they made up games like cowboys and American Indians. Carmel had always wanted to be the Indian and have him chase her.

He had loved watching her long auburn curls bob up and down as she ran across the field. He never caught her, although they both knew he could. Liam reddened when he thought about it now.

Without warning, the door of the Monks' Table pushed open and Detective Inspector Reedy appeared.

Saved, Liam thought.

"Come in, Liam," Reedy called. "It is way past time for a bite. I could eat the back door buttered," he said. "He'll see you later, Carmel."

Liam felt his cheeks burning again as Carmel's giggle filled the air.

"Will I see you after a while?" Carmel asked. "Will you be at Rafferty's tonight?"

"What's going on at Rafferty's?" Liam asked, wondering if he should continue speaking to her while he was on duty. Why not? he reasoned. He was only guarding the pub door, not Buckingham Palace.

"A whist game for the older folks and a dance for us," Carmel called.

"She's quite a beauty," Reedy remarked, watching Carmel hurry down the street.

Liam pretended not to hear his superior officer as he followed him into the Monks' Table.

"Sit down, lad." Detective Inspector Ernie White indicated a place on the bench next to him. Without a word, Liam took off his hat and sat. Hugh Ryan, the publican, came with a tray piled high with cheese and tomato sandwiches, some bags of crisps, and three tall glasses of Guinness to wash it all down. Without a word, he returned to his position behind the bar.

Liam hadn't realized how hungry he was until he saw the spread. They had taken no more than a bite or two and a sip of Guinness when Ernie White cleared his throat.

"Sorry, lads," he said, "but this will be a working lunch, although I know it's not good for the digestion." He took another bite of his sandwich and swallowed. "This morning I heard from the deputy commissioner in Dublin.

Seems that nationally, Willie Ward was a bigger name than we realized. The commissioner is desperate to find his murderer."

Liam's face burned. *Is he talking to me, too?* he wondered.

Narrowing his eyes, White swung them from Reedy to Liam and back again, making it clear he was. "It's up to us to listen and hear what is being said about the murder. Nothing is too small or too insignificant. We never know what unlikely slip may give the murderer away."

Brian Reedy frowned as he searched his partner's face and slowly chewed a crisp. "Do I take it you've heard something?" he asked.

White gave a sad smile. "Not a'tall. Not a damn word," he said, running his fingers through his haystack of hair.

"How did they get in?" Liam's voice surprised even him. It was small and high-pitched.

"Are you saying something, Liam?" Reedy asked.

Liam cleared his throat. "How did they get in? Mr. Ward and his murderer?"

"What is it, lad?" White frowned.

Liam felt three pairs of eyes boring into him. Even Hugh Ryan was staring. "I'm just asking." Liam wished he had kept his gob shut. "How did Willie Ward and his murderer get into the Monks' Table?" He turned toward Hugh. "Did you see them come in?"

Scowling, the publican rewiped the already spotless bar top. "If you are asking me, I'd swear they didn't come in a'tall," Hugh said. "As God is my witness, I didn't see them, and I would have. The place was nearly deserted. The hangers-on, the servers, the cook had all gone. Only the two American nuns were still here." Hugh wadded up the bar rag and tossed it into the sink.

"And they claim they didn't see anyone either," White mumbled to himself.

"The only way a living soul could have come in without anyone seeing him," Hugh said, "is through the service entrance in the back. I wouldn't have seen anyone from here. No one would." He slapped down the palm of his hand for emphasis.

The four men silently chewed on that possibility.

"Wouldn't they be taking an awful risk being so conspicuous? Someone standing in the road might notice them coming in the wrong door." Reedy finished off the last of his Guinness and looked happy when Hugh walked over with another.

"Not if they were conspicuous already." The words were out of Liam's mouth before he thought.

"What's your meaning, lad?" White asked, frowning.

Liam's mouth felt dry and his cheeks were hot. For a moment the room was so quiet you could have heard a bee belch. Had he spoken out of turn?

No, White looked genuinely interested. "Suppose they were dressed in Tommy Burns's Grim Reaper costume?" he said, at last. "Everyone might notice, but who would think it odd? They would think it was just the I Believe Team having a bit of fun."

"That would explain why someone cracked poor Tommy on the head and left him in the field," Reedy said.

"Good point, lads," Detective Inspector White downed his Guinness. "Maybe the first order of business is to find the whereabouts of that costume."

When the two nuns came out of the old convent school auditorium, Paul Glynn, arms crossed, was leaning against the hackney looking the picture of long-suffering.

Above him dark clouds rolled across the sky, looking as if they might bump and burst at any minute. Mary

Helen shivered. It had started out to be such a nice, sunny day.

"Did ye enjoy yourselves?" Paul asked, opening the car door for them.

"It was interesting, Paul. Very interesting," Eileen said as the two nuns settled in the backseat.

"And what exactly is your meaning?" Paul asked, starting the motor. "What was so interesting? Jake, the tinker, always wins. He's the only one in the village with any real talent. Even a blind man can see that."

"That is just it," Eileen said. "There were two winners, really three. Jake and the Lynch twins."

Paul turned around in his seat. Behind his rimless glasses his hazel eyes were full of disbelief. "The Lynch twins?" he repeated. "Noreen and Doreen? Are ye sure?"

"Sure I'm sure," Eileen said. "You should have heard the roar that went up."

"I can imagine." Paul shook his head. "The Lynch twins, was it?" he asked again, as though he were unable to take it in.

"That's who," Eileen assured him.

"They're talented, are they?"

"Not a bit of it, as far as I could tell," Eileen answered truthfully. "Although I'm no art critic," she added quickly.

"I doubt if art has much to do with it," Paul said. "Over the years, there have been them who wanted someone else besides Jake to take first prize. Willie Ward, God rest him, among them," he said. "Not to speak ill of the dead, but I would be surprised if our departed Willie hadn't stuffed the ballot box. It's been out since the display went up on Saturday."

"Why?" Mary Helen asked.

"Why what?'

"If Jake was clearly the most talented, why would Willie want someone else to win?"

"It was just his way," Paul said.

"I see," Mary Helen said, although she didn't see at all. "But if he or someone else did stuff the box, why wouldn't Mr. Lynch just disregard a big block of votes that looked suspicious?" It seemed a sensible question to her.

"Lynch had nothing to do with the counting. Father Keane heads the committee that tallies the votes, and he's straight as an arrow. Where is it you two want to go?" Paul asked, backing out of his space in the car park.

Without so much as a backward glance, Mary Helen thought, tensing for the crash. When none came, she relaxed.

"What is the next event on the Oyster Festival schedule?" she asked.

"Right now?" Paul started to rustle through some papers next to him on the front passenger's seat.

It was all Mary Helen could do to keep from shouting, "Mind the road!" She scooted forward on her seat so that, at least, he wouldn't have to turn around to talk.

"There doesn't seem to be anything right now," he said, holding up a paper in front of him on the steering wheel. "Ah, tonight there is whist at Rafferty's Rest, starting at eight. And for those who haven't had enough punishment, there's a dance." He glanced at the road, then back at the paper. "Right now, for those with any sense, it's probably time for a lie down. What's your pleasure?" he asked, studying them in the rearview mirror.

"Why don't you drop us at the mews," Eileen suggested, "and take a bit of a rest yourself? Then"—she looked at Mary Helen for approval—"if you'll pick us up about eight."

Mary Helen nodded, although she hadn't the slightest idea how to play whist (pinochle was her game). But perhaps Eileen did, and at any rate, Mary Helen would enjoy watching the dancing.

"My nerves couldn't stand another minute of his driving," Eileen said, fumbling with the key to the gate that led to their mews. Mary Helen was glad to hear it. She had thought only her nerves were thin.

Once inside, they settled in comfortable chairs and put up their feet. Through the front window the late afternoon sky looked bruised with dark clouds, but so far there had been no rain. In fact, Mary Helen noticed one radiant shaft of sun piercing the cloud cover.

A flock of tiny wrens lit on the grass and flicked their tails as they busily searched for their supper. She checked her wristwatch. It was dinnertime.

"Are you hungry?" she asked Eileen.

"I could eat." Eileen sat up. "Which reminds me, we've nothing in the house."

"A perfect excuse to go out to dinner," Mary Helen said.

"Who needs an excuse, old dear? We are on holiday." Eileen pushed up from her chair. "The Ballyclarin Hotel is within walking distance, and I'm told the salmon there is delicious."

"If we go now, we can easily be back before Paul comes for us," Mary Helen said, picking up her umbrella, just in case.

Liam O'Dea was knackered. He had led a small army of gardai called up from Galway City on a search of every yard, every lane, and every field in Ballyclarin. They had looked beneath every hedge and down every alley. They had spent the remaining daylight trying to find the missing I Believe costume.

Dogs barked and a cloud of crows wheeled into the air as they tramped through muddy pastures, peering behind stone walls. They had even sifted through household trash left out for the trash man. They had found not a thing.

"Would we know it if we saw it?" one weary fellow asked as the lights began to go on in the houses up and down the main street of the village. Smoke from chimney fires rose into the damp air.

"Sure enough," said Liam, although he was not at all sure. "It looks like a very long bedsheet."

"Next thing you know, the chief inspector will be having us search the beds," one fellow joked.

"Or the clotheslines. Maybe the murderer washed it and hung it on the line to dry."

Even Liam laughed.

"Very funny, lads." In the settling darkness, they had not seen Detective Inspector White approach the group. "You've had no luck then?"

"None, sir," Liam answered.

A soft rain had begun to cover them all. "Good work, lads," White said, although Liam wasn't sure what was good about a search that turned up nothing. "Time to go home for a hot supper and a good night's sleep."

"Yes, sir," the gardai answered in unison, then headed for their cars before he changed his mind.

After a quick hot shower, Liam decided to go to Rafferty's Rest for a pint and to have his supper. The food was decent, cheap, and fast—three qualities that Liam always looked for in a restaurant.

Besides, Carmel Cox had practically invited him to the dance there tonight. It was only right that he should go.

When the two Sisters arrived at the dining room of the Ballyclarin Hotel, it looked empty. In fact, Mary Helen began to wonder if it was open. Even the maître d' seemed surprised to see them. And the young man behind the bar looked as if he'd just stepped out of the shower.

"What is it?" Mary Helen asked, once they were seated in a comfortable booth by a window. "Where is everybody?"

"We're early," Eileen explained. "Nobody but a tourist eats this early in Ireland."

As if to prove her point, a party of Americans was the next to arrive, followed by a small group of Germans.

Eileen had been right about the salmon. It was delicious—the entire meal was. The rain began as they waited for their dessert. The dining room and bar were starting to fill.

A tall man in a dark rain slicker passed their table, his movements strong and sure, like the gait of a prowling cougar, Mary Helen thought. His straight black hair, wet with rain, was combed back and reached the collar of his jacket. Something about him was familiar. Where had she seen him before? The gala, was it, shouting at Owen Lynch?

"How ye keeping, Jake?" the barman called.

The man shrugged, shook his head, and straddled the bar stool.

Silently the barman pulled a pint and set it before him. "This will be good for what ails you," he said.

Mary Helen leaned toward Eileen. "That must be Jake, the tinker," she whispered.

It took Eileen several seconds to peek without appearing to be peeking. "I think so, too," she whispered finally. "I wonder if someone's told him that he tied for first prize with the Lynch twins?"

"From the look of him, I'd say somebody did." Mary Helen tried not to stare.

From nowhere their waiter appeared. "Sorry to keep you waiting, Sisters," he said with an apologetic smile. "But the crème brûlée is taking a little longer than the chef intended. While you are waiting, may I get you more coffee or, perhaps, some Baileys Irish Cream?"

"No, thank you," Eileen answered for both of them.

"Anything a'tall ye want?" The waiter gave a toothy grin and was preparing to leave.

"Anything?" Mary Helen asked.

The waiter paled a bit but nodded good-naturedly.

"Would you mind asking Mr. Jake to join us for a moment?" she asked.

The waiter seemed surprised, but not as surprised as Eileen. "What in the world . . . ?" she muttered, watching the waiter approach the bar.

"I'm very interested in purchasing one of his photographs to bring home as a little gift for the convent. I'm simply going to ask him if they are for sale and the price."

Much to Mary Helen's delight, Jake came right over. In fact, he looked almost happy to have been invited. Pint in hand, he smiled down at them.

"The Yanks I've been hearing about all day," he said without a bit of reticence.

Meeting his eyes, Mary Helen was struck by how enormous they were and how blue and sparkling, as if they were taking in everything. *The eyes of an artist,* she thought. *No wonder he can capture such detail in his photographs.*

Quickly she introduced Eileen and herself. "Will you join us for dessert, Mr. . . ." Suddenly she realized that she had no idea of the man's last name. All she'd ever heard was Jake, the tinker. Calling him Mr. Tinker would never do!

"Powers, Sister. My name is Jake Powers, but please, just call me Jake," he said, his brilliant blue eyes seeming to look right through her. "Everyone else does."

"Pleased to meet you, Jake," she said, feeling a little foolish. She probably should have found out where he lived and made an appointment with him.

"Won't you join us? Perhaps you'll have some dessert or a cup of coffee? Or another Guinness?"

Jake examined his nearly empty glass as though he were seeing it for the first time. Then he sat down in the booth next to Eileen. "That would be grand," he said, lifting his glass so the barman could see it. "A bird cannot fly on one wing alone."

That settled, he turned his enormous eyes on Mary Helen. "What is it you want, Sister, besides to buy me a pint?" Jake asked, a broad grin on his face. "To ask me if I murdered Willie Ward?"

The bluntness with which he blurted out the question startled Mary Helen.

"Why, no," she stammered.

He took a swallow of the dark liquid and looked at her sideways. "No?" he said with a hollow laugh. "Then, I guess, you'll be the only one for miles around who doesn't. You and the murderer, of course. But the rest of them! I'm a tinker, and for any crime committed you have no further to look than the nearest tinker. Besides I had a bit of a brawl with old Willie at the wine tasting."

Jake finished his Guinness and traded glasses with the barman, who had just arrived with another.

"Certainly, just because you argue with someone doesn't mean you kill him," Eileen added sensibly.

Jake spread his elbows wide on the table and stared into his glass. "You'd think, wouldn't you?" he said.

Sister Mary Helen was glad to see the waiter reappear with two small bowls of steaming crème brûlée. "What I do want to ask you about, Jake," she said, anxious to change the subject, "are your photographs."

Jake frowned, as though he had no idea what she was talking about.

"I was so impressed with your work at the art show in the old convent auditorium."

Jake lifted his head and studied her with glassy eyes.

"And I was wondering," she went on, "if any of them are for sale?"

Jake gave a sharp laugh. "They're all for sale," he said, "to those who're willing to pay the price."

Sister Mary Helen was almost afraid to ask the price. Apparently he was done talking. Draining his glass, he set it on the table, then stood and pulled a business card from his pocket. He placed it beside the glass.

"It's there you'll find me tomorrow. All afternoon," he said, pointing to the card. "We can chat." Without another word, he left the hotel dining room.

"I'm sure Paul will know where this is," Eileen said, reading the small card. "Speaking of whom, we had better hurry."

Mary Helen nodded. Quickly the two nuns finished their dessert. Mary Helen resisted the temptation to scrape the bowl.

One look at the whist game in progress at Rafferty's Rest and Sister Mary Helen knew there was no room for an amateur. Except for the slapping of the cards and a low mumble of players bidding, the room was eerily quiet.

Standing in the doorway, she recognized a number of faces, although she could not put a name on most of them. Many of the whist players were the same smartly dressed women who had been at the wine tasting.

Zoë O'Dea sat at a table with a view of the entire room. Her sharp dark eyes swept across it like prison searchlights taking in everything.

She smiled stiffly and waved one hand when she spotted Mary Helen and Eileen. Her partner turned to see whom she had acknowledged.

Sister Mary Helen was surprised that Zoë was playing with Patsy Lynch, although she wasn't really sure why. She didn't know either one of the women, but from the little she had seen, she never would have picked them for friends.

"Now, would you join us?" Owen Lynch's voice startled Mary Helen. For such a large man, he seemed to be able to appear without a sound.

"I think not," Mary Helen said, catching her breath, then turned toward Eileen. "How about you?" she asked.

Eileen, too, declined. Mary Helen had the strange feeling that Chairman Lynch was relieved. "They're a friendly enough lot," he said with a chuckle, "until it comes to whist. Then they take no prisoners."

The sound of a small band warming up lured the two nuns to the back room of Rafferty's where straight chairs lined the walls. At one end of the nearly empty room, a fiddler plucked a few notes while a man with a great mountain of white hair played a quick tune on his flute. A tall thin lad with a happy grin stood ready with his goatskin bodhran.

All three seemed to be following the lead of an an-

cient fellow with eyes at half mast. He was holding what
Mary Helen's old granny used to call a squeezebox.
Tapping his foot, he pulled open his instrument and at
the count of three, although only a few people were beginning to drift into the room, the band broke into a
lively reel.

"We wouldn't have lasted two minutes with the card
players," Eileen said as they settled into two chairs.
"They'd have eaten us alive."

"I hope there will be dancing." Mary Helen leaned
toward Eileen to make herself heard.

"Don't worry," Eileen assured her. "It's early yet.
They'll come along soon." And the two nuns clapped in
time with the music.

Eileen proved to be correct. The music seemed to
draw the crowd, and soon the dance floor was full of
men and women of all ages.

Quickly they formed small sets, their flying feet
moving to the rhythm. Mary Helen watched, fascinated,
as the dancers went through the intricate steps, twirling
and tapping, never missing a beat. To her amazement,
they never ran out of breath either. She was tired just
watching.

She noticed Oonagh Cox was on the floor with . . .
She strained to see. Could that be Owen Lynch with
her? For a large man, he could dance quite well. She
wondered why his wife had chosen whist.

And Paul Glynn and his redheaded missus were
twirling with the best of them. After he'd dropped the
nuns off he had said he was going to fetch her. He
hadn't wasted any time.

A laughing Carmel Cox was a partner with the young
red-faced garda. What was his name? Liam O'Dea?
Poor fellow looked terribly ill at ease. Despite his shy-
ness, he, too, could dance.

Tara, the Oyster Queen, was still wearing her emerald-green taffeta dress. *Surely, she must air it out,* Mary Helen thought. Tara looked exhausted as she took her place in the set.

When the musicians finally stopped for a break, Oonagh Cox nearly fell into the chair next to Sister Mary Helen. "There was a day, mind you, when I could go on all night," she said, pressing a clean handkerchief to her brow. "But, no more. I fear," she said with a wink, "that I'm getting old."

"You looked just fine to me," Mary Helen said, and she meant it.

"And your partner, Owen Lynch," Eileen added, "is a fine dancer, too."

Oonagh nodded. "And the shame of it is that his wife, Patsy, grand girl that she is, has two left feet," she said, which satisfied Mary Helen's curiosity as to why Mrs. Lynch had chosen whist.

"But his Patsy"—Oonagh stood and ran her fingers through her damp gray hair—"is brilliant when it comes to whist. She wins nearly every game she plays. So as the old saying goes, 'God shares the good things.' "

Mary Helen was thinking about that when the band started up again. "A slip jig," Oonagh said, hurrying out to the dance floor. "Ladies only."

Sister Mary Helen watched the women both young and old dancing with an energy and grace that amazed her.

"They lift themselves and leap like deer, don't they, now?" Father Keane said, sitting down on the empty chair next to Sister Eileen. "Are ye enjoying yourselves?" he asked, leaning forward so he could see them both.

"Indeed," Eileen said, and Mary Helen nodded. "Are you a dancer yourself, Father?" she asked.

"Not a'tall! You'll not find me anywhere near a dance floor," he said. "All I'd need is to choose one of the ladies in my parish as a partner and rumors would be flying like pillow feathers in the wind. They'd have it on every tongue. Besides," he added, "the bishop frowns on the priests dancing, and it's a perfect excuse for me."

"Then you're here for the whist?"

"No, not that either. Those whist players show no mercy even to the clergy," he said with a laugh. "Or should I say, especially to the clergy. No"—he lowered his voice—"I'm here because I'm expected to be. To tell you the God's honest truth, I'm home to bed as soon as possible."

"Father Keane," an older man called, "I'd like you to meet my brother. He's here on holiday."

"Happy to, Donal," the priest said. "On holiday from where?" His voice trailed off.

On the dance floor, a reel or two followed the slip jig, and finally the band broke into a waltz. The twirling couples, the music, the warmth in the room, and the full supper began to take their toll on Sister Mary Helen. Her eyes felt heavy. To be honest, she could scarcely keep them open. She glanced sideways at Eileen, who didn't seem to be having any problem at all.

"I think I need a breath of fresh air," Mary Helen said.

"What?" Eileen bent toward her, but the music made it difficult to hear.

"I'm going outside," she mouthed, "for a breath of air."

Eileen smiled and nodded but didn't seem eager to go along. "I'll be back in a few minutes," Mary Helen said.

The contrast between the warm back room of Rafferty's and the crisp night air nearly took her breath away. The wind slapped at her face and tore at the edge of her sweater. She shivered, yet it felt refreshing.

Overhead the sky was brilliant with stars. The wind must have blown the storm clouds out over the Atlantic and left the heavens sparkling. She pushed up her bifocals on the bridge of her nose and gazed at the beauty. The words of the ancient psalmist echoed in her mind. "You fix the number of the stars and give to each its name."

She was so enthralled that she nearly missed the smell of smoke, cigarette smoke. It was coming from somewhere close. Who else was out here? She edged toward the back door of Rafferty's. She didn't want to startle anyone.

Peeking around the corner of the building, she spotted what she thought was a couple—a tall man and a much shorter woman. In the darkness she saw the orange tip of a burning cigarette. The hand that held it seemed to be around the other person.

Despite the brightness of the stars it was difficult to make out what they were doing. If she had to venture a guess, she'd say that they were embracing.

Sister Mary Helen squinted into the darkness. She watched the burning cigarette tip drop to the ground as the man pulled the woman to him in what looked like a passionate kiss.

Oh, my, she thought, edging backward. Talk about being in the wrong place at the right time! Although considering how engrossed they were, she didn't think that they would even notice her.

Standing very still, she wondered exactly what she should do—slip back into the building, or make some noise so that they'd know she was there?

"We can't continue to do this," she heard the woman whisper. She sounded frantic. "I'm nearly beside myself with worry she'll find out. Then what?"

That voice! Mary Helen recognized it, although it took her several seconds to put a name to it. Oonagh Cox! But who was the large man she was with? It couldn't possibly be Owen Lynch, could it?

"To hell with it," the man muttered.

"Owen," she heard Oonagh say softly. "Get ahold on

yourself. You've got to go back inside. They're probably looking for you right now."

"Not to worry, love." Owen's voice was thick with emotion. "No one suspects. I'm sure of that."

"That's what you say, but we both know Willie Ward was onto us."

"Willie Ward!" Lynch gave a nasty laugh. "He'll not be bothering anybody ever again. God saw to that."

"Tell me you didn't play God's helper," Oonagh whispered.

Mary Helen's heart plummeted, and she felt a little queasy. Was she about to overhear a murder confession?

"Of course I didn't, much as I'd have liked to have. You know I didn't." Owen's words had the cold clink of ice. "But I am terribly grateful to whomever did."

The night air was beginning to chill Mary Helen to the bone. Were these two ever going to go back inside? She clenched her teeth so they wouldn't chatter from the cold. Just when she thought she could stand it no longer, she heard someone make a move. Was there another person out here? She peered into the darkness but saw nothing. It must have been one of them.

"You go first," Oonagh said very softly. "I'll follow."

Mary Helen stood still until she thought the coast was clear, but her mind was racing.

Oonagh Cox and Owen Lynch were having an affair! Could that be? They both seemed so upright, so proper. Not that upright and proper people are immune to emotions.

And Willie Ward. . . . Had Oonagh actually asked Owen if he had killed the man? That was an odd question for one lover to ask another. Mary Helen's teeth began to chatter uncontrollably. She needed to go inside. She needed to tell someone what she had just heard.

Back home in San Francisco, she would have given

Homicide Inspectors Kate Murphy and Dennis Gallagher a call. But here there was no Kate or Gallagher, and Detective Inspector White had made it clear that he didn't want her meddling in his business . . . quite clear! Yet she felt she should tell someone. But whom?

Without warning, the back door of Rafferty's Rest swung open, and a young man stepped out. He looked startled to see her.

Garda Liam O'Dea, perfect! Mary Helen thought. What was the old saying? "Chance is a nickname for Providence."

Liam O'Dea spun around with surprise. He hadn't expected to find anyone else standing outside. "Who's that?" he called, feeling his heart beating against his ribs.

"Sorry, I didn't mean to startle you," a voice said.

It had an American accent. Liam frowned. *Could it be one of those nuns from San Francisco?* he wondered. But what was she doing out here in the cold? "It's Sister, is it?" he asked.

"Yes." Sister Mary Helen's voice was low. "I just stepped out for some fresh air."

"I did myself," Liam admitted, sticking both hands in his trousers' pockets. "That Rafferty's can get as hot as the hinges of hell."

In the darkness he heard her chuckle. "Especially when you're dancing," she said. When Liam didn't comment, she went on. "Actually, I was just on my way to— of all things—find you," she said with a shiver.

"Find me?" Liam felt his face redden. Sure, what did she want with him?

"Is there someplace we can talk privately?" she asked.

Staring into the darkness, he wondered what place would be more private than this.

"Someplace a little warmer?" she said through chattering teeth.

Back inside Rafferty's, Liam miraculously found a quiet spot near a broom closet where he was almost sure no one would disturb them, for a few minutes anyway. "Does this suit you?" he asked.

Sister Mary Helen nodded and then got right to the point. "While I was out back, I overheard something that I think I should tell to someone in authority."

Liam's stomach knotted. Go on, now! Why him? He had only been a garda for six months. "Detective Inspector White," he said quickly. "He's the man in charge."

The old nun's eyes widened, and she studied him over the top of her spectacles that seemed to have slipped down her nose again.

"Under ordinary circumstance, I would, Liam—may I call you Liam?" she asked softly.

He nodded.

"But you were there," she continued. "You must have heard what the detective inspector said about my getting involved with his case." She paused, waiting for some reaction.

Liam felt the heat rise from his jawbone straight up to his scalp. Of course he'd heard. He wasn't a deaf man, was he? But should he have been listening?

"Well, if you didn't hear him," she said, clearly impatient to get on with her story, "the detective inspector made it quite clear that he wouldn't tolerate anyone who wasn't a garda interfering in his homicide case. Clearly, he meant Sister Eileen and me.

"But what I overheard out there"—she pointed toward the back lot of Rafferty's—"might be quite important, and"—she lowered her voice—"I would feel very guilty keeping it to myself."

Liam's mind was racing. Sure now, do I need this headache? he wondered, not quite sure how he should react. Not that it would make any difference. Clearly she was going to tell him whether he wanted to hear it or not.

And why shouldn't she tell him? After all, he was a garda, and he was assigned to the case. Yet, if the truth be told, it was his first murder case, which was not surprising. There weren't that many murders a year in the whole country. A man could be a garda his whole life and never be involved in solving one. But that was neither here nor there, was it?

"It seems to me," the nun was saying in that schoolteacher voice that most nuns have, "that this could be valuable information that your superior would be glad to hear."

Something Detective Inspector White would be glad to hear? Liam perked up. Hadn't he this very day been thinking that someday he'd like to become a detective inspector himself? What better way than to glean some information about the case and pass it on to the famed Ernie White, who would be grateful? "Fine work, lad," he could almost hear the man say. "Fine work, indeed."

Liam felt the nun's eyes on him. He threw back his shoulders and tried to look official. If only he had a notepad to write it all down. Not that he'd forget. Even at school he'd had a splendid memory. It just looked more professional with a notepad.

He cleared his throat, then said in the deep solemn voice that Father Keane used in the confessional, "What is it now, Sister, that you want to tell me?"

Without any further hesitation, Sister Mary Helen told him about stumbling on Mrs. Cox and Mr. Lynch and her suspicion that they were having an affair.

Liam's stomach cramped. Mrs. Cox, Carmel's

mother, and Owen Lynch, one of the area's most re-
spected businessmen! He felt numb and scarcely able to
believe his ears. He wished she'd stop, but, no, she had
more to say.

Liam's mind was whirling as she repeated the conversation that she had heard about Willie Ward's murder. "But he did say 'no,' he hadn't killed Willie, didn't
he?" he asked when he could finally catch his breath.

"Yes, he did," Sister said, "and I hope he was telling
the truth. But the very fact that she asked . . ." The old
nun paused and studied his face, obviously waiting for a
reaction.

Liam wanted to put his hands over his ears and run,
but he knew he couldn't do that. "Thank you, Sister. I'll
see to it," he said, hoping he sounded as if he had everything under control.

"You'll see to it?" Mary Helen repeated, as if she expected him to lay out his plan.

Well, first off, he didn't have one. And if he had, he'd
keep it to himself. "Tell one person and next it will be on
every tongue," Liam's da often said, and he was right.

"Very well, then," Sister Mary Helen said finally. She
looked a little bit disappointed, but that couldn't be
helped. It was all the garda could do to contain himself.

"Thank you, Liam. I feel a great deal better." She
smiled, and Liam forced himself to smile in return.
That's all well and good, he thought, *that you feel better,
but, sure, I feel like someone has filled my pockets with
stones.*

Liam O'Dea's head was swimming as he watched
the old nun move off to the hall where the music had
started up again. Eyes closed, he leaned against the
broom closet door. Maybe he was hallucinating and
this would all go away!

Carmel's mother, the doctor's wife, having an affair

with the garage owner. It was preposterous! No one would believe him if he did tell them. And if Carmel heard, she'd never forgive him for saying such things about her mam. And her brothers! Liam didn't even want to think about what they'd do if they heard a word.

Yet, he had a duty. He had some information that might prove useful to solving a serious crime.

Yerra, he felt the perspiration under his arms run down his sides. He better keep his gob shut. Maybe look around on his own, be sure of his facts when he did present them to Detective Inspector White. That would be the safest thing to do. On the other hand, maybe the best thing to do was to tell him straightaway.

"Oh, there you are," Carmel called, bouncing up to him. "I've been looking all over for you and I'm nearly hoarse from calling your name." Reaching out, she put her hand on his forearm, and Liam felt a shock rush all the way to his toes.

"Come, dance with me," Carmel begged, her bright eyes teasing, "before someone else asks me. You know you'd hate that."

Liam allowed himself to be led onto the dance floor.

"Is something bothering you?" she said, lightly touching his shoulder.

"No. Nothing," Liam lied. But after a few steps with Carmel's supple body pressing against his, Willie Ward's murder and his duty to help solve it seemed far, far away.

"Oh, you're back," Sister Eileen said when Mary Helen slipped into the empty chair next to her in the hall. "I was beginning to get worried."

"What time is it?" Stifling a yawn, Mary Helen glanced down at her wristwatch. It was nearly midnight, and Rafferty's Rest was still packed with people, young and old.

"You can't even count on the old people to go home early," she whispered.

Eileen's gray eyebrows shot up. "What? And miss something?"

Just when Mary Helen thought that she could not sit upright another minute, Paul Glynn, their driver, appeared with his wife on his arm.

"We've a babysitter," he said, "so I have to take the wife home. Shall I come back for you or are you ready to go?"

"Ready!" Eileen said, even faster than Mary Helen could.

Once inside their mews, the two old nuns changed quickly into their nightgowns, bathrobes, and slippers.

"Where were you for so long tonight?" Eileen asked, handing Mary Helen a cup of steaming hot cocoa. "To help you sleep," she said, as though either of them needed any help.

"You won't believe it." Mary Helen took a cautious sip of the foaming drink.

"Try me."

"Well, you remember I went outside for a breath of fresh air?"

Eileen nodded.

"And apparently I wasn't the only one with that idea. There was a couple out there in the dark, kissing, I think."

"Oh?" Eileen blew on her cup of hot cocoa.

"You'll never guess who!" Quickly she told her friend about Oonagh Cox and Owen Lynch and what she had overheard.

For once Eileen was speechless.

"Just when I was wondering what to do with the information, who should come outside but that young garda, Liam O'Dea."

"You do remember what Detective Inspector White said about getting involved?"

"Of course I remember," Mary Helen answered, a bit testily. "How could I forget? And that is why, when I saw Liam O'Dea, I decided to put the whole thing in his hands."

"Good for you." Eileen collected both empty cups, putting them in the sink to soak. "And what did he say?"

"Not much," Mary Helen admitted, "just that he'd take care of it."

"Splendid." Eileen yawned. "And you'll let him, right?"

"Right," Mary Helen said. "I couldn't help what I overheard," she said a little defensively, "but now the whole thing is out of my hands." She brushed her palms together to make her point. "I want nothing more to do with it."

And when she said it, she truly meant it.

Tuesday, September 2

May your glass be ever full,
May you always have a roof over your head,
And may you be in heaven
Half an hour before the devil knows you're dead.
—Irish blessing

A sharp rap at the front door of the mews woke Sister Mary Helen.

"I'm here to hoover," a woman's voice called cheerfully. "Are ye up yet, love?"

"Yes, indeed," she heard Eileen answer. "One minute, please. We'll be right there."

Abruptly Mary Helen's bedroom door flew open, and Eileen whispered, "It's Tuesday. The cleaning lady is here."

"Cleaning lady?" Mary Helen mumbled. "We haven't been here long enough to get anything dirty."

Still fuzzy with sleep, she dressed quickly and walked into the front parlor just as a woman who introduced herself as Judy, the cleaning lady, turned on the vacuum.

"Don't bother with the beds," she called above the hum, "I'll change the linens, and mind you, take a sweater."

Fortunately, Eileen had been able to rescue two cups of coffee and two scones from the kitchen and was settled on a bench just outside the mews. Despite the fact that the sun was out and the morning sky was colored with streaks of ripe apricot, there was a nip in the air. Mary Helen was glad she'd heeded Judy's advice and brought her sweater.

Clouds were already forming billowy white hills along the horizon. The soft *churr*ing of a wren in the ivy, the scratchy song of a brown dunnock, the hum of the hoover, and the rumble of a lorry on the main road were the only sounds in the yard.

The two nuns sat in companionable silence, sipping their coffee, each lost in her own thoughts, when Paul Glynn came round the corner. "Ah, there ye be," he said with a wide grin. "And what's on the schedule for today?"

Mary Helen had no idea and was glad when Paul produced the bright yellow Oyster Festival brochure.

"Tuesday," he read. "Guinness Country Golf Classic." He looked at them inquisitively. "Are either of ye golfers?"

"Lord, no!" Eileen said.

"Where is it being played?" Mary Helen asked. She didn't remember seeing a golf course in the area.

"At Athenry Golf Club," Paul said. "It is located midway between Athenry and Oranmore."

All that Mary Helen remembered hearing about Athenry was the famous ballad "The Fields of Athenry."

Eileen seemed to know a little more. "It's a medieval town," she said, "the only walled town in Ireland where some of the walls are still intact."

"Then, it might be worth our while to go even if we don't play golf," Mary Helen said, and Eileen agreed.

That settled, they made arrangements for Paul to pick them up after the morning Mass.

• • •

With Paul at the wheel they seemed to fly along the carriageway through rich farming country. *These must be the famous fields of Athenry,* Mary Helen thought, but she didn't dare ask. She didn't want to take their driver's attention from the road, not even for a second.

Before long they spotted the still-intact walls. "Here we are," Paul said, pulling into the nearest car park to let them out. "You go on ahead," he said, "I've some business and I'll catch you up."

"Business, indeed," Eileen said, watching the man hurry away toward the nearest pub. "That reminds me of an old joke," she said. "The justice asks the defendant, 'Were you intoxicated?' 'That's my business,' the defendant answers. Then the justice asks, 'And, ould son, have you any other business?' "

Strolling in a leisurely manner through the small town, the two nuns thoroughly enjoyed exploring the ruins of the castle, the Dominican priory, and an ancient arch, which had been one of the gateways to the town.

They stopped for a bite to eat at a cozy sandwich shop in the town center and were about to buy some homemade berry jam when Paul caught up with them.

"Shall we drive over to the golf course?" he asked. "See if we can find who's winning? It's said to be the most challenging and scenic course in all of Ireland," he added proudly.

After a few minutes' ride, Paul pulled the hackney into a crowded car park near the clubhouse. Set against a backdrop of beech and pine trees, the course lived up to its reputation for beauty, anyway.

"Look who's here." Paul pointed to a large-boned woman leaving the clubhouse.

"It's Patsy Lynch, and a grand player she is, too," Paul remarked, clearly in admiration of her skill. "She's a good, clean stroke."

Watching Patsy start across the lot, Mary Helen felt a twinge of sadness. *That poor woman has no idea what her husband's up to,* she thought, feeling strangely guilty that she did. *Should I be the one to tell her?* she wondered, although of course, it was the last thing in the world she intended to do. There was a lot to be said about knowing when to mind your own business.

Yet it didn't seem fair. Patsy was a pleasant enough–looking woman in an outdoorsy sort of way, with a long face and her thick gray hair pulled back and fastened with a tortoiseshell clip. Clearly she was no match physically for the beautiful Oonagh Cox.

"Shall I let you two out?" Paul asked, turning in his seat.

All at once, as if to answer his question, large drops of rain hit the windshield.

"No," Eileen and she said in unison.

"Where to, then?" Paul asked.

"What about visiting Jake?" Eileen said. "Didn't you want to see his photographs?"

"Jake, the tinker?" Paul seemed to be struggling to keep from laughing.

"Yes," Mary Helen said. "Is there any reason we shouldn't?"

"None a'tall." Paul turned the key in the ignition, and the hackney roared into action. "I was just wondering how long it would take your visit to get on the wire."

Mary Helen must have looked puzzled.

"You've heard the saying, have you? 'Tell it to Mary in a whisper and Mary will tell it to the whole parish.' Well, Sister, we've a lot of Marys in this village."

◆ ◆ ◆

Garda Liam O'Dea caught a glimpse of Paul Glynn's hackney passing the Monks' Table. The two American nuns were on board, sitting just as proper as you please in the backseat.

What are they up to now? he wondered, watching the car turn down a lane. Could they be on their way to Jake Powers's studio? It was off that lane, but so were dozens of other homes.

"Garda, can you give me a minute?" One of the men from the Dublin Technical Bureau interrupted his thoughts, and it was just as well.

Those two nuns had been on his mind all morning. If the truth be told, they had been on his mind all last night as well. Ever since that one with the slippy spectacles had dropped her bomb about Carmel's mother and Owen Lynch.

He had tossed and turned most of the night, unable, at first, to fall off to sleep. When he did, he had dreamed about those two old gals looking on as Carmel's brothers chased him, threatening to break his head if he dared to say a word.

Detective Inspector Ernie White's brown eyes pinned him like a specimen to a tack card, insisting that he tell all he knew. The beautiful Carmel, her bright blue eyes pleading with him, faded in and out, while Auntie Zoë and her scissor lips clipped away at him.

In the distance, his death bell rang out. He struggled to get away from the sound, which fortunately turned out to be only his cell phone playing a tune.

Detective Inspector Brian Reedy was on the horn to remind him that the forensic team from Dublin would be at the Monks' Table early. As if he could forget!

For several minutes, Liam stared into the bathroom

mirror. The face that stared back at him was the color of pale cheese, and there were small dark circles under both of his eyes.

Squinting, he spotted a few gray hairs sprouting from his thick sandy mop. He could swear that they had not been there when he went to bed. Dread slid down his back like a chill. He had to tell White, and the sooner the better. Even if he wanted to, he couldn't keep what he knew to himself.

Liam pulled up in front of the Monks' Table about the same time the team from Dublin arrived. After shaking hands all around, they went to work immediately.

"These lads are all business," Reedy said, raising his eyebrows at Liam. "The Monks' Table should be able to reopen by this evening or tomorrow at the latest."

The publican, Hugh Ryan, standing not too far away, looked anxious. "But will anyone come?" he asked. "Might they be afraid, with a murderer on the loose?"

"Not to worry, Hugh, me boyo," Reedy assured him. "We'll have the murderer caught soon, as well."

Liam felt his mouth twitch with tension. His cheeks burned as he visualized Oonagh Cox being led away in chains.

Inside the pub, cold and damp from being closed, cameras flashed while men and women dusted and searched and generally went about the complicated business of trying to uncover clues.

All the while, Liam watched with a pain in his stomach, knowing full well that he might be sitting on the biggest clue of all.

For the next few hours, everyone including the two detective inspectors was so caught up in what was going on that there seemed no time for a decent chat. Each time Liam thought he could buttonhole Detective Inspector White, someone or something interrupted him.

Finally the technical bureau began to wind down. Carefully they packed up everything and readied to leave.

"We'll have the results to you very soon, indeed," the man in charge said. Then, making a U-turn on the main street, the team departed for Dublin. With a sinking feeling, Liam watched them go.

Inside the pub looked almost deserted with just the two detectives, a few of the local gardai, Hugh Ryan, and himself. A wind off the Atlantic caught the end of the tape that had cordoned off the murder scene and slapped it against the building.

"Will one of you lads take that bloody tape down?" White shouted.

Which is not a bit like him, Liam thought, frozen in his spot while the others rushed to the door.

"It hardly takes four men to take down a tape, now does it?" White asked, giving Reedy a desperate look.

"You most likely scared them to death with your bellowing," Reedy said. "What seems to be bothering you, Ernie? What's happened?"

White ran his fingers through his dark hair and perched himself on a bar stool. He looked exhausted. *Maybe he isn't sleeping too well either,* Liam thought.

"Would you believe that I got a message from the commissioner himself? He heard complaints from some of the locals that this murder has put a damper on their bloody Oyster Festival. To hear him tell it, you'd think we murdered the poor blighter ourselves." He stared at the ceiling. "We are missing something, Brian," he said at last. "For one thing, that costume couldn't have just disappeared. We need to start over. Requestion everyone. Someone saw something or heard something. Maybe they'll remember it now. Maybe there was something they forgot to mention. That happens."

Liam's shirt collar squeezed his neck until he could scarcely catch his breath.

White checked his wristwatch. "It's time to go home, lads," he said to the gardai who had just reentered the pub. "All ye get a decent night's rest. We'll start fresh tomorrow."

The place emptied. "Before he changes his mind," one wag said aloud.

His mouth dry, Liam lagged behind the rest, waiting for just the right moment to inform his superior about what the old nun had told him.

"What is it, Liam?" White eyed him. "Don't tell me you don't want to go. I hear they are having a lovely barbeque tonight."

"Sir." Liam cleared his throat. Now was no time to lose his voice or, heaven help him, stutter. Avoiding his superior's eyes he said, "May I have a word?"

"You can have a dozen words, son," White said, "if they will help solve this case."

All at once a vision of tiny Oonagh Cox behind bars in a cold prison cell flooded Liam's mind. His stomach cramped. What if the American nun was wrong about what she had heard? Wouldn't it be the better thing for him to check on it himself?

And then there was Owen Lynch, the chairman of the Oyster Festival. If the locals were complaining now about a damper on their festival, how would the arrest of their chairman set? Liam bit his lip, wondering what he should do.

A ragged ring of a cell phone broke the flat silence. "What now?" White grumbled, digging in the pocket of his rumpled jacket. "Will they give a man no peace? White, here," he barked into the phone.

When Liam dared to look up, White's face was crimson. Liam feared for a minute that he was having a stroke. What do you do when someone is having a stroke? Frantically he searched his memory. All that came to him was to call an ambulance, which was probably the best thing he could do anyway.

"Bad news?" Reedy asked when White snapped the phone shut.

White shook his head. "Not really, Brian, but not good news either. It seems as if the knife that killed our Willie was a common kitchen knife. It could have come out of anyone's kitchen drawer."

Liam felt his face flush. *Even the Coxes',* he thought.

"Sorry, Liam. You wanted a word?" White said, but his mind seemed far away.

"Sir." Liam could hear his voice quivering. "It's nothing really. It can wait."

"He probably wants a day off," Reedy joked.

"There'll be no days off until this is solved." White wagged his head as though he were dog-tired.

"I need a cuppa tea," he said to Hugh Ryan, who hadn't moved from behind the bar all day.

"A drop of anything stronger?" Ryan asked.

"Not yet. I still have some work to do. Garda." He turned to Liam, who was trying to look invisible and hoping to slip away unnoticed.

"Will you tell those two Americans that I'd like a word?"

Quickly Liam told his superior that earlier he'd seen their car go down the lane.

"You don't miss much, do you, lad?" White's dark eyes focused on him.

Not knowing what to reply, Liam tried not to squirm.

"The moment you spot Paul Glynn's automobile, stop him and tell him to take those two nuns home. Then, let me know and I'll meet them there."

"Yes, sir," Liam said smartly.

"What are you thinking, Ernie?" Reedy asked.

"As I said, I think I'd be wise to question everyone again. I'll start with the American Sister first. She did find the body, didn't she? Maybe she'll remember something she forgot to mention the first time around. Then, I need to question anyone else who came in contact with the victim that day."

"That's a lot of folks," Reedy said, and then he laughed. "I've a marvelous grasp of the obvious," he said.

White didn't seem to hear his partner. "Somebody must know something," White said. "In a village this size, it's hard, near impossible, to keep a secret. Let's hope, this time around, we'll stumble onto something."

The blood pounded in Liam's ears and he felt his face grow hot. *Somebody knows a secret, all right,* he thought, *and sooner or later it's got to come out.* Oh, how he wished he'd never gone to Rafferty's Rest at all.

Sister Mary Helen was a little surprised when Paul pulled up near a brightly painted wooden caravan, the horse-drawn kind that is featured in all the tourist souvenir shops.

"Surely Jake doesn't live here," she said, knocking on the side of the flower-painted wagon. All she heard was a hollow sound.

"No, indeed." Paul pointed to a small modern house with large picture windows built just behind it. "As it happens," he said, "Jake lives there. The caravan is just for show. I doubt if he could even move the thing.

"Shall I wait for you here?" Paul asked, making no effort to get out of his car.

"We shouldn't be long," Mary Helen assured him,

but their driver had already leaned back in his seat and closed his eyes.

Making their way around the caravan, the two nuns approached the front door. They were about to knock when it swung open and Jake stood in the threshold. With his hair uncombed, the stubble of a beard on his chin, and rumpled clothes, he looked for all the world as if he had just rolled out of bed. Yet his blue eyes shone brightly, too brightly, almost as if he had a fever.

"So, you did come," he said in a near growl. "I thought for certain that you'd be afraid to come to the house of a murderer."

Narrowing his eyes, he peered out at Paul. "I see you've brought along a bodyguard. Lot of good he'll do you fast asleep."

Mary Helen frowned. What on earth had gotten into the man? She thought they had made it abundantly clear at the hotel last night that they had no reason to think he was the murderer.

"So, do you want to come in or don't you?"

"We do," she managed to say.

"So you're not afraid?"

"Not at all," Mary Helen said.

"Not afraid of the man who might have killed Willie Ward?"

Mary Helen shook her head. The poor fellow didn't seem to be able to get off the subject.

"Well, are you coming in or aren't you?" he nearly shouted.

"If we are disturbing you," Eileen put in quickly, "we can come back another time. Maybe we should call before we come."

"Not a'tall," Jake said, and his anger seemed to melt as suddenly as it had come. He stepped back to let them in. "What time is it?" He glanced at an ornate grandfather clock against the wall in his front parlor. "Half three. I've been up all night working in my darkroom. I just realized I was hungry. You'll have a cup of tea? Or maybe something a little stronger? And a bite to eat?"

"Please don't go to any trouble for us," Eileen said. "We won't be staying long. As we told you last night, my friend is interested in your photographs."

"The tea is brewing and I've something already on a plate. Come in and sit."

Obediently the two nuns sat on the sofa he pointed out in the parlor.

"Well, if you're having something yourself," Eileen said.

"Indeed." Jake left the room and quickly reappeared with a tray containing a pot of tea, cups, cream and sugar, and plates of small sandwiches and assorted cookies.

"I've a woman who does for me," he said, setting the tray on a low coffee table next to a burning candle. The fresh woodsy scent filled the small room.

"She does for you quite well," Mary Helen said, biting into a delicious salad sandwich.

"As well she might," Jake said. "I pay her a king's ransom just to come in."

Mary Helen stiffened. His voice was becoming strident again.

"God knows what she'll ask for now that I'm not only a tinker, but a suspected murderer." His eyes were blazing now as they locked on the two nuns. He stared at them as if he expected them to cower.

Mary Helen felt her cheeks grow warm as her own temper rose. Who did this man think he was, anyway? It would take more than a stare and a few hot words to cow her. If he wanted to talk about murder, she'd talk. "What exactly were you angry with Willie Ward about?" she asked bluntly.

For a moment, Jake looked as if he had been punched in the stomach, then a small laugh rattled out of him and soon became a roar. "You are a cheeky one, you are," he said finally, wiping his eyes.

"Be that as it may," Mary Helen said, still a bit piqued. "It doesn't answer the question."

For a few seconds, Jake seemed to be mulling over his answer. "I was not only angry, I was furious when he printed that I was one of the travelers involved in the brawl at the Monks' Table, with no proof and no consequences for his libelous statements." His eyes were blazing now, and his nostrils flared. "He was a maggot. He deserved to die. And I say, God bless the man who killed him!" The small parlor rang with his rage.

Mary Helen's mouth went dry, but she had another question. She figured she might as well ask it. She might not get another chance.

"And at the gala?" she said. "What were you and the chairman arguing about?"

Jake seemed distracted. He rubbed his eyes. "That was a cruel blow, even for Willie," he said.

Mary Helen was startled by the sadness in his voice.

"Not enough that he tried to ruin my good name, but word had it that he stuffed the ballot box. I tried to tell Owen, but he'd hear none of it. Willie must have had a hold on Owen."

Quite a hold, Mary Helen thought, her heart racing.

"I don't know why, but it rankled him that I won every year. So this year, there were two winners." He shrugged.

An awkward silence filled the parlor. They had eaten everything on the two plates and drunk all the tea. Suddenly the grandfather clock chimed a melodious four.

"Now, about my photographs," Jake said. "You said

you were interested in bringing one home to America as a gift?"

"Yes," Mary Helen said. "I know the Sisters I live with at the convent would really love having one of your beautiful photos."

Jake seemed lost in another world. "Let me think about it," he said. "When do you leave?"

"Not until Friday," Mary Helen said.

"And this is Tuesday?" Jake asked, as if he truly did not know.

Eileen and she nodded.

"I'll contact you," he said, and they were clearly dismissed.

"That man is as odd as two left shoes," Eileen whispered on their way to the waiting car. "But surely someone who can capture such beauty can hardly be a murderer, can he?"

"You wouldn't think so," Mary Helen said, "but unfortunately one does not necessarily rule out the other."

As Paul drove the two nuns back into the village, Sister Mary Helen was surprised to see Garda Liam O'Dea standing by the side of the road. He looked as if he was waiting for someone.

She was even more surprised when he stepped into the cobblestone street, waving wildly for them to stop.

"What is it, Liam?" Paul asked, rolling down the window.

"It's the American nuns," Liam said, sticking his head into the cab.

The poor fellow looks as if he's been up all night, Mary Helen thought, wondering if he had passed on her discovery to his superior and what the detective's reaction had been. She knew he'd warned her to stay out of his business, but it was only natural to be curious. Anyone should understand that.

"Sisters"—he looked directly at Sister Mary Helen—"Detective Inspector White would like to meet you in your mews," Liam announced.

He was all business, and Mary Helen hesitated to ask him any questions.

"Has something else happened?" Eileen obviously did not share the same hesitation. "You look like death warmed over."

Liam stiffened. "I am not at liberty to speak for Detective Inspector White," he said.

"Besides, he probably doesn't know," Paul mumbled, rolling up his window.

Having sent the driver home, the two nuns sat in the living room of the mews, waiting. An anxious-looking Liam had followed them.

"What is it, Liam?" Mary Helen asked. "Did you tell the inspector what I overheard?"

Liam stiffened. "No," he said.

"No?" Mary Helen couldn't believe her ears. "May I ask, why not?"

Liam hesitated for a long minute, as if he were gathering up his courage. "Suppose you were mistaken about what you heard," he said finally. "I'd never forgive myself if . . . if . . . if."

Was he stuttering? Mary Helen tried not to show her annoyance. "I see," she said. "And just when do you intend to tell him? You know I can't. He made that quite clear." Was she mistaken, or did the young garda look relieved?

"We'll talk later," Liam said nervously. "Are you going to tonight's barbeque?"

Mary Helen glanced over at Eileen. "That sounds like fun," her friend said.

"I'll see you there, then," Liam said. "Now, I need to tell Detective Inspector White that you've arrived. You'll not have to wait for him long."

White was as good as Liam's word, and in just about five minutes they heard a knock on the mews' door.

"Come in, Detective Inspector," Mary Helen called politely.

As soon as he was comfortably seated, Eileen offered him a cup of tea, which he refused. Mary Helen was glad. She'd drunk so much tea today that she felt as though her back teeth might be floating.

"What can we do for you, Detective Inspector?" she asked.

"I hate to trouble you," White said, "but I wonder if you two would tell me, once more, about finding the fellow from Dublin in the field." Then he focused on Sister Mary Helen. "And then about your discovery of Willie Ward in the ladies'?"

Mary Helen sighed and took a deep breath. "I don't know what more I can tell you," she said. *About that, anyway,* she thought. "But I'll be happy to repeat it if it might help."

The clean fresh scent of aftershave alerted her that Detective Inspector Brian Reedy had slipped into the room. He joined White on the couch.

With Eileen chiming in here and there, Mary Helen repeated the story of discovering the near-naked Tommy Burns, stumbling on Father Keane, and finally notifying Owen Lynch. It was basically unchanged.

"What was the parish priest doing in the field?" White asked.

"You'll have to ask him," Mary Helen replied. Then, trying not to visualize the scene in the toilet stall, she retold how she had come upon Willie Ward.

When she had finished, all Detective Inspector White said was, "Thank you, Sister."

The moment she had closed the front door on the two inspectors, Eileen turned, narrowed her eyes, and put her hands on her hips. "Why didn't you tell him about overhearing Oonagh Cox and Owen Lynch?"

"For the very reason I told the young garda instead. Detective Inspector White gave me strict orders to stay out of his case."

"Since when has that ever stopped you?" Eileen asked.

"Besides," Mary Helen said, ignoring the question, "I want to talk to that young garda first at the barbeque tonight and find out when he intends to inform his superior."

"Barbeque!" Eileen reached for the Oyster Festival brochure. "It begins at nine p.m.," she read. "At the Court Hotel. *Craic,* it says—that means 'lots of fun'— with live music. Shall I give Paul a jingle and ask him to pick us up?"

"Nine o'clock!" Mary Helen adjusted her bifocals on the bridge of her nose. "If you think we'll still be awake at nine o'clock."

"We will if we take a nap now," Eileen said, holding the receiver. "Do you feel like taking a little snooze?"

With a yawn, Mary Helen nodded her head. There were some answers she didn't have to think about twice.

The sound of music and the smell of barbeque greeted Sister Mary Helen and Sister Eileen as Paul Glynn's hackney rolled into the circular driveway of the Court Hotel.

Dropping them off, Paul left to pick up his wife, who,

if he was to be believed, never was ready on time for anything. The two nuns joined the crowd milling around the entrance.

"Welcome, Sisters," Father Keane called out. The priest's gray curly head rose above the crowd standing in the ornate lobby. He was shaking hands and greeting his parishioners by name.

Mary Helen was impressed. He seemed to know everyone—and enough about him or her to carry on some sort of a conversation.

As Eileen returned his greeting, Mary Helen caught herself wondering what more, if anything, he did know.

"Tonight's dinner might remind you of home," Father Keane interrupted her speculation. "Don't you have lots of barbeques out west?" he asked.

Mary Helen smiled, thinking of the last barbeque the nuns had in San Francisco. With dripping fog rolling in from the Golden Gate and the drone of foghorns in the distance, anyone with an ounce of sense brought their meal indoors.

"Yes, indeed," she said. There was no reason to dispel his illusion.

"Ah, Sisters, welcome to the Oyster Festival Barbeque." Owen Lynch, a frozen smile on his drawn face, ushered them into a large room that had no trouble serving as a ballroom. A bar was set up against one wall, with creamy pints of Guinness and lager waiting to be drunk. Against another wall, barbequed seafood, grilled tomatoes, butter, soda bread, jam, clam chowder, oysters, and an array of desserts filled a table. The ever-present tea occupied a place of honor at the table's end.

"Help yourself," the chairman said. "More hot barbeque will be off the grill in a few minutes."

"Thank you," Mary Helen said, fighting down the

urge to ask him how he could betray his lovely wife. She deliberately avoided looking at the man, afraid that the expression on her face might give away what she'd overheard.

The large room was filling quickly. A dance floor had been set up in one corner, and the band was beginning to play something that sounded very much like Glenn Miller's "In the Mood."

Couples filled the wooden floor. Most were content to do the fox-trot. Despite the crowd, there were a few brave souls who attempted to jitterbug.

Sister Mary Helen scanned the room wondering when, if ever, she would have the chance to talk to Garda O'Dea. She saw that Carmel had arrived, looking lovely, as usual, in a filmy lavender dress of the softest toile. But there was no Liam. Had something come up? Had he decided, maybe, to tell Detective Inspector White tonight about what she'd overheard and not wait until tomorrow?

She was so deep in her own stewing juice that she didn't hear the young man come up behind her. In fact, when he said her name, she jumped, and for several seconds her heart beat like a jackhammer.

"If I had a heart, I'd be dead," she managed to say, finally. But Liam had no time for humor.

"Follow me into the lobby," he whispered. "I'll meet you by the hotel telephone"—he checked his wristwatch—"in five minutes."

Five minutes later, having explained to Eileen where she was going, Mary Helen came face-to-red-ruddy-face with Liam O'Dea. He smelled of sporty after-shave lotion, which was possibly why his face was fire-engine red.

"Why didn't you say anything to Detective Inspector White?" Mary Helen asked, before she'd even said "How do?"

Liam coughed and sputtered and sounded, for a moment, as though he might choke. Finally, with his eyes glued on the toes of his shoes, he stammered, "I feared you might be mistaken."

"Most likely you were afraid I was not mistaken," she said, trying to keep at least a civil tone. After all, this surely was his first murder case. "Besides," she said reasonably, "all you had to do was tell the detective inspector and leave it to him to investigate."

Mary Helen watched the red spread up Liam's neck and onto his clenched jaw. He ran one finger around his shirt collar. "When I finally came to that myself, it was too late. He would have murdered me with his bare hands for keeping the information from him all day, like that."

"Excuse me," a thick voice interrupted, "but if you're not going to use the telephone, may I?"

"Sorry," Mary Helen said to the tall man who obviously had an important call to make.

She watched Liam's blue eyes search the smoky room, most likely looking for a safe place to talk. When he didn't find one inside, he muttered, "Will I meet you outside then?"

"Good idea," Mary Helen said. Making sure that Liam was behind her, she threaded her way through the crowd until she reached the side exit. A strong push on the door, and they stepped out into the dark.

A cup of heavy clouds covered the sky, blotting out any stars that might have appeared. And a shrieking wind tore around the corner of the hotel.

This is going to be a very quick conversation, Mary Helen thought, shivering. "Let me get this straight," she said. "First you weren't sure I was right, and then, by the time you figured I might be, you'd kept it too long. Does that about sum it up?" she asked with a touch of starch.

"Yes, Sister," Liam answered softly.

"And, now what?" she asked, trying to keep her teeth from chattering.

"I'll tell Detective Inspector White what you over-heard first I see him tomorrow."

"Good enough," Mary Helen said, although she wasn't so sure it was. Not that she could really do any-thing about it.

Turning on her heel, she hurried into the warmth of the Court Hotel. If anything, the crowd had grown.

"Over here, old dear." She was glad to hear Eileen's voice and to see that her friend had fixed her a wonder-ful plate of barbeque.

"You only need two eyes to see that you two are enjoy-ing yourselves." It was Patsy Lynch. "May I join you?"

"Certainly," Eileen said, making room at the table to accommodate the chairman's wife. "This is a lovely party," she said, once the woman was seated.

Patsy sighed, and Mary Helen noticed deep, dark cir-cles under her eyes. Absentmindedly, Patsy pushed her thick gray hair back over her ears. Mary Helen caught the faint scent of perfume that she must have dabbed on her wrists.

"I'll be very glad when the whole thing is over," Patsy said, playing with an oyster on her plate. "Poor Owen's run ragged." She looked up.

Poor Owen, nothing, Mary Helen thought, scarcely able to meet the woman's gaze. How much, if anything, did she know about her husband's affair?

"Run ragged," Patsy repeated, shaking her head. "Out until all hours almost every night, and the calls never stop. Some one of these days I'd like to crush that

little phone with a rock until not a beep comes from it."
She almost seemed as if she were talking to herself.
"His daughters rarely see their father anymore." She bit
into a slice of soda bread and chewed noisily.

Can she really be that naïve? Mary Helen's thoughts
crept in like a chill. *This is such a small village. Surely
someone must have noticed something.*

"How did you do at the golf tournament?" Eileen was
asking.

Patsy seemed to perk up before their very eyes, like a
plant that had been watered. Her whole demeanor
changed.

"It was brilliant," she said with a triumphant smile.

"You won, then, I take it," Eileen said.

Patsy nodded, her eyes enormous now. "I can't wait
to tell Owen. He'll be so proud."

Mary Helen said nothing, but she felt as if her heart
had just turned over and sunk.

"And now"—it was Owen Lynch's voice booming
from the microphone—"we have a special treat for you
tonight. All the way from Dublin . . . Danny Short."

A roar went up from the crowd. "Who?" Mary Helen
bent toward Patsy and asked.

"Danny Short, a comedian," Patsy said. "Although
he's not nearly as funny as he thinks he is."

Short, who was, in fact, rather tall, grabbed the mike
and wasted no time getting started. "Ole Pat Clancy
rushes into the church, enters the confessional, and
confesses his sins. When he's finished the priest says
nothing.

" 'Father?' he whispers, but he gets no answer.

"After a few minutes, he leaves his side of the box
and goes to the other side.

" 'Do you know where Father went?' he asks the penitent kneeling there.

" 'Can't say as I do,' the fellow answers, 'but if he heard what I just heard, he's surely gone for the garda.' "

A drum roll and a roar of laughter followed Short's joke. Mary Helen glanced around, wondering what Father Keane must be thinking.

A few minutes of Short from Dublin were enough, even for Sister Mary Helen. She was glad when the band began to play again.

"Patsy." It was Owen Lynch, standing at the end of the table. "There you are. I was wondering where you'd gone to."

His wife rose immediately at the sound of his voice. "Yes, love?" she asked.

"Shall we try this dance?" he said. "It's a slow one."

Blushing like a schoolgirl, Patsy let herself be led away. Mary Helen watched them rather awkwardly disappear into the crowd, unable to shake the sympathy she felt for Patsy Lynch. She was so obviously in love with her husband. The cad!

In one sense, Mary Helen hoped Patsy never did find out about the affair. Maybe she wouldn't have to. Mary Helen had clearly overheard Owen and Oonagh each deny that they had anything to do with Willie Ward's death. They had not known anyone was listening, had they? So what reason would they have to lie?

When someone uncovered the real murderer, Patsy might never be the wiser. The possibility sounded slim, even to her, but why not hope?

Tilting back her head, Mary Helen closed her eyes. Days and events and people tumbled like bits of colored glass in a kaleidoscope: the market day with the farrier and the dancers and Father Keane; Jake, the tinker; Tara, the Oyster Festival Queen; Owen Lynch, the chairperson of the event; the women at the wine tasting; Tommy Burns and the I Believe Team; the Monks' Table and Hugh the publican; the weary waitress; Oonagh Cox and Zoë O'Dea. Round and round they went.

Suddenly her mind focused on Zoë O'Dea. On her first day in Ireland—was it only five days ago?—she had overheard Zoë talking to Willie at the Monks' Table.

What were her exact words? "I'm surprised someone hasn't killed you already." She'd thought it an odd thing to say when she heard it, but in view of the events of the last few days, had it been a threat or a warning?

Mary Helen felt a hand on her arm. "Are you falling asleep on me, old dear?" Eileen whispered.

Her eyes popped open and she sat up. "Not a'tall," she said, pushing her slipping bifocals up where they belonged. "I was just thinking, is all."

"And?" Eileen studied her. "I can tell by your expression that you're up to no good."

Mary Helen frowned. "I don't know what you mean," she said. "When can thinking not be good?"

"To quote a famous bard, 'Yond, Cassius. He thinks too much. . . . Such men are dangerous.'" Eileen's gray eyes twinkled. "Although I could never accuse you of having a 'lean and hungry look.'"

"One night with Danny Short and everyone's a comedian," Mary Helen muttered, laughing in spite of herself.

"How about dessert?" Eileen asked, gathering up their dinner plates. "What would you like? I see all kinds of sweets on the table, and I noticed someone with ice cream."

"Surprise me," Mary Helen said.

"That's the spirit, Sister," said a voice from behind her.

Mary Helen turned quickly and found herself face-to-face with Zoë O'Dea. *Speak of the devil,* the nun thought, although she hadn't actually been speaking of Zoë. It was more like think of the devil. Not that it really mattered.

Zoë's dark eyes seemed to be scrutinizing everything about Mary Helen, jumping nervously from her face to her hands and back again.

"Is our barbeque to your liking?" she asked, then answered her own question. "It was lovely, wasn't it?"

"Yes, indeed," Eileen said, and she joined the two women. She had a dish of rich creamy gelato in each hand. Crazily, Mary Helen felt saved.

Zoë smiled a satisfied smile. "And I see you've a sweet."

"We do, thank you," Eileen said, "and it looks delicious. May I get you something?"

"Not a'tall. I couldn't eat another bite. But you go ahead. I'll just sit with you a minute, rest my feet." Zoë sat and began to study her thumbnail, as if she was about to say something and was not so sure she should.

"It's a pity we had a murder," she blurted out finally, as if it were somehow her fault. "I hope it didn't spoil your holiday."

Mary Helen could scarcely believe her ears. The woman was worried about their holiday being spoiled. Shouldn't she be concerned for the murdered man?

"Not a bit," Eileen answered. Mary Helen was shocked her friend could be so unemotional. "We were feeling sad for Mr. Ward and for his family. Surely that was a brutal way to die."

"No more than he deserved," Zoë uttered. "He was a brutal man, was our Willie," she said, almost as though she were talking to herself. "And he had little concern for anyone else's feelings. He didn't care who he hurt."

Zoë's words tumbled on. *Like poison oozing from a lanced boil,* Mary Helen thought. The woman's sharp eyes focused on her. "Willie Ward was a cruel man. He never minded what he said in his column about people, never gave a thought to their feelings.

"Last year he wrote about my Tara when she didn't win the Oyster Queen contest. He made very hurtful remarks about her hair. She has lovely long chestnut brown hair, does my Tara," Zoë said, putting a hand to her own Clairol-colored curls. "My poor child cried for days about his calling it a horse's tail." Her eyes narrowed. "I can tell you what part of a horse our Willie is . . . was," she corrected herself. "Mark my words, there will be many a dry eye at his wake, as the old saying goes." Zoë stopped for breath. "Oh, I could tell you tales about our Willie, I could, if I had a notion."

Her eyes scanned the dance floor as if she was searching for someone. "He's a long legacy of upsetting people, even someone as sure of herself as our Mrs. Oonagh Cox."

Mary Helen noticed a hint of contempt in Zoë's voice when she mentioned Oonagh Cox. *There must be some history there,* she thought. There was more to it than both having lovely daughters running for Oyster Festival Queen. Hadn't someone told her that Zoë and Patsy Lynch were friends? Did she perhaps know that Oonagh and Patsy's husband were lovers?

"And Owen Lynch!" Zoë said, her eyes clamping on the chairman, who was slowly steering his wife around the dance floor. "He couldn't abide Willie."

"Why was that?" Mary Helen wondered aloud.

"Because Willie always poked his nose into festival business, no matter who the chairman was. He fancied himself sort of the last word on how things should be done. The year my Bertie was chairman, he came down with an awful case of the hives."

"Bertie?" Mary Helen asked.

"Mr. O'Dea," Zoë said. Her nose lifted slightly as if she smelled something unpleasant. "I thought everyone knew *himself*. Bertie, the undertaker. *Let O'Dea send you on your way*," she said, without skipping a beat.

Although Mary Helen knew she might be getting in farther than she should, she couldn't resist. "Mrs. O'Dea," she began cautiously.

"Zoë. Please call me Zoë."

"Zoë, I wonder if you have any idea who was responsible for Willie Ward's death?"

All at once, Zoë O'Dea's brown eyes were wary, and her mouth twitched. She stood and pulled herself up to her full five feet. "No idea a'tall," she said so emphatically that Mary Helen was almost positive she did.

Even from across the ballroom, Liam O'Dea could tell by her demeanor that his Auntie Zoë was stirring the pot. The woman had a God-given talent for starting trouble.

Liam sniffed. *Look at her chatting up the American nuns, telling them God knows what,* he thought, running his finger through his thick sandy hair.

Why couldn't he have been a garda in Roscommon or Cork instead of Oranmore—any place away from this woman? She was making a holy show of herself, standing like a bantam rooster crowing away.

Sure, he didn't need another headache, and if anyone could give him one it was his Auntie Zoë. What Bertie O'Dea saw in her, Liam would never know. Poor man, stuck with a harridan of a wife. No wonder Bertie stayed in the family business. At least he had a little peace and quiet at work.

Although Liam tried not to look obvious, he couldn't take his eyes off the women. He was dead curious to know what they were going on about. *You don't suppose that the old nun is telling her about Owen Lynch and Mrs. Cox?*

At the thought, Liam's throat felt as if it were closing, and a trickle of perspiration slid down from his underarm to his waist. God help him. She had to be smarter than that!

Zoë would have it on every tongue by the noon Angelus tomorrow. If it got back to Detective Inspector White before he had a chance to tell him! Liam didn't even want to think about it.

Nor did he want to think about the mess he'd be in if Mrs. Cox really was involved. Would Carmel ever speak to him again if she found out that he had implicated her mother?

Stupid woman, having an affair with Owen Lynch, of all people! A married man—and everyone loved big-hearted Patsy, his wife. If the villagers found out, he'd be considered worse than a murderer, now wouldn't he?

Liam dabbed perspiration from his forehead with a clean handkerchief. He'd swear that this room was as hot as one of those saunas he'd seen on the telly.

Where was Mrs. Cox, anyway? Liam scanned the room, but she was nowhere to be seen. He'd be wise, wouldn't he, to observe her and Owen Lynch like any good detective might, to get a take on their relationship?

He spotted Owen Lynch easily enough. Much to Liam's relief, he was dancing a slow one with his wife. Patsy, for her part, looked a bit uncomfortable being led around the floor by himself. Something about her rhythm seemed a half beat off.

The chairman's face was pinched, but that was no crime. He was dancing with the missus. *A good sign,* Liam thought.

And there was always the hope that the technical

team would turn up some evidence pointing to the real killer. Willie Ward must have had dozens of enemies. And they didn't have to live in Ballyclarin, did they? Could it be that the villain wasn't after Willie at all? That might be an explanation for why Tommy Burns from Dublin was attacked in the field. The fellow was after Tommy and was interrupted.

Liam shook his head. That made no sense. Why kill Willie if you were after Tommy? And why take his costume?

Liam groaned. They'd have their fill of that old sheet tomorrow. If Ernie White was as good as his word, which Liam felt sure he was, they'd search again for that bloody thing.

With all the crowds coming into the village for the Oyster Festival, someone could have slipped in, stolen the costume, put a knife in the man's chest, and slipped out again, just that quickly. Someone who was a total stranger.

That could have been it. Liam hoped it was, but it didn't help him with the mess he found himself in right now. Why had the old nun told him about what she'd overheard? Why not tell one of the other gardai or Brian Reedy? Tall, handsome Brian Reedy would have been the logical one to approach. He was White's partner, after all.

Then Reedy could deal with Auntie Zoë. And the way Reedy was gawking at Liam's cousin Tara these days, sometime soon he'd have to deal with her mother. Poor *divil*! He had no idea what he was in for, and Liam wasn't about to tell him. Liam had enough trouble of his own.

"Oh, there you are!" Liam recognized the voice, and a chill raced down his spine, as if someone had put an ice cube down his collar. It was Carmel.

Turning, he found her gazing up at him. Her face was

the color of fresh cream, and her cheeks were rosy. Her enormous blue eyes sparkled with fun, and her thick auburn curls bounced freely to her shoulders. At the sight of her, his stomach knotted.

"I've been all over for you," she said, gently touching his arm. A tiny shock ran up to his elbow. "Do you want to dance?" she asked with a smile.

"Well," he stammered.

Her lower lip stuck out ever so slightly. "If you don't, Liam O'Dea, there are others that do."

"Ah, Carmel, you know I do," Liam said as quickly as he could catch his breath. Carmel was already leading their way to the dance floor, where the lads were playing another slow one.

Liam would have much preferred something fast so they would not be able to talk. He didn't want to take the chance that anything might come up about her mother.

But Carmel didn't seem interested in talking, either. She snuggled close to him and put her head against his shoulder. He caught the sweet, flowery scent of her hair and felt her soft warm body against his.

All at once, his Auntie Zoë, the American nuns, Willie Ward's murder, and even his meeting with Detective Inspector White tomorrow didn't seem that important.

Sister Mary Helen's eyes burned, and she wondered if this might have been the longest Tuesday of her entire life. "Are we ever going home?" she whispered to Eileen, who was looking a little weary herself.

"My thought exactly," Eileen said, checking her watch. "Can you believe it's only eleven o'clock?"

Mary Helen suppressed a groan. "We've been here two hours. It's not as if we ate and ran."

"Right you are." Eileen stood and looked around. "I don't see Paul anywhere," she said. "God only knows where he's gone to, and God isn't telling."

"Do you see anyone else who might give us a ride?"

"I was looking for Oonagh Cox," Eileen said, "but I don't seem to see her anywhere."

Mary Helen frowned. She hadn't seen Oonagh all night. Curious! The woman had been at every other event.

"Ah-ha." Eileen sounded triumphant. "What about Father Keane? As luck would have it, he's coming our way."

Within minutes the two nuns, having left a message for Paul with Owen Lynch, were seated in Father Keane's black Mazda.

"I hope this is no bother," Eileen said as the priest pulled out of the car park.

"Not a'tall," he answered. "I was hoping for a reason to make my excuses, and you two were the perfect answer."

They drove in silence past the old convent school, the church, and the Monks' Table. There didn't seem to be a light on anywhere. And, except for one stray dog, the village looked absolutely deserted. The only sound was the hiss of their tires on the macadam.

It must have rained a bit while they were at the barbeque. Although now the night sky was clear and brilliant with sparkling stars.

"Will I leave you here, then?" Father Keane asked, as he pulled up and parked in front of the gate leading to their mews.

"This is fine," Mary Helen said, climbing out of the car. "Thank you so much."

Eileen had pushed open the heavy gate and was waving.

Carefully making their way toward their front door,

Mary Helen was very glad they had remembered to
leave a light burning. Even so, the stone path was difficult to see.

"Next time, we should bring a torch," Eileen said.

"Next time, we will," Mary Helen agreed as her foot hit
against something soft. What could that be? She pushed
her glasses up the bridge of her nose and tried to make out
what was on the grass. A faint groan sent goose bumps up
her arm. "Eileen," she whispered, "did you hear that?"

"Indeed, I did," Eileen said, opening the front door
and throwing on all the lights. "Who's there?" she called
loudly.

Blinking at the sudden brightness, Sister Mary Helen
bent forward, trying to get a better look. Her scalp
prickled as a rush of panic shot through her. "It's a
woman," she stammered, her mouth furry, as she bent
closer still to the crumpled form.

Gently touching the shoulder, Mary Helen noticed a
faint flowery fragrance. She rolled the body toward her.
Another moan ripped through the stillness.

With a queasy feeling in the pit of her stomach, Mary
Helen stared down at the round face. She recognized it
immediately. The short curly gray hair was matted with
blood, but at least the woman was breathing.

"It's Oonagh Cox." Sister Mary Helen's voice
sounded distant even to herself.

All at once Oonagh's eyelids fluttered, and she attempted to get up on one elbow. "Ooh," she moaned.

"Lie still," Mary Helen said softly. "We'll get someone."

"It's freezing on this grass," Oonagh said, her teeth
chattering. She reached out for Mary Helen's hand.
"And I'm getting my new dress all dirty. I paid a fortune
for it in the city."

Although a dirty dress seemed to Mary Helen to be the least of Oonagh's problems, the nun tried to steady her.

"Ooh, my head," Oonagh groaned, struggling to her feet.

"Eileen, help," Mary Helen called, but Eileen was already on the telephone.

Trying desperately to remember what she'd learned of first aid, Mary Helen led Oonagh to a comfortable chair in their parlor and wrapped her in a blanket in case she went into shock.

"Ouch," Oonagh said when Mary Helen put a cold compress on her head for swelling.

"Do you remember what happened?" Mary Helen asked gently.

Oonagh shook her head and then let out a sharp yelp. "Not entirely," she said. "But whatever happened, it hurts."

"How about a nice cup of hot tea?" Eileen asked, putting on the electric kettle. "That might help."

Oonagh gave a weak smile. "That would be grand," she said. "Ta."

The tea water had just boiled when Detective Inspector White arrived at their front door. His face was puffy with sleep, and his dark hair stood out like iron filings on a magnet. He had on exactly the same clothes he'd worn earlier today. From the look of his suit, Mary Helen wondered if he might have slept in it.

"The ambulance is on its way," he said, pulling up a chair and sitting across from Oonagh Cox.

"That's not needed," Oonagh started, but White interrupted her.

"Better be safe than sorry," he said, crossing his legs. Mary Helen noticed that the man's socks were two different colors. At least he had changed those.

"Before they get here," White said, his dark eyes

studying Oonagh, "can you tell me everything you do remember about what happened?"

"I was on my way to the hotel for the barbeque," Oonagh hesitated, obviously in pain, "when . . ." Her voice began to tremble.

"No hurry, love," White said. "Take your time."

Oonagh swallowed hard. "I was on my way," she repeated, "and I was just passing the mews, when I heard someone behind me. When I turned around to greet whoever it was, I nearly wet my knickers." Her cheeks reddened. "Sorry," she said. "But I was met by Death, or at least by someone dressed in his long white gown and his black mask. I thought he was playing with me. I didn't think anything of it. 'You ought to be ashamed of yourself, scaring an old lady,' I said, joking.

" 'It's I that ought to be ashamed?' the person said, almost as if it were a question. And he just kept coming. All at once, I felt something hit my head."

She put her finger on the spot and grimaced. "After that, I don't remember a thing until the Sisters were here helping me off the wet grass."

"Why do you suppose he left you here?" White wondered aloud.

"Maybe someone came along and surprised him," Oonagh said. "Or maybe he ducked in here so he wouldn't be seen."

White did not comment, just stared up at the ceiling. Mary Helen wished she knew what he saw up there.

"You didn't recognize his voice or notice anything familiar about him?" White asked.

"It all happened so fast," Oonagh said, "and his voice was muffled. It was as though he were trying to sound different."

"Was he tall?"

"Taller than I am," she said.

Which covers most men and quite a few women,
Mary Helen thought. Oonagh must be only a little over
five feet tall.

"Did he say anything else, besides asking 'It's I that
ought to be ashamed?'" Detective Inspector White ac-
cepted the cup of tea Eileen offered him.

"Not a word. That was what was so frightening."

"And you said he changed his voice. Can you be sure
then it was a man, or could it have been a woman?"
White asked.

"No, not entirely sure," Oonagh admitted, "but I did
think it was a man. It doesn't sound like anything a
woman would do, now does it?"

"Have you any idea of the time that this happened?"
White tried to stifle a yawn.

"I was running a little late," Oonagh said. "So, I'd say
about half nine."

"And did you see anyone else on the street?"

"No one," Oonagh said. "Everyone seemed to be at
the Court Hotel already."

Everyone but our murderer, Mary Helen thought.

The sound of doors slamming and voices outside announced that the ambulance had finally arrived.

"Tomorrow, then," White said as the attendants helped
Oonagh Cox onto the gurney. "We'll talk. Maybe you'll
remember something that slipped your mind tonight."

Putting his empty teacup on the sideboard, Detective
Inspector White turned to face the Sisters. "I'll be head-
ing off now," he said. "Tomorrow, then." He glanced at
his wristwatch. "It is tomorrow. Later today we can talk,
too. Maybe you saw something. . . ." He let the thought
trail off.

Maybe, indeed, Mary Helen thought with a twinge of
guilt. Just when was Liam O'Dea going to get around to
talking to his superior? Mary Helen couldn't help won-

dering if the attack on Oonagh Cox had something to do
with her affair with Owen Lynch.

Sister Mary Helen could scarcely keep her eyes open
when she was getting ready for bed. Once she had
climbed in, however, and her head touched the pillow,
she found herself suddenly and absolutely awake.

Shadows scooted across the walls of the small room,
creating a moving mural of shapes. The wind, which
had come up quite unexpectedly, lashed the tree
branches against her window. She half expected to hear
raindrops hit her windowpane, but none came.

She stared up at the ceiling wondering, once again,
what Detective Inspector White saw up there. All she
noticed was a small water stain that made her wonder if
the mews' roof had a leak.

She took a deep breath, trying to relax and coax
sleep, but her mind would not turn off. Instead, her
thoughts swam like fish in a small bowl.

At first glance, Ballyclarin had seemed to her like
such a perfect little village. But villages were made up
of people. At her age, no one needed to remind her that
there are no perfect people.

On her longest day, however, she had not expected to
stumble into a murder here. But stumble she had, right
into the body of Willie Ward.

Every murder, she knew, had a motive. Who, she
wondered, had motive enough to kill Willie Ward? Certainly Oonagh Cox had a grudge, she'd been told, from
when Oonagh's husband had been in agony and Willie
threatened to expose her for giving him cannabis for
his pain.

Then there was Jake, the tinker, an angry man who
resented Willie for sullying his name and whose talent

Willie seemed to resent. Was that motive enough for murder?

And Zoë O'Dea, an odd duck at best, whom Mary Helen had heard tell Willie that she was surprised that no one had killed him yet, implying that a number of people might have a reason.

Sister Mary Helen plumped up her pillow, hoping to get comfortable. She tried to picture green fields, ocean waves, anything peaceful. But her thoughts kept jumping to Tommy Burns nearly naked in the field and Oonagh unconscious on the grass and the horrible shock of finding Willie dead.

What was the connection, if there was one? Why had all this hatred come to a head at the Oyster Festival? Mary Helen's own head began to ache. She needed to get some sleep. What had triggered the violence? What was going on behind the scenes? When she found that out, surely the motive and the murderer would come clear. Not that finding the murderer was her responsibility, she told herself firmly—in fact, quite the contrary.

You know very well that Detective Inspector White has forbidden you to get involved, a small inner voice reminded her.

I'm already involved, she reasoned. *Besides, he never said a word about passing on information to Garda O'Dea.*

He would have if he'd known you intended to, the voice countered.

She turned on her side, trying to relax. "Oh Lord, how did I get into this mess? Help me," she prayed as she felt sleep quickly overtaking her. "Help me!"

She could have sworn she heard the Lord reply. "I'm really trying to, old dear. Now get some rest."

Wednesday, September 3

May God grant you always . . .
A sunbeam to warm you,
A moonbeam to charm you,
A sheltering angel, so nothing can harm you.
—Irish blessing

When Sister Mary Helen woke on Wednesday morning, her small bedroom was exceptionally bright. So much so that she wondered if she had fallen asleep with her light on. It took her a few moments to realize that the room was flooded with sunshine.

Peeking out the side of the drape, she saw that the sun was, indeed, shining and that the sky was a bright scrubbed blue. During the night the wind must have blown the clouds away, leaving Ballyclarin sparkling.

The brightness made Mary Helen's eyes burn, and she realized she had a dull headache, probably from lack of sleep. Nothing, she was sure, compared to the headache Oonagh Cox must have this morning.

Hearing Eileen moving about in the kitchen, she slipped into her robe and slippers and joined her friend.

"How are you this morning?" Eileen asked the moment she saw her. "You look awful."

"Tell me what you really think," Mary Helen muttered, taking the cup of coffee Eileen offered her. She settled down at the kitchen table.

Eileen sat across from her. "I was thinking what a glorious day it is. That it's much too beautiful to be in the house and that we ought to go visit Oonagh Cox to make sure she is all right."

"I agree," Mary Helen said.

"I thought you would, and so while you were still asleep I called the Coxes," Eileen continued. "It seems that the doctor decided to keep her overnight in the hospital as a precaution. And although the son who answered the telephone was very polite, it was apparent that he was discouraging visitors."

"You can't blame him," Mary Helen said. "What the poor woman probably needs is rest."

Mary Helen sipped her coffee in silence. "What's on the Oyster Festival schedule for today?" she asked finally.

"I looked that up, too," Eileen said. "As luck would have it, today is a free day. That is, until early evening, when there is a hurling match."

"Hurling?" Mary Helen stifled a yawn. "Do you know anything about hurling?"

"Next to nothing," Eileen admitted.

"Maybe today should be our day to rest," Mary Helen suggested. "To tell you the truth, at the rate we've been going, we'll have to have a vacation after our vacation."

"And you are to meet with Detective Inspector White this morning," Eileen reminded her, as if she needed to be. "By the time you are finished with him, a day of rest may be very much in order."

Since the morning was so beautiful and Detective Inspector White had not yet come by, the two nuns decided to have breakfast in the backyard. When Mary

Helen had dressed she helped Eileen move out orange juice, warm raisin scones, and second cups of coffee.

The sunlit garden was aflame with bright sturdy fuchsias, long-stemmed orange montbretia, and oxeye daisies. Marigolds and buttercups appeared among the shrubs. And a plump wood pigeon cooed softly in the distance.

Ah, peace! Mary Helen sighed, feeling the warmth of the sun on her feet. At the moment she was unable to fit Willie Ward's murder or the attacks on both Tommy Burns and Oonagh Cox into this idyllic scene. Maybe it had all been a dream. Detective Inspector White had not yet sent for them. Perhaps he had caught the culprit already.

The deep rhythmic *bong* of the church bell rang through the village calling the faithful to morning Mass. Compelled by it, the two nuns quickly brought their dishes into the kitchen and hurried across the road to the church.

A small congregation was already gathered, and one of the women was leading the Rosary. Mary Helen had never in her life heard it recited so quickly. Eileen had told her long ago that the Irish prayed that fast so that the devil couldn't get a word in. *Even an angel, let alone a human being, would have a tough time,* Mary Helen thought, trying to keep up.

When Father Keane finally did walk onto the altar, nearly ten minutes late by Mary Helen's watch, he looked as if he hadn't slept a wink. She felt sorry for him. Had he been on a late night sick call, or was he just unable to sleep?

Even the few words he did say after the Gospel reading were short and stiff, as if his mind was somewhere else.

Could it be on Oonagh Cox and Owen Lynch? Had he learned about their affair in the confessional? She couldn't help wondering as he gave the final blessing. Did murderers really confess their crimes, or was that just in the movies?

She'd never know. By the time the church ordained women, she'd be long gone.

Coming out of church, Sister Mary Helen spotted Detective Inspector White's automobile parked near the Monks' Table.

"Should I report in or should I wait to be summoned?" she wondered aloud.

"Probably the most prudent thing would be to report in," Eileen said, "but since when has prudence been your long suit?"

Before Mary Helen had a chance to argue, Detective Inspector Brian Reedy came toward them, his short red hair still wet from the shower.

"Sisters, good morning," he called cheerfully, "and a marvelous morning it is, too. You slept well, did you?"

"Yes, indeed," Eileen answered for the two of them.

"I've a message from Ernie White," he said. "He wants to know if it would be convenient for you, Sister Helen, to meet with him at half one this afternoon?"

"Surely," Mary Helen said, not bothering to correct her name. She was eager to get the interview over. "Where would the Detective Inspector like to meet?"

"Your mews will be fine," Reedy said. "He'll be at your door at half one, then?" With a quick smile, Reedy turned and left them standing in the road.

"It doesn't seem right to sit in the house on such a lovely day," Eileen said, watching the handsome detective disappear into the Monks' Table. She checked her wristwatch. "And we've almost two hours before you are to meet the inspector. How about a little walk? And then we can get some lunch."

Mary Helen readily agreed. The air was warm, and the sky was scoured clear. The day was perfect for a walk.

The whole village seemed to be taking advantage of the fine weather, Mary Helen thought as the two sauntered along a side street. Every house, large or small, had its windows thrown open, and linens like white sails hung on lines to dry.

"Everybody must have changed their linens yesterday," Eileen noted, watching the breeze gently flapping the bedsheets. "Or maybe they did it when they saw the sun this morning."

"Out for a walk, I see, and 'tis a grand day for it altogether," Zoë O'Dea called from her front garden. Her sharp, dark eyes fastened on the two nuns. "You've been to Mass, have you?"

Mary Helen was hard-pressed to tell if that was a question or a statement of fact.

"And who'd blame you? We ought all to be saying our prayers after the mischief you stumbled on last night by your mews."

Sister Mary Helen was stunned. How in the world had the woman found out? She hadn't told anyone and neither, she knew, had Eileen. She felt sure the police inspectors hadn't. At the moment even Eileen was speechless.

Zoë must have noticed their surprise. "Oh, it's all over the village, on every tongue," she said. "Yes, indeed." She pushed back a lock of chestnut hair that had managed to fall over her forehead. "Poor Oonagh," she said, sounding sympathetic. "How is she feeling this morning?"

"We haven't seen her," Mary Helen said when she managed to get her voice back. "She's still in the hospital."

"Everyone knows that," Zoë said impatiently. "Didn't you ask that Reedy lad when he stopped you by the road?"

The woman misses nothing, Mary Helen thought, shaking her head. "No," she said finally. "I didn't." From the expression on Zoë's face, she felt as if she had somehow shirked her duty.

"Well." Zoë leaned against her front gate. "I suppose it could have been a lot worse. Poor love is not as young as she once was. A hit in the head is not easy to get over when you're getting on in years."

"Zoë!" A man's voice roared from the cottage. "Are ye going to fix me breakfast or are ye going to stand around all morning long flappin' your lips?"

Zoë's face hardened, and her dark eyes snapped with anger. "That's *himself*," she explained, her cheeks flushed. "And he's helpless.

"Hunger makes good sauce, Bertie," she called back, not moving an inch.

A door slammed in the house. "You ladies are lucky, indeed," Zoë said, still not moving. "As me ould mother used to say, 'There are no trials till marriage.' "

Without another word Zoë turned on her heel and stomped back into the cottage, slamming her front door.

"Ye right *eejit*!" Her angry voice tore through the quiet morning and a heavy pan hit the stovetop. "It's breakfast you want, is it? I'll show you breakfast."

There was another crash and an unidentifiable thud as Sister Mary Helen and Sister Eileen moved quickly down the road.

"Oh, my," Eileen said when they were passing a thick hedge that shielded a neighboring house and its gardens from view. "It sounds as if poor Bertie is going to get more than he bargained for."

"She's a good heart, has our Zoë," a strong voice came from over the hedge. "She's only the one chick, you know, not enough to keep her busy."

Patsy Lynch appeared by the front gate. Her thick hair was pulled back and fastened with a tortoiseshell clasp. She smelled as if she'd just stepped out of the shower. "Out for a walk, are ye?" she asked pleasantly. "And a grand day for it, too."

Behind her, Mary Helen noticed a carefully tended garden full of rambling roses, yellow flag iris, and healthy bushes of heather. Next to the house was a clothesline heavy with laundry.

Patsy must have noticed her looking. "No one can resist washing on a fine drying day like today," she said. "Everything smells so clean and fresh from the sunshine. I've every bed in the house stripped."

Mary Helen could see that this was true. There must be at least a half dozen sheets hanging on Patsy's line.

"'Twas a terrible thing, I hear, happened to Oonagh Cox last night," she said. "Poor love, her husband gone and all. She's had enough troubles. And Oonagh herself wouldn't harm a fly." Her voice trailed off, as if she was waiting for them to reply.

Mary Helen's mouth felt dry. *If you only knew,* she thought, hoping her face didn't give anything away. She didn't dare look at Eileen.

"Yes, indeed," Patsy Lynch said, her voice full of compassion. "God love Oonagh. She has had more than her share."

Liam O'Dea pulled back the heavy wooden door of the Monks' Table. Once he stepped inside he stood still, waiting for his eyes to adjust to the sudden darkness of the place.

"Good morning, lad." He recognized Detective Inspector White's voice, and the man actually sounded cheerful. Had he discovered the murderer overnight? Wouldn't that be grand?

"Good morning to you, sir," Liam answered, then realized as his vision cleared that White was not alone. Next to him, Brian Reedy sat on a stool, obviously enjoying a coffee.

Hugh Ryan was behind the bar, looking especially glum. Liam glanced around the pub, expecting to see gardai from the neighboring villages. Hadn't White asked them to come back and help with the search for the missing costume?

"Good day to you, Liam," Hugh said, rewiping the bar top. "Can I get you something? A cuppa? A wee drop?"

Liam noticed that he deliberately turned his back to White.

"Thanks, no," Liam said, wondering what the tension was between the two men.

"I might as well be serving somebody as standing around losing a fortune," Hugh mumbled.

"Hugh is annoyed that he can't open just yet," White explained.

"But Reedy himself told me that he thought I'd be able to open last night, today at the latest," Hugh complained.

White raised a hand, cutting him off. "Brian told you that before Oonagh Cox was found."

"Oonagh Cox, found?" Liam's stomach dropped. Had he heard correctly? He cleared his throat. "Found, how?" His voice cracked and his cheeks were burning.

Turning, White studied him until Liam felt like a bug under a microscope.

"Not dead, thank God, if that's what you're worried about," White said at last.

Liam wished that Hugh would offer him a cuppa again or better yet, a wee drop. He could use it now.

"How, then?" Liam asked, trying to keep his tone of voice all business.

"With a very painful bump on her head. Not unlike the one Tommy Burns received. She was left on the lawn of the American nuns' mews."

Carmel must be frantic, Liam thought anxiously, trying to figure out a way he could get to see her. "Is Mrs. Cox in hospital?" he asked, hoping he sounded professionally concerned.

Detective Inspector White nodded. "The ambulance took her to emergency last night. Although she said that she was perfectly fine, the doctor decided to keep her overnight. Just a precaution," White added quickly.

"Like Tommy Burns, Mrs. Cox was knocked quite unconscious. Her attacker wore a white sheetlike costume and apparently was pretending to be Death." White thought for a moment, then added, "It is more imperative than ever that we find that costume."

His eyes locked on Liam. "I know you and the lads said you looked everywhere, but that costume was somewhere in the village and ended up on a very dangerous individual. I want it found!"

Although Liam knew he probably shouldn't ask, he couldn't help himself. "Where are the rest of the lads?"

Reedy gave a bark of a laugh.

"That's the bad news," White said. "Some visiting dignitaries are coming to Dublin for a bloody meeting with the Taoiseach, and all personnel who can be spared are being called to come to Dublin.

"I threw a regular fit, mind you, but it did no good.

You, Liam, are my only helper." He grabbed Liam's shoulder and gave it a friendly squeeze. "Now, the good news."

Thanks be to God there's some good news, Liam thought.

"First, a couple of lads from the tech team are coming to check the yard at the mews. I must tell the American nuns. And second: the sun. It's a mighty glorious day out there, and every woman in the village has her clothes on the line. That should be to our advantage."

"How so, sir?"

"Everyone knows that the perfect place to hide something is where everyone can see it because if you can see it, no one will look." White looked pleased with himself and waited for Liam's reaction.

The man is daft, Liam thought, but he knew better than to say that.

"Sir," Liam swallowed. This was as good a time as any to tell his superior about Mrs. Cox and Owen Lynch, even if it was only hearsay. White may be angry that he'd kept it to himself for so long, but even a reprimand seemed better than looking through blasted clotheslines.

"Get to it, Liam," White said, pulling his cell phone from the pocket of his rumpled jacket. "I've got to ring the hospital to ask if Oonagh is up to seeing me."

"But, sir," Liam protested.

"Later, lad," White said impatiently. "Go find me that costume."

"The sun is to our advantage, indeed," Liam grumbled to himself as he began his walk through the village. If anyone asked him, the only thing the sun was, was blasted hot. If you considered sweating in one's blue woolen uniform useful, then he guessed the sun was an advantage. What in God's name made the man tick?

Liam felt like a right fool walking down the side streets staring at clotheslines. Detective Inspector White had been right about one thing. Every line in the village had wash drying on it.

There were sheets, yes, but also towels and socks and women's personals. He felt his face redden as he stared at a large pair of women's underdrawers. What kind of a pervert would the villagers take him for? Sure, if his Auntie Zoë caught sight of him, he'd never hear the end of it.

Deliberately avoiding her block, he walked in the direction of the Cox home, hoping Carmel would be there so that he could tell her how sorry he was to hear of her mother's accident.

Standing by the front gate to the Cox's garden, Liam removed his hat. His head felt as if he had just lifted a pot of hot water off it. He ran his fingers through his thick hair. It was damp.

Carmel must have seen him coming. The Coxes' front door flew open, and she nearly threw herself at him.

"I'm so glad to see you," she sobbed into his chest. He wondered if she could hear his heart beating against his ribs.

"Are you here about my mam?"

"Yes. No," Liam stuttered.

"Is it yes or no?" Carmel asked, her big blue eyes staring up at him.

"It's yes. Of course, it's yes. Finding out who did this to your mam is our top priority," he said, puffing out his chest a little. "We can't have our women attacked."

"She could have been killed," Carmel moaned.

"Indeed," said Liam, trying to soothe her, "but I understand she'll be fine. Have you spoken to her this morning?"

Carmel shook her head. "I called the hospital, but the Sister in charge said that she was asleep. I didn't want to wake her. I'm just on my way over now."

She pushed back from him and smoothed down her curls. "What are you doing?" she asked.

How could he tell her that he was checking clotheslines? He'd rather die. He put his hat back on and said nothing. Maybe she'd think what he was about was top secret.

"Liam," she wheedled. "What is it you are doing?"

He smiled, trying to imitate that I-know-something-I-can't-tell smile he had seen on television detectives. A trickle of sweat slid down each of his sides as she continued to study him.

Finally she looked away. "It's something you can't tell me, isn't it?" she teased.

Liam held his know-something smile.

"It is," she said gleefully. "I best go and see mam, now. And, Liam," she added softly, batting her bright blue eyes at him, "I'm so very proud of you. You must be tremendously useful to those detective inspectors for them to send you out to investigate on your own."

Liam walked away quickly. The collar on his uniform shirt seemed to have shrunk. His telltale face must be crimson by now. Tremendously useful, indeed! If she only knew! Right now he felt about as useful as a chocolate teapot!

Sister Mary Helen took a deep breath. "This walk really was a good idea," she said in a soft tone.

The two nuns had deliberately lowered their voices when they left Patsy Lynch's house. As Eileen had wisely observed, "You can never tell who's on the other side of these hedges, listening."

"_y f__ _uch better than I did when we started," _y Helen declared. "Nothing like a brisk walk to clear your head."

"And a good sit to get your breath back." Eileen pointed to a vacant bench near a bus stop sign.

"Another grand idea!" Mary Helen said, joining her friend. The sky was still a clear bright blue and the sun was warm. The wind sent the fuchsias dancing on the large bushes that grew along the road. All the scene needed to make it postcard perfect was a green-suited leprechaun hiding behind a tree.

Quickly Mary Helen looked both ways before she spoke. They seemed to be alone. At least, she didn't see another living thing except for a lone cow in a large emerald-green pasture on a nearby hill. And the cow didn't seem to be paying any attention to them.

"Do you suppose that the young police officer has told Detective Inspector White about Mrs. Cox and Mr. Lynch yet?" she asked.

Eileen's gray eyebrows shot up. "I thought you said that this walk had cleared your head."

"It has. Unfortunately, it has also made some of the questions ricocheting around in my head more clear, too."

"Ricocheting questions?" Eileen frowned. "That sounds dangerous, old dear."

Mary Helen adjusted her glasses on the bridge of her nose and studied her friend. "Don't tell me you don't have questions. For example, what do Willie Ward, Tommy Burns, and Oonagh Cox have in common that made someone attack all three of them?" She paused in case Eileen had an answer.

For several seconds her question hung in the air. "You've got me," Eileen said, at last. "Wait a minute," she said. "They were all involved in the Oyster Festival."

"So were hundreds of other people."

"True." Eileen looked disappointed.

"And another thing," Mary Helen whispered, in case someone had slipped unnoticed into hearing range. "Why was Willie Ward killed while the other two were not? We know he made enemies, but why would someone have to kill the man?"

"To silence him, maybe?" Eileen asked.

"Very good," Mary Helen said. "I thought of that, too. To keep him from telling something . . . something you'd commit murder not to have known."

"Or maybe to keep him from writing about it in his column?" Eileen ventured. "There can't be too many things that serious."

"What could he possibly know that would be bad enough to make someone kill him?"

Eileen shrugged. "You told me that he knew about Oonagh Cox and the chairman having an affair."

Mary Helen mulled over that for a minute. "But I also heard them both say that they hadn't done it."

"Isn't that what all murderers say?" Eileen asked.

"But I'd bet my life that they had no idea I was overhearing their conversation. Why wouldn't they tell the truth to one another?"

"Maybe you're right," Eileen agreed. "And where does Jake, the tinker, fit in? If he does fit in."

"We know he feels as if Willie made sure he wouldn't be the only winner of the art contest this year."

"Odd that Willie wielded that much power," Mary Helen reflected. "And I also somewhere picked up the feeling that it was Carmel Cox, not Tara O'Dea, who should have been the Oyster Festival Queen. Was that Willie's doing, too? I ask you, how did he have so much pull?"

"You-hoo, Sisters!" An unfamiliar car slowed across the road. Mary Helen squinted. Was that Owen Lynch behind the wheel?

"Are you waiting for a lift?" he called.

"No, thank you. We are just catching our breath. We've been out for a walk." Eileen checked her wristwatch. "It's about time for us to head back to our mews." She smiled sweetly.

"Let me drop you," Owen Lynch insisted, hopping out of the driver's seat to open the back door. They had little choice but to get in.

Strange, Mary Helen thought, slipping into the back. Chairman Lynch had never before offered them a ride. *Why now?* she wondered.

"Lovely day," Lynch said as he turned the car around and headed toward the center of the village.

"Indeed," Eileen said.

"And you had a nice walk, did you? My wife says you found your way to our house."

"And such a lovely garden you have," Eileen said.

"It's all her doing," Lynch was quick to give his wife all the credit.

"You've been busy with the festival, I'm sure," Eileen said, "and a lovely affair it is, too."

Mary Helen stared at her friend in disbelief. Was the sun getting to her? A lovely affair? Really! Had she forgotten a murder, two assaults, and adultery? Or was this just the Irish way?

Owen seemed surprised, too. "I understand you were the ones who stumbled upon Oonagh Cox last night. After she'd been attacked, I mean."

Ah-ha, Mary Helen thought. *Now we are getting to his point, and it only took him two blocks to arrive there.*

"Yes, we did find her," Mary Helen said. "Poor dear probably has the grandmother of all headaches this morning, I'm sure."

"Why would anyone do that to Oonagh?" Lynch seemed to be talking to himself. "She is such a lovely

sively. "Is it our fault that someone left Mrs. Cox practically on our doorstep?"

She hesitated and then decided to give it a shot. "It is almost as if it is God's will that we get involved."

"Oh, pl-ea-se." Eileen dragged out the word while staring at her with raised eyebrows. "Don't tell me you are going to blame this on God?"

Sister Mary Helen smiled sheepishly. "Under the circumstances," she said, "who better?"

The two nuns were just finishing their bowls of clam chowder when they heard a rap on the mews door.

"That must be Detective Inspector White." Eileen checked her wristwatch. "And he's right on time."

Mary Helen shoved the last bite of soda bread into her mouth and put both of their bowls and spoons into the kitchen sink to soak.

"Come in, Detective Inspector," she heard Eileen call, followed by an offer of a cup of tea.

"Thank you, but I've just finished one," the inspector said, and Mary Helen detected a let's-get-down-to-business edge in his voice. *Someone or something must be putting pressure on him to get this crime solved.*

"What can we do for you, Detective Inspector?" Mary Helen asked once the three of them were comfortably settled in the cozy parlor.

"First off, the tech people are coming from Dublin to search your lawn," he said, then slipped a small notebook from the pocket of his suit jacket and opened it. He seemed to be studying one page. Several seconds passed before he looked up. The small pouches of flesh under his dark, bloodshot eyes reminded Mary Helen of two tiny blimps. Obviously this poor fellow had had very little sleep.

"If you will, Sister," he cleared his throat, "I'd be grateful if you'll tell me again what you remember about finding Mr. Ward's body."

He paused, waiting, no doubt, for her reaction. When she gave none, he went on. "I know you've told me before . . ."

"Twice before," Mary Helen muttered.

"And I have written it all down," he said, pushing the little notebook toward her in case she needed proof. "But sometimes, when a person tells it again, something comes out that the person inadvertently left out in the first telling."

"I know, Detective Inspector," Mary Helen said, and then wished that she hadn't.

His face reddened. "I realize that you are not a novice at this kind of thing," he said rather sharply.

"I'll be happy to repeat my story," Mary Helen blurted out before he could say any more. She hoped she sounded duly humble and helpful. There was no sense getting the man's hackles up. After all, they were on the same side, weren't they?

"Very well, then," White said, sounding somewhat mollified. Sister Mary Helen closed her eyes visualizing the scene she was not likely to ever forget. She gave an involuntary shiver.

She had gone down the hall to the ladies'. Entered. Thought that its one stall was occupied. Then, she had stepped back into the hallway. Waited. When no one came out and she heard no sound, she wondered if it really was occupied. After that, she had gone back in and pushed open the stall door.

Her stomach turned as she remembered the scene. It was more than her mind wanted to take in. A man fully clothed, wearing an old Donegal tweed cap, sat on the closed toilet seat. A knife protruded from his chest.

Blood soaked his shirtfront. His head rested against the water tank, an old-fashioned chain hanging from the tank, and the smell. What was that smell?

"Smell?" Detective Inspector White's voice startled her. "You hadn't mentioned a smell before," he said. "What was it? Blood, perhaps, or . . . ?"

"Yes." Mary Helen's eyes were still closed. "But there was also a pleasant smell, like flowers."

"Flowers?" Detective Inspector White sounded incredulous. "Flowers at a murder scene?"

Mary Helen's eyes shot open. "I didn't say there were flowers, Detective Inspector, I said something smelled like flowers."

"What kind of flowers?" he asked.

"I'm not really sure," she admitted. "In fact, I'm not sure I ever smelled that scent before, but it made me think of flowers."

"You are not sure," White repeated, as if he was making certain that his ears were not deceiving him. "But you say you think you smelled flowers?" His eyes narrowed as he studied her.

"I smelled something fragrant," she said, wishing that she had never mentioned it at all. "It might have been bathroom spray. Actually, at the time I remember thinking of bathroom spray. But it may well have been the soap."

"I see," White said curtly, writing something in his notebook. Mary Helen wondered if he might have jotted down, "Nutter—smells things" after her name.

Looking up, he said offhandedly, "I'll ask Reedy to check with the publican to find out what kind of spray and soap is in the ladies'. Is there anything else you remember?"

"Nothing," Mary Helen said.

Seemingly satisfied that he'd learned all he could

about her finding Willie Ward, he focused his attention on Sister Eileen. "And it was the two of you, then, that found Tommy Burns?" he asked.

"Yes, Detective Inspector," Eileen answered.

"Can you tell me, again, how you happened upon Tommy?"

Mary Helen was grateful that this time Eileen took the lead, explaining how they'd slipped out of the Monks' Table after the wine tasting; how they felt lost in the field and then stumbled upon Tommy Burns.

"The poor fellow was freezing," Mary Helen added sympathetically.

"Murderers usually don't much care about their victims catching a chill," Detective Inspector White said.

"We went to find help," Mary Helen continued, ignoring his remark, "and came across Father Keane and Owen Lynch."

"The whole point of attacking Mr. Burns," Eileen swept on, "seems to have been stealing his Death costume."

Without uttering a word, Detective Inspector White turned his dark eyes, sharp as pins, on her. Mary Helen noticed a vein in his forehead stand out like a cord.

"Sister, please, just tell me what you remember. Let the detectives work out the reasons."

Eileen's cheeks reddened and her lips were set in a tight line—a sure sign that she was angry.

"Excuse me, Sister, if I'm a little direct," White apologized.

He must have mistaken Eileen's sudden coloring for embarrassment. "Some detective," Mary Helen wanted to say, but she thought better of it.

Detective Inspector White took time to read his notes while the two nuns sat in silence.

"You two best stay indoors," he said, obviously trying

to dispel the tension that had crept into their conversation. "You never know what you're going to run into out there!"

If you only knew the half of it, Mary Helen thought, giving an obligatory chuckle. *And you will, my man, as soon as Garda O'Dea finds an opening to tell you.*

"And then, last night," White was saying, "you found Mrs. Cox on your lawn?"

"Yes, Detective Inspector," Mary Helen answered, and she told him about getting a ride home from the barbeque with the pastor, Father Keane, and walking across the darkened lawn only to find Oonagh Cox on the ground.

"She said that she had been attacked by someone in Death's costume," Eileen added. She seemed determined to have the detective inspector at least acknowledge her theory about the costume's importance.

This time it was Detective Inspector White's face that colored. "Right," he said at last, obviously just as determined not to give the costume its due.

Why in the world not? Mary Helen wondered, stealing a furtive glance at his face, which revealed nothing.

"Do either of you remember anything else?" he asked at last. "Any more flowers?"

Now that he mentioned it, Mary Helen had noticed a fragrance when she rolled over Oonagh's body. One look at Detective Inspector White's thunderstorm face, however, and she decided to keep it to herself. She was in no mood for his ill humor. Abruptly White slapped his notebook shut and rose from his chair.

"Is that it, Detective Inspector?" Mary Helen asked.

"For now," the detective said. "If you think of anything else, I'll be in the village for the rest of the day."

"How is Oonagh this morning?" Eileen asked as they walked White to the door.

"I understand she's in pain, but that she'll be fine. I intend to go to the hospital this afternoon and see what she remembers."

With a smile, Eileen shut the door behind White. "Isn't he a right pain in the neck today?" she asked. "*Narky,* as the Irish would say."

"What do you suppose is bothering him?" Mary Helen peeked out the window and watched the detective return to the Monks' Table. He was shaking his head and looking for all the world as if he was carrying on a heated conversation with himself.

"Most likely he is getting a great deal of pressure to solve this case, and instead of his wrapping it up, more people are getting hurt. That can't be good for the detective inspector's nerves."

"I don't suppose that the young garda has told him about Oonagh and Owen Lynch." Mary Helen turned on the water in the sink and began to wash the lunch dishes. "Surely he'd have mentioned it if he knew."

"I wonder." Eileen picked up a towel to wipe. "And what was that about a fragrance? I don't remember you mentioning that before."

"I didn't remember it before," Mary Helen admitted, "what with the shock of finding the man and all. And from Detective Inspector White's reaction, I wish I hadn't thought of it yet. He acted as if I were imagining it, at best, or making it up, at worst. What did you think?"

"I don't know what to think," Eileen said. "I guess I would have expected the man to be happy to have another clue. Although you must admit, old dear, that smelling a fragrance you can't identify isn't much of a help to the poor fellow."

"If he'd just let me sniff around," Mary Helen said wistfully.

"But he won't," Eileen said, "and I suspect if we even try we'll get the rough side of Detective Inspector White's tongue, which I imagine is something to behold."

"What about the young garda, Liam O'Dea?" Mary Helen asked brightly, although she didn't have much faith in him herself.

"Don't even think about it," Eileen said.

"What harm, I ask you, can thinking possibly do?" Mary Helen asked.

The expression on Eileen's face was all the answer she needed.

Liam O'Dea had canvassed the entire village. No longer could he avoid the lane where his Auntie Zoë lived.

Taking a deep breath, he fervently hoped that Zoë was in the back of the house or, better yet, watching the telly. But even he knew that was too much to hope for.

The Lynch house was the first he passed on the lane. He stopped by the gate leading to the garden and took a quick look inside, then gave a sigh of relief when Patsy Lynch was nowhere to be seen. Sure if she caught a glimpse of him, she'd be on the horn with his auntie, as quick as a wink.

He'd often wondered why those two were such fast friends. Patsy seemed so loving and sweet while Zoë could drive a body to drink without a penny in his pocket.

Liam looked around the Lynch garden. Like so many of the village women, Patsy Lynch had her washing on the line. It looked to him as if every sheet, pillowcase, and towel in the house was being sun dried.

He half wondered if the beds of Ballyclarin would ever have clean linens if the sun didn't come out once in a while. Not that he'd say that to any ladies in the vil-

lage, including his mother. He knew better than to criti-
cize their housekeeping.

Patsy's line had several flowered sheets that he figured must belong to the twins, Doreen and Noreen.
Hanging among the towels and pillowcases were a number of large white sheets—he counted seven—from a
double bed, no doubt.

Staring at them, he wondered if Owen ever felt a
twinge of conscience when he was sleeping on them beside his wife. Or maybe he had the twinge when he was
in bed with Oonagh Cox. At the thought of it, he felt his
face grow hot.

That is, he reminded himself, if what the American
Sister told him she'd overheard was true. How was he
going to find out for sure? He couldn't just walk up to
Mr. Lynch and ask, now could he?

But why not? He was a garda, wasn't he? Owen
Lynch, on the other hand, was chairman of the Oyster
Festival and an important businessman in the county.

But nobody is above the law, are they? Liam took off
his hat and mopped his forehead. This heat was a killer.

Chairman or no, no one is above the law, he repeated
to himself. And he was the law.

Liam was dredging up the courage to knock on
Lynch's front door when his uncle Bertie stormed out of
the house next door, slamming the front door behind
himself.

Even from this distance Liam could see that his face
was crimson. "Don't get married, son, if you can avoid
it," Bertie shouted at him. "Above all, avoid a woman
with a sharp tongue!"

"Are you all right?" Liam asked, but Bertie O'Dea
didn't seem to hear him. Or, if he did, he wasn't answering.

Making a sharp turn by the front gate of his cottage, Bertie jumped into a waiting black funeral hearse, revved up the ignition, and raced away as if the devil were on his tail.

"And what is it you're gawking at?" It was Zoë's voice coming from the open front window. "Don't you have anything better to do than to snoop into decent people's business? If I remember correctly, there's been a murder in our village and one of our leading citizens has been attacked. Shouldn't you be trying to find the one who did these things?"

In case he hadn't heard her, she flung open the front door and stood with her hands on her hips. Her face was contorted with anger. "Well," she said, "has the cat got your tongue? Or are you so high and mighty in that uniform that you don't speak to your own relatives?"

Liam fought down the urge to arrest her, clamp handcuffs on her skinny arms, and drag her off to Mountjoy, then throw away the key. Instead, he walked slowly into the front garden and moved ever so purposefully among the laundry hanging on her lines.

"What in God's name do you think you're doing?" she shouted as he deliberately picked up one of his uncle's shirts and examined it.

Her small dark eyes stared unblinking, and her mouth twitched with fury.

Without a word, he examined her towels, bedsheets, and three pairs of cotton stockings.

"Don't you dare touch my laundry, you bold stump!" Zoë screeched, but Liam acted as if he hadn't heard her. Instead, with two fingers he picked up each side of a pair of her knickers and pulled them as wide as they would go. Raising his eyebrows, he looked from Zoë to the knickers and back again as if measuring them for a fit.

"Be Jaysus," Zoë screamed, her voice swollen with rage. "Leave those be and get out of my garden, you *ee-jit*, before I murder ye!"

Her words had the cold chill of ice, and Liam wondered for the first time if his Auntie Zoë could be the one.

Walking quickly back to the Monks' Table, Liam could not shake the feeling that Zoë was a possible suspect.

Just because a person says that she wants to murder you doesn't mean she will do it, he reminded himself.

And just because she's your auntie doesn't mean she's innocent, he countered.

"How did the sheet search go?" Detective Inspector White asked when Liam stepped into the pub. "Did you uncover anything unusual?"

Brian Reedy laughed at his wording, and the expression on White's face made it difficult for Liam to tell whether or not the pun was intended.

The young garda hesitated, not sure exactly what to say. "Well, sir," he said at last, "I'd say that we'll not find one made bed in the whole of the village."

"But you found nothing?"

Liam shook his head. "Sorry," he mumbled.

"It was a long shot," Reedy said, grabbing Liam's shoulder and giving it an encouraging squeeze. "We are just on our way to hospital to visit Mrs. Cox. Maybe we'll have better luck."

Liam felt Detective Inspector White's eyes studying him. "Join us, lad," White said. "Three heads are surely better than two."

"Yes, sir," Liam said, trying to hide his pleasure and relief. Surely Mrs. Cox was no longer a suspect. She was a victim, wasn't she? And hadn't he been right, after all, not to say anything about her and Owen Lynch? What a fool he'd feel, now that Mrs. Cox had been attacked.

Carmel would be at hospital, too, with her mam. He wondered what she'd think when she saw him keeping company with the detectives. He hoped she wouldn't get all giddy. Sure he didn't need another headache, now did he?

Sister Mary Helen could not settle down. She tried reading. But she couldn't concentrate. She flipped through several magazines left on the bookshelf by previous guests at the mews, but she'd be hard-pressed to tell anyone what she looked at.

Out the window, she noticed a brilliant white cloud bank forming along the horizon, and the sky was beginning to show patches of steel gray. A sudden wind slammed the trees in the backyard, sending a flock of crows cackling and wheeling into the sky.

Mary Helen shivered. Was that all the sunshine they were going to have?

Eileen, too, seemed unsettled. Maybe it was the weather.

"I can't seem to get Oonagh Cox off my mind," Eileen said finally. "Regardless of what her son said, I think we should pay her a visit."

"You do?" Mary Helen was surprised.

Eileen nodded. "We're only going to be here a couple more days, you know. And since she was attacked nearly on our very doorstep, I think we owe her, at least, a short visit."

"I couldn't agree more," Mary Helen said, gathering up her jacket and her umbrella.

"Have you any idea where the hospital is?" she asked.

"That's what Paul is for," Eileen said, dialing their driver's number.

• • •

Thirty-five minutes later, the two nuns were on their way to Bon Secours Hospital outside Galway City. *Good Help,* Mary Helen thought, *what a perfect name for a hospital.*

"Her husband, may he rest in peace, was on the staff," Paul Glynn told them as he sped along the dual carriageway, taking the roundabouts in his stride. "Everyone loved the old doc. Not even the pope himself could have had such a big funeral. So, she'll be treated like visiting royalty. You can't blame her for not wanting to come home."

The traffic picked up as they neared the city. And, much to Mary Helen's relief, Paul seemed to have to pay more attention to the road.

"About tonight," he asked finally, "are ye interested in the hurling match?"

Mary Helen hesitated. She knew by his tone when he asked the question that their answer should be yes.

"Do you think we should be?" Eileen asked.

Mary Helen marveled. Eileen had mastered the Irish knack of answering a question with a question.

"Indeed," Paul said, turning half around in the driver's seat.

Wondering if he could hear her heart thudding, Mary Helen resisted the temptation to close her eyes. Someone should be watching where they were going.

"Hurling is one of the fastest and most skillful games in the world," he said proudly. "It's an ancient Gaelic sport played before the coming of Christianity, and even the Great Famine could not stop it."

Mary Helen was impressed.

"There were no rules, you know, until the Gaelic Athletic Association was founded in the late 1800s." Paul was on a roll. "They say that ten thousand Irish people play hurling," he said with a smile in his voice, "and I am one of them."

"Then, it's settled," Eileen said. "We'll go."

Paul left them at the entrance to the hospital and promised to pick them up in thirty minutes. More than enough time, they reckoned, to visit a sick person.

When they arrived at her room, Oonagh Cox was sitting up in a chair that seemed to dwarf her. Even the top of her curly gray hair was hidden. Bouquets of red roses, hot pink and white carnations, and golden chrysanthemums surrounded her. A bright orange begonia plant was sharing a wicker basket with a box of Butler's Irish Chocolates. A potted calla lily rested on the windowsill alongside a small yellow box of what looked like perfume.

"You're up, I see," Eileen said.

Oonagh turned her head slightly, as if her neck was stiff. A bruise on her cheek where she had fallen was beginning to color, and a scratch on her chin looked red and sore.

"I can't bear to lie down surrounded by all these flowers," she said, her blue eyes dancing. "It's too much like being laid out."

"Oh, mam, really!" Carmel Cox entered the room carrying a vase filled with Peruvian lilies. "How you do go on!"

"You know my cheeky daughter, Carmel," Oonagh said. "She came to visit me, but she's spent most of her time arranging flowers."

"People love you, mam," Carmel said, gently planting a kiss on her mother's forehead. "And I do, too."

"Which is why someone banged me on the head," Oonagh protested. A flat silence filled the small room, and a ray of sun bounced off the windowpane.

"Why don't you get yourself a cup of tea, love," Oonagh said finally. "I know you can use one. Let me visit with the Sisters."

Unless she was mistaken, Mary Helen thought the girl looked relieved.

"I apologize," Oonagh said as soon as they were alone. "I'm in a fierce mood and my head is throbbing."

"No need for apologies," Mary Helen assured her. "Maybe we shouldn't have come at all. We were just concerned, but if you'd prefer—"

Oonagh put up one small hand to stop her. "I'm glad you did," she said. "I wanted to thank you for your care last night. What must you think of Ireland?" Sudden tears flooded her eyes. "You come for a holiday and we give you instead two attacks and a murder."

Mary Helen was about to assure her that violence is universal and as statistics go, Ireland is way below the norm, when a young delivery boy came through the door with a bunch of long-stemmed roses. They were a pale yellow and surrounded with maidenhair.

"Please put them there," Oonagh said, taking the enclosure card from the lad and pointing to the window ledge. "Wherever you can find space."

Once he was gone, she tore open the small envelope, and Mary Helen watched all the color drain from her already pale face. She looked for a moment as though she might faint.

"What is it?" Mary Helen asked. "Are you all right?"

Eileen stepped closer. "Do you need some water?"

Trying to catch her breath, Oonagh said nothing, only stared at the card.

Taking it from her trembling hand, Mary Helen read the message aloud. "I SHOULD BE ASHAMED?" was written in bold capitals. No name was attached.

"That is what my attacker said," Oonagh whispered. "These roses are from the person who struck me."

Mary Helen's stomach turned over. *Whoever it was is as bold as brass,* she thought. And she wouldn't be a bit surprised if he tried it again.

"Can you remember anything else?" Mary Helen asked. "Anything at all that might help the police find out who this person is?"

Eyes closed, Oonagh seemed to be thinking. "Nothing," she said finally.

"Have you any enemies?"

"Enemies?" Oonagh repeated. "The first person who pops into my mind is Willie Ward, but he's dead now, isn't he?"

Mary Helen remembered hearing that Mr. Ward had threatened to report Oonagh to the authorities for trying to purchase cannabis for her ailing husband. But her husband had been dead for several years now.

"Have you any idea why Willie Ward disliked you so?" Mary Helen asked.

Oonagh gave a wry smile. "You've heard it said, I'm sure, that 'Heaven hath no rage like love to hatred turned, Nor hell a fury like a woman scorned'?" she asked.

Mary Helen nodded.

"Well, it goes double for an Irishman."

"You scorned him?" Eileen asked.

"It's ancient history, Sister," Oonagh said wearily. "We must have been about fourteen years old at the time." She smiled sadly at the memory. "I refused him a dance. Not meaning to, I humiliated him, I guess, and he never let it go. He took every chance, every way he could to get back at me. Willie was a vengeful lad and he grew into a vengeful man."

"And was he that way, as well, with Jake Powers?"

Oonagh gave a rueful laugh. "Jake, the tinker? If anything, he was worse to Jake."

"Why?"

"Not only was Jake a tinker, but he took all the top honors when we were at school, which Willie thought rightfully belonged to him. Jake has been paying the price ever since."

Oonagh closed her eyes. "Now there's the person who had a reason to kill the bastard, not that he did. Jake is really a gentle sort."

"You look tired," Eileen said, checking her wristwatch, "and we've probably overstayed our welcome, but before we go, is there anyone else besides Willie that you can think of who might have a reason to hurt you?"

Oonagh caught her breath and looked up at Mary Helen. Her eyes were full of pain. "The one person who has reason to hate me," she said sadly, "doesn't even know it."

Again, a heavy silence hung in the small hospital room. Obviously Oonagh Cox thought she was speaking in riddles, unaware that the two nuns knew she was referring to Patsy Lynch.

But Patsy couldn't have attacked her, could she? Mary Helen had seen her at the barbeque, dancing with Mr. Lynch. Did Patsy have the time—and ability—to attack someone, knock her unconscious, and then go dancing with her husband as if nothing had happened? It seemed almost impossible.

Mary Helen was teetering on the verge of telling Oonagh what they knew when she heard a commotion in the hallway. The Sister in charge was explaining that Mrs. Cox already had company, too much company, and that she mustn't get overtired.

"This is official business."

With horror Mary Helen recognized the voice of Detective Inspector White, the last person she wanted to run into at Bon Secours. He'd consider her presence there anything but Good Help.

Liam O'Dea couldn't believe his eyes. The American nuns, if you please, were standing, as big as life, in Mrs. Cox's hospital room.

Stealing a quick look at his superior's crimson face, Liam thought the man might be having a coronary. *What better place for it than a hospital?* he mused, wondering, in the event that there was no heart attack, where this little meeting would be going.

Both Sisters stood their ground, speechless. Obviously, they had not expected Detective Inspector White.

Tension nearly crackled in the small flower-filled room. Oonagh Cox, looking frail and tiny in her chair, didn't seem to notice. "Inspectors, Liam," she said. "How nice of you to come." She turned slowly and stiffly. "You know the Sisters, of course."

With a face like a thundercloud, Detective Inspector White nodded. "Indeed, we do," he strained through clamped teeth. "I am, however, surprised to see them here."

"And we were just about to leave," Mary Helen said quickly. "We just wanted to make sure Mrs. Cox was doing well. It isn't every day that you find someone unconscious on your lawn."

Good point, Liam thought, looking from the old nun to Ernie White. He had the feeling that he was watching a match of sorts. What he couldn't decide was if it was going to be a full-out battle of wits or just a little friendly scrimmage.

White said nothing, which in itself was unusual, Liam noted.

"You know, Detective Inspector." Sister Eileen tilted her chin slightly.

Uh-oh, Liam thought, *two against one.* "We are leaving for home in a few days."

Although he saw no lips moving, Liam could have sworn he heard someone mutter, "Thanks be to God."

"Surely we couldn't be expected to leave without checking on Oonagh," Sister Eileen added reasonably.

"Surely not," White agreed.

"So then, good-bye, Oonagh dear," she said. "We hope you are feeling better soon."

Silently, hands in his pockets, Ernie White watched the two nuns leave. When he was sure they were out of earshot, he turned to his partner. "I ask you, Brian, was I clear or was I clear? Didn't I tell those two to stay out of police business?"

"You can hardly say they were in police business," Oonagh spoke up, "when all they were doing was checking to see how I was feeling. And who can blame them? It's just common courtesy, really. I was, after all, literally left in their backyard."

Liam watched his superior officer open his mouth, then close it again, leaving Oonagh Cox with the last word. *Amazing,* Liam thought, even though he knew from experience that women have a tendency to band together, particularly against a man.

"Oh, look who's here now," Carmel called from the doorway. Her cheeks colored as her eyes fell on him. "Are you going to find out who did this to my poor mam?" she asked.

White answered for him. "We are trying our best, Carmel," he said, sounding surprisingly fatherly. "Now, we need to ask your mother some questions, if you wouldn't mind giving us a few minutes."

Carmel's smile faded. "But—" she started to protest.

"Go on, love," Oonagh coaxed. "Be a darling and go home now and fix your brothers something for supper. They'll be hungry, I'm sure."

Carmel frowned and her face crumpled as if she was about to complain, but Oonagh patted her hand. "That's a good girl, now," she said. "If you hurry, you can catch the same lift down with the Sisters," Oonagh said.

Detective Inspector White shut the hospital room door behind Carmel. For a moment, the room seemed unnaturally quiet. "Well, well," he said, surveying the place, "if I didn't know better, I'd think this was a florist shop."

Oonagh sighed. "I know what you mean, Detective Inspector. Too many flowers, really. My knock on the noggin must have made the florist's day."

"Never mind day," Reedy said. "I'd say month."

Quietly the three of them admired the beautiful bouquets. Outside dark clouds tumbled across the sky, dulling the sun. Deep shadows filled the corners of the room.

Oonagh cleared her throat. "This came with the last bouquet, the pale yellow roses and the maidenhair," she said, handing the detective the small white enclosure card.

White read it, turned it over, then handed it to Reedy.

Silently, Liam stood by, wondering what in the devil was on that little card that could be so important. When Reedy kindly handed it to him, he knew.

Neither detective said anything, so Oonagh spoke up. "Those are the exact words the person who attacked me said. You remember what I told you last night?" She sounded frustrated.

"As I recall, you said that you weren't really sure to what the sender was referring," White said softly as if he were thinking aloud.

Oonagh averted her eyes and Liam couldn't tell if she nodded or simply adjusted her head on the pillow.

As he took the card back from Liam, White's whole

face brightened. "Oranmore Florist," he said. "As soon as we have a chance, we'll give him a call. With any luck at all, the florist will remember who ordered these flowers. Yellow roses and maidenhair, you say?"

Liam watched White take in all the bouquets around the room. "That was the only one with yellow roses?" he asked.

Liam heard the optimism in his voice.

"Maybe our murderer finally made a mistake. They all do eventually, lad," he said, giving Liam a friendly punch on the upper arm.

"Yes, sir," Liam said, trying not to wince. It seemed almost too simple. The murderer orders flowers in the village from a florist who most surely would recognize him, then sends a card practically giving himself away. *No murderer is that thick, is he?* Liam wondered.

From nowhere, a nurse appeared in the doorway of the room, the picture of an avenging angel in white. "Pardon," she said softly, "but it is time for Mrs. Cox's medication." She held a small tray in front of her like a battering ram.

"We'll be on our way, then," White said, taking his notebook out of his pocket. He flipped it open and read down the page. Then he snapped it shut and put it back in his jacket pocket. "Is there anything you may have remembered about last night that you may have forgotten to tell us?" he asked.

Oonagh seemed to be thinking. "No, Detective Inspector," she said finally. "Except that if Willie Ward wasn't dead himself, he'd be my first suspect."

"Maybe we should be looking more closely into Willie's enemies," Reedy said as they waited in the hallway of the Bon Secours for the lift.

"He seems to have had so many," White said. "What do you make of it, Liam?"

At the sound of his name, Liam jumped. Both sets of eyes were on him. Liam could feel his face growing warm and his shirt collar pinched his neck. He hoped neither of them asked him what he was thinking about. Sure, they'd not expect him to say Carmel Cox, but he was. He was hoping she'd come to the game tonight, even if her mother was in hospital. He would be playing in the match, and after it, he'd ask her for a drink. And, maybe if he were lucky, she'd let him walk her home. Liam felt his face redden as he thought what else they could do.

"Well, what do you make of it?" White sounded impatient.

"The case?" Liam asked, stalling for time.

"Of course, the case." White grumbled.

To be honest, Liam didn't know what to think. He knew he was glad he hadn't told his superior about Oonagh Cox and Owen Lynch. Since Mrs. Cox was attacked, she could hardly be the murderer. Someone had used the Death costume as a disguise and then murdered Willie Ward and attacked Oonagh Cox.

Somehow it all fit together, although for the life of him he couldn't think how.

Maybe the answer was with the florist. He'd be glad not to have to search anymore for that costume. It was humiliating to have to pick through people's clotheslines.

And wait until his Auntie Zoë told his mam what he had done to her. Now he wished he hadn't, but it was too late. She had driven him to it, hadn't she, the old bat? His mam would be furious with him and he'd never hear the end of it, now would he? He knew his da would think it was funny, but that wouldn't save him from his mother's tongue.

Something else was bothering him about today's search. To save his soul, he could not put his finger on what it was. Maybe if he stopped thinking about it, it would just come.

"I don't know what to make of it, sir," he said at last and was glad when the lift door opened.

When Sister Mary Helen and Sister Eileen arrived back at the mews, they were surprised to find two young men crawling around on their lawn. The late afternoon sky looked bruised as the sun flittered in and out, creating dark shadows on the grass.

"They must be the technical bureau from Dublin," Eileen whispered.

"I hope so," Mary Helen replied. "How do?" she called aloud.

Both men stopped and sat back on their haunches. She could swear that neither of them looked a day over twenty. *You'd have to be young to crawl around like that for long,* she thought.

"Good day to you," one of them answered pleasantly.

She noticed that he was holding what looked like a plastic bag and a large pair of tweezers. Several bags had been sealed, labeled, and set in a pile near the edge of the lawn. It was impossible to tell what they contained. Even close up Mary Helen doubted that she would recognize what was in them.

"Are you finding anything?" she asked.

"We are," the man answered, "although it's hard to tell what or if it's important till we get it back to the lab."

"Can we get you anything? Tea? Coffee? A cold drink?" Eileen offered.

"That would be grand," the same fellow admitted,

"but we've no time. The detective inspector wants our report tonight."

Without any further conversation, the two men went back to work and the two nuns went inside.

"What time did Paul say that he's picking us up for the hurling?" Mary Helen asked.

"He said that it starts at seven and that he needs to be there a bit before, so half six would be fine. He'll take us to the pitch."

Mary Helen must have looked puzzled.

"That's what they call the field," Eileen explained.

Sister Mary Helen checked her wristwatch. "Why don't I make us some supper and you see if you can find something on that bookshelf about hurling?"

A quick search of the small refrigerator yielded enough to make a delicious omelet. Served with soda bread, real butter, and tea, it would be perfect for supper.

Eileen uncovered a short but comprehensive article on hurling, written, no doubt, with tourists in mind.

By the time Paul stopped by for them, they knew that hurling was best compared to lacrosse. They had learned that it was played with a "hurly"—a wooden stick made of ash—and a small ball, on a field larger than a soccer field. It was a seventy-minute game with fifteen players, two halves, and a ten-minute intermission in which the teams changed sides.

The point, they discovered, was to drive the ball either into the goal or over the bar. The goal was worth three points, the bar, one.

When they arrived at the Ballyclarin Pitch, a high-spirited crowd had already gathered and was quickly filling in the bleachers. Despite the fact that the seats were sheltered, Mary Helen was glad they had dressed warmly.

"Sisters, over here." They turned to find Father Keane beckoning them. He seemed to have saved them seats.

"Thank you, Father," Mary Helen said, settling down among the enthusiastic fans.

They were barely settled when a loud roar went up as the Ballyclarin players in gray and black came onto the field. An equally loud cry rose when the opposing team from a neighboring town appeared, dressed in blue and gold.

The voice of Festival Chairman Owen Lynch came over the loudspeaker. He welcomed everyone and introduced the referee, two linemen, and four umpires in white coats. Finally he yielded the microphone to what must have been the Irish equivalent of a sportscaster. Everyone seemed to know him, because a cheer rose from the crowd at the mention of his name.

"We're in for quite a night," the man began. Or at least, that was what Mary Helen thought he said. He spoke so rapidly and with such a thick accent that she could not understand much of what he said. Considering a few of the words she did catch, it was probably just as well.

The players moved so quickly that it was difficult to tell who was who. She thought she recognized Paul zipping down the field. She asked Father Keane to make sure it was he.

"Indeed," the priest answered. "He's a fine player, though he'd never be the one to tell you. One of the stars, is our Paul."

Mary Helen felt a little reflected glory watching him race toward the goal. The way the sticks were swinging and the ball was speeding through the air, she was especially glad he was wearing a helmet.

And wasn't that Liam O'Dea running close to him? If she wasn't mistaken, she thought she heard the announcer say, "He's the last person to let you down. His people are undertakers."

A roar went up and the crowd went with it. Someone must have scored, although Mary Helen couldn't say who and Father Keane seemed so engrossed in the game that she didn't want to bother him.

Looking around, she realized that the bleachers were packed. If she wasn't mistaken, the hurling match was the best-attended event of the festival so far. She wondered if Carmel Cox had come to the match. There were familiar faces from the wine tasting, the art contest, morning Mass, and the gala.

It wasn't hard to spot Patsy Lynch sitting with Zoë and Bertie O'Dea. Tara, who had mercifully abandoned her green taffeta dress for a pair of blue jeans and a jacket, was there with Detective Inspector Reedy. Hugh Ryan, the publican, had actually left the Monks' Table for an hour. And there among the spectators was Jake Powers, the tinker, whose face looked as if he was studying a thing of beauty. Paul's wife sat close to the field. Her red hair was pulled back and tied with black and gray ribbons.

Only Oonagh Cox, who was in hospital, and Detective Inspector White were missing. Possibly he was the only fellow in the west of Ireland who was still working. Sister Mary Helen hoped that the technical bureau had uncovered something in the grass.

The minutes passed quickly, and Mary Helen was surprised when an official called the end of the half. The players filed into the clubhouse for a well-deserved break.

The crowd used the intermission to move around, get tea and chips from the vendors, and visit with their friends and neighbors. Eileen set off to get them each a hot drink.

"Sister Helen."

Mary Helen was startled to hear someone call her
name. She turned around to find Jake directly behind
her. His straight black hair was slicked back and fell to
his shoulders. His brilliant blue eyes studied her.

She hadn't heard him coming, but with all the noise,
how could she?

"How do?" she said, smiling.

"I came by your place last night," he said, his voice low.

"Oh!" Mary Helen was taken aback. Had he seen
Oonagh on the lawn? If so, why hadn't he called the
police?

Hesitating, Jake frowned. "About my photograph," he
said. His mouth tightened. "You are still keen to have
one, are you?"

"Yes! Yes, indeed," Mary Helen said quickly. What
was the matter with her? She didn't even know what
time Oonagh was attacked, let alone what time he had
dropped by. Was she getting to be as suspicious of him
as he claimed others were?

She felt Jake's eyes boring into her. "What is it? Is
something gone wrong?" he asked.

He had picked that up, Mary Helen thought.

"No, not really. Can you sit for a minute?" She patted
the bench beside her.

Still frowning, Jake settled in Eileen's seat next to her.

No sense beating around the bush, Mary Helen
thought, taking a deep breath. "You must be the only
one in the entire village who doesn't know," she said.

"Doesn't know what?" Jake pulled up his coat collar
against the crisp wind.

"That Oonagh Cox was attacked last night and left on
the lawn behind our mews."

Jake's face drained of color, and his eyes seemed to

grow even larger. "On your lawn?" he asked. "I was there about half eight and I didn't see anyone at all. In fact, the entire village looked deserted. Only when I realized that you weren't at home either did it occur to me that everyone must be at the barbeque."

He stopped. "You don't think that I . . . ?" Abruptly he rose to his full height. Reaching up, Mary Helen grabbed the sleeve of his coat and pulled him back down.

"Of course I don't," she said with as much conviction as she could manage. "What I was thinking was that if you were at our mews at eight thirty and we found Oonagh about eleven, that narrows down the time frame." She smiled. "We had better tell Detective Inspector White. He seems to need all the help he can get."

With a rush, the color flooded back into Jake's face. His eyes flashed anger. "Detective Inspector White, indeed! That's all he needs, a tinker to blame this on."

"Jake," Sister Mary Helen said soothingly, "I'm sure that the detective inspector—"

Without letting her finish, Jake shot to his feet. "You don't know what you're sure of," he said angrily. "You don't know shite about a tinker's life."

"Wait!" she sputtered, but he didn't seem to hear her. Feeling a little sick, Mary Helen watched his tall sinewy body move cougarlike down the bleachers and out of sight.

"What was that all about?" Eileen asked, handing her a cup of tea that she had managed to find.

The hot, sweet aroma rose and warmed Mary Helen's cheeks. "Jake was at our place last night at about eight thirty," she said, "and he says he didn't see anyone there, which means that surely Oonagh could not have been there."

"She would have been hard to miss," Eileen agreed.

"I suggested we tell Detective Inspector White—to pin down the time," she explained. "Obviously it was the wrong thing to say."

"He went ballistic, then, did he?" Eileen asked.

"Right."

"Thought he'd be blamed, did he?"

"Right again," Mary Helen said. "How did you know?"

"I'm just guessing from our conversation with him at his home."

"I thought he had some valuable information to pass on to the inspector." Mary Helen shrugged. "But he didn't see it that way."

Eileen blew on the tea. "Why was he there?" she asked.

"At our place?"

Eileen nodded and cautiously took a sip of the hot liquid.

"To offer us one of his pictures, I think," Mary Helen said. "He stalked away before I could ask him more about it."

"Do you think he'll be back?" She scanned the bleachers and the sides of field, but Jake seemed to have completely disappeared.

"It's difficult to tell," Eileen said. Her words were scarcely audible over the roar from the crowd that greeted the returning teams.

"There's Liam O'Dea," Eileen said, pointing to the young garda running down the field.

"Oh, yes," Mary Helen said, but her mind was not on the game. All she could think about was Jake Powers. Such a talented fellow and so angry. Poor man! How had she been so insensitive to his feelings? She wondered if she would have a chance to see him and apologize before they left for home.

And should she tell Detective Inspector White about Jake being at the mews at 8:30? It sounded like a valuable bit of information to her, but he had told her several times in several ways to stay out of his business. Maybe she should pass this latest discovery on to young O'Dea, who was, at this moment, on the ground. But O'Dea hadn't been too reliable conveying the one bit of information that she had given him to pass on. What reason had she to believe that he'd be any better with her second discovery?

Frustrated that she couldn't make up her mind what to do, she figured that she might as well try to enjoy the game. Hard as she struggled, she couldn't seem to keep her mind on it.

Frankly, she was relieved when the crowd rose to their feet and started picking up their belongings. At last, the whole thing was over.

"We won!" Eileen, her cheeks red with excitement, informed her.

"Hooray!" Mary Helen said, assuming that "we" was Paul's team.

"Let me take you two home," Father Keane offered. "Paul will no doubt be doing a bit of celebrating with the lads." He turned and looked at them inquisitively. "Unless you two want to stay and join in the fun."

"Thank you, no," Mary Helen answered quickly. "Home is fine." She glanced at Eileen to make sure.

"Home, James," Eileen said with a grin, "and don't spare the horses."

It had been a long, full day, and all that fresh air and sunshine had done them in. Sister Mary Helen did not remember anything at all after she climbed into bed and pulled up the soft down quilt.

Thursday, September 4

May the Lord keep you in His hand
And never close His fist too tight.
—Irish blessing

On Thursday morning, both Sister Mary Helen and Sister Eileen overslept. When Mary Helen finally did wake up, she lay in her bed listening, hoping to hear familiar sounds, but there were none.

The mews was eerily quiet, as if it were deserted. In fact, the whole village sounded deserted. Even straining, she could not pick up the sound of a voice or tires on the macadam or even a lorry door slamming.

She checked her bedside clock. Ten fifty! Was it possible that she had slept through the church bell calling the villagers to morning Mass?

Silently, she slipped out of bed and into her slippers, anxious to check on Eileen. She was surprised to find her still in bed, too.

"Is that you?" Eileen asked groggily as Mary Helen tried to back out of the bedroom without waking her.

She was tempted to say, "No," but it was too soon after waking to try to be funny.

"What time is it?" Eileen asked, her eyes still shut and her blanket around her ears.

"Nearly eleven," Mary Helen said.

Eileen's gray eyes popped open and she sat up. "Oh dear," she said. "We've missed the field trip to the Burren. I think the coach was leaving at ten."

She fumbled on her bedside table for the list of Oyster Festival activities. "Sure enough," she said, sounding a bit disappointed, "this morning was the trip to the Burren with," she read from the brochure, "the naturalist Ignatius D'Arcy."

"The Burren?" Mary Helen didn't remember Eileen mentioning it. "What is the Burren?" she asked.

Getting out of bed, Eileen slipped into her bathrobe. "I'll put on some coffee," she said.

Mary Helen followed her into the kitchen.

"The Burren," Eileen explained, sounding like the schoolteacher she had been, "is a section of western Ireland, about one hundred square miles, to be exact, which resembles nothing as much as a moonscape with miles of polished limestone stretching in every direction. It is an archaeologist's delight with megalithic tombs and Iron Age stone forts. Botanists are amazed to find arctic, alpine, and Mediterranean plants growing there together. At this time of the year they bloom." Eileen stopped. "If you want to go, we can give Paul a buzz," she said. "I'm sure he'd take us."

Although it was tempting, Mary Helen didn't know if she was up to driving on the opposite side of another narrow road with Paul at the wheel. "Maybe we should take the morning off," she said, "unless you want to go."

Eileen considered it for less than thirty seconds. "We need a holiday from our holiday," she said and began to hum a few bars of "The Old Gray Mare, She Ain't What She Used to Be."

Pulling back the kitchen curtain, Mary Helen checked the morning sky. To her amazement it was bright blue and cloudless. "It's another glorious day," she said, watching a pair of black jackdaws hopping across the lawn as several Great Tits, their large white cheeks standing out, flitted among a cluster of magenta foxgloves.

"Two in a row." Eileen opened the back door and took a deep breath. "What a blessing," she said.

With nothing special to do and nowhere in particular to go, the two decided to enjoy a leisurely brunch in their garden.

Eileen was just taking several strips of crisp bacon from the frying pan when the telephone rang.

"Sister." Paul sounded anxious when Mary Helen picked up the receiver. "Did you miss the bus to the Burren?" he asked.

"Yes, Paul, I'm afraid we did." Rolling her eyes, she said it loud enough for Eileen to hear.

"Do you want me to take you, then?" he asked.

"No. No, thank you. Not at all," she answered quickly. "We decided to take it easy today."

To her surprise, Paul didn't insist. Actually, he didn't even offer a second time. If the truth be told, he sounded downright relieved.

"You've saved me a bloody fortune," he said in a low whisper.

"How's that?" Mary Helen asked, straining to hear.

"My wife loves that perfumery that they have there. According to herself, they have a special smell that she goes daft about. She'd want me to bring some back, and it costs an arm and a leg."

"What is so special about it?" Mary Helen asked, feeling a little sorry that they were depriving Paul's wife of a treat.

"You've got me there," Paul said. "It looks like yellow water to me. She says it captures—that's the word she uses, mind you, captures—the scent of wild orchids and an Irish summer."

"I see," Mary Helen said, although she didn't. For the life of her, she couldn't remember ever smelling a wild orchid, nor had she the faintest idea of what the aroma of an Irish summer might be.

"To me it smells like fern and moss with a few bits of old wood thrown in for good measure. They even sell a yellow candle that smells the same way." He was talking louder now; his wife must have gone out of earshot.

Mary Helen watched as Eileen scrambled the eggs, adding a few slivers of creamy white cheese. "Well, if she likes it," she said, anxious to hang up before the eggs were done.

"If you ask me, what she likes about it is the fact that some of the ladies in the village wear it. You know, the ones whose husbands have money." He lowered his voice again. Obviously, the wife was back. *Good,* Mary Helen thought. *He can't go on much longer.*

"So you don't want to go, then?" He quickly changed the subject. "I'm home, then, all day, if you change your mind. Or if you need me for anything at all, just ring. Oh, and I'll ring you later to see if you want to go to tonight's jamboree."

The receiver slammed down before Mary Helen could even congratulate him on last night's victory and his brilliant playing.

"Perfect timing," Eileen said, dishing up the eggs and bacon. "Butter the toast, will you please, old dear? Let's eat while it is piping hot."

Hugh Ryan was like a new man, and it hadn't taken much. Detective Inspector Ernie White had given him permission to reopen the Monks' Table today at eleven, on the condition that the detective inspector and his men could use Hugh's small office as headquarters for their investigation.

Arrangements were quickly made. The news of the pub's reopening had traveled through the village almost faster than the speed of sound, if such a thing were possible.

A record crowd arrived by noon for a bite to eat or for just a pint and a look around at the murder scene. The waitresses were run ragged, and Hugh himself could scarcely keep up with the Guinness orders.

Old Terry Eagan was back. He had managed to claim his usual bar stool and was full of bad jokes to tell to all who would listen. Over the din, his voice could be heard. "Paddy, Sean, and Seamus were stumbling home from the pub late one night," he said, "and found themselves on the road which leads past the old graveyard.

" 'Come, have a look over here,' says Paddy. 'It's Michael O'Grady's grave. God bless his soul. He lived to the ripe old age of eighty-seven!'

" 'That's nothing,' says Sean. 'Here's one named Denis O'Toole. It says here he was ninety-five when he died.'

"Just then Seamus yells out, 'Good God, here's a fella that got to be one hundred forty-five.'

" 'What was his name?' asks Paddy.

"Seamus stumbles around a bit, awkwardly lighting a match to see what else is on the stone marker. 'Miles from Dublin,' he says."

"That's a good one," Hugh said, sounding happy that business would soon be back to normal.

As agreed upon, Detective Inspectors Ernie White and Brian Reedy set up headquarters in Hugh's small office, which had a door leading to the field behind the Monks' Table. That is, if you could call bringing in a couple of chairs and clearing off the desktop setting up headquarters. Simple as it seemed, it had taken most of the morning to do it.

"Reporting for duty, sirs," Liam O'Dea said smartly when they had finished. He glanced surreptitiously around the room. By this time, he had hoped to find more gardai on the scene. He tried not to show his disappointment when only White, Reedy, and he were on board. Maybe the others were still coming.

"Good morning, lad," White replied, scarcely looking up from the desk. "As you can see, the men are still needed in Dublin, but we can't let our small number stop us, can we?" He looked up, and his brown eyes caught Liam off guard.

"No, sir," Liam answered quickly, wondering if his face gave him away.

"No, indeed. Have a seat, Liam." White pointed to the one empty chair left in the room. "Let's go over what we know and what needs to be done to solve this case."

"Yes, sir," Liam answered stiffly, sitting straight-backed in his chair. The muscles in his arms and legs ached from yesterday's hurling match. He had no idea he was in such bad shape. But they had won, and Carmel, in her excitement, had given him a great big victory kiss, which made his pain a small price to pay.

"Good game last night," Reedy said, raising his teacup in a toast.

"We've no time for games," White cut in.

Uh-oh, Liam thought, catching a glimpse of the frown on the detective's face. *Today is not going to be a good one.* "Yes, sir," he said.

White ran his eyes down his notebook page. "Let's see now," he said.

It's as if he expects something to pop off the page and hit him in the eyes, Liam thought, watching the man's dark scowl.

"The search for Death's costume went nowhere, then?" White grumbled.

Liam couldn't tell if it was a question or a statement, so he said nothing. Actually, there was not much he could say. He knew that most of the families in Ballyclarin were now sleeping on clean sheets, but that hardly seemed pertinent to the investigation.

"Ah." White stopped and looked up suddenly. "We did have one complaint. One," he repeated, "from Ms. Zoë O'Dea."

Liam's stomach cramped, and he could almost feel White's dark eyes boring into him.

"It seems that you touched her unmentionables."

Reedy snickered, and Liam felt his face grow hot. *Damn woman,* he thought, averting his eyes.

"Was there a reason?" his superior asked, rationally. "There had better be a good reason, lad."

Liam needed to think of something. Desperately, he searched for a reasonable explanation. "I was just being thorough, sir," he said finally.

"Thorough? How so?"

Dear God, don't let me stutter. "Well, sir," he said, "she seemed reluctant and I wanted to make sure she wasn't hiding anything."

"In her knickers?" White roared.

This time Reedy laughed out loud.

"This is not a joke, Brian," White cut back at his partner.

"Sorry," Reedy mumbled, biting his cheeks.

"This woman is your aunt, is she not?" White asked.

"By marriage," Liam answered.

"And you were afraid she might be hiding something?"

Liam didn't know whether to answer yes or no. Either way, he was caught.

Fortunately, Reedy saved the day. "She's his aunt, all right," he said, "and one colossal pain in the arse. You can't blame Liam for doing his job." That seemed to mollify the detective inspector, at least for the moment, and he went back to studying his notebook.

"Anything else on your search?" he asked after a few minutes. "Anything significant?"

Not a damn thing, Liam wanted to say, but he knew that wasn't the answer. The Lynch twins have flowered sheets, he remembered, but he knew White would have his head if he mentioned that.

"Well, garda?"

Liam fidgeted. Would White ever get off him? Probably not until he had another bone to chew. Now was as good a time as any to tell him about Mrs. Cox and Owen Lynch.

"Well, sir." Liam's Adam's apple felt enormous in his throat, and he was sure beads of perspiration were popping out on his forehead.

"Well, what?" White narrowed his eyes.

With as few words as possible Liam told the detective about what Sister Mary Helen had overheard.

"Oonagh Cox and Owen Lynch?" White repeated in disbelief. "And you say Willie Ward knew?"

"Yes, sir, that's what the American nun said."

"And why didn't she tell me?" White muttered to himself.

Liam knew the answer, but he also knew better than to give it. He was glad when Reedy spoke up. "Be reasonable, Ernie. You told her to stay out of your business."

"But she didn't, now did she?" His eyes swung back to Liam. "Is there anything else she told you that you've not told me?"

"No, sir," Liam said, dreading the next question he knew was coming.

"And when did she tell you this?"

Liam cleared his throat. He was sure his voice was gone. The sharp ring of the telephone shattered the silence. Liam jumped.

White stared at it as if he'd never seen it before, then reached over to the edge of the desk and picked up the receiver. "Hello," he shouted into the phone. "Yes, this is he," he said, then listened.

Liam would have liked to get up from his chair, but he wasn't sure his legs would hold him. The temperature in the small office seemed to have soared, and at the moment, he could scarcely breathe. Whoever was on the line had given him a short reprieve, but he knew that it wouldn't last long.

How would he tell his da that he had been let go, which he surely would be when White found out he'd kept the information from him for three days? What would he do with himself? He supposed he could get himself a position in the family business, maybe as a hearse driver. But he had always wanted to be a garda.

And what would he tell Carmel—that he'd been fired? She'd want to know the reason. And how would he tell her about her mother and Owen Lynch? Maybe this was a good time to go to America.

"That was the florist in Oranmore," White said, frowning.

"Good news, I hope." Reedy perked up. "Could he tell you who sent the yellow roses and the note to Mrs. Cox?"

"No," White answered. "It seems that his records show that whoever sent them paid in cash and must have given him the signed card to enclose."

"And he can't remember who it was?"

White shook his head. "Not at all. He says there were

so many orders that day all going to Oonagh Cox that he can't remember one from another."

"But not everyone pays in cash, I'm certain. And we only saw one bouquet of yellow roses." Reedy frowned. "You'd think he'd remember that."

"Right. He does remember several people giving him cash. Most of them women, but he can't be sure this one was. But it could be."

White rose from behind the desk, put his hands in his trousers pockets and stared into space. "A woman," he repeated. "This case is getting stranger and stranger."

"Now what?" Reedy asked.

White shrugged. "Let's talk to the American nun," he said. "And"—he looked at Liam—"you stay here, lad, and wait for the tech team to call from Dublin. Please God, they will have found something useful."

"Yes, sir," Liam said, feeling a little sick to his stomach. Watching the two inspectors walk toward the mews, he thought he knew how a condemned man feels when his death sentence has just been commuted.

"Uh-oh," Mary Helen said softly, nodding her head toward the gate leading to the mews.

Eileen turned and quickly rose. "Good morning, Detective Inspectors," she said. "We were just finishing up. Will you join us for a cup of coffee or a cup of tea?"

Reedy looked as if he might be tempted to accept, but White spoke up before he had a chance.

"Thank you, no," he said with a voice from the deep freeze. "We need a word."

"A word?" Eileen asked, her gray eyes wide.

"Can we go somewhere?" White looked around the garden as if he suspected the hedge sparrows skulking around in the underbrush of being bugged.

"It's such a lovely day," Eileen began to protest, but White had already pulled open their front door and stood aside waiting for them to enter.

Silence fell like a stone as the four settled into comfortable chairs in the living room.

"What can we do for you?" Mary Helen asked finally and noticed that her question had made White's face redden. Was it anger or embarrassment? She couldn't tell.

"We understand from Garda O'Dea," White began.

Mary Helen felt a sudden relief. *That's what this is all about,* she thought. *The young fellow has finally told his superior.*

"I wish that you had come to me," White was saying in a rather snappish tone, which made Mary Helen's backbone stiffen. Her jaw tightened, and she pushed up her bifocals onto the bridge of her nose as she studied the man. *How quickly we forget!* she thought.

White must have noticed her expression for all at once his voice softened. "No harm done," he said with largesse.

As though I were the one at fault. Mary Helen bristled.

"What's important is that we find who murdered the poor blighter." White looked directly at her. "Don't we agree?"

Mary Helen nodded. How could she disagree?

"Lovely, then," White said.

Without warning a towering bank of black clouds covered the sky, darkening the room. A sudden wind bent the trees and rain spit against the windows.

"Maybe we will have that cup of tea," White said, watching the rain. "Then you can tell me exactly what you overheard."

Sipping tea and chatting for a few minutes about last night's hurling match did wonders for the meeting. Sister Mary Helen calmed down and Detective Inspector White seemed friendlier.

Eileen refilled their cups as Mary Helen related what she had overheard outside the hall.

"You are sure it was Mrs. Cox and Mr. Lynch you heard?" White asked.

"Positive," Mary Helen said, "but as I told you, both of them denied doing Mr. Ward any harm."

White leaned back in his chair and studied that spot on the ceiling again. "But someone did," he said, as though it were news. "Why would someone attack Tommy Burns, steal his costume, kill Willie Ward, and attack Oonagh Cox wearing the costume? It all must be connected somehow, but how?"

Reminding herself that this was probably a rhetorical question, Mary Helen bit her lip.

All at once, White's dark eyes focused on her. "And the note that was sent to Oonagh in the hospital. It had the same words on it that her attacker said to her. Sure, that must fit in somewhere. What do you think, Sister?"

"What do I think?" She repeated the question making sure she had heard correctly. *Poor fellow must be desperate,* Mary Helen reckoned with a twinge of sympathy. She wished she could help.

White's face burned red as he nodded his head. This time she had no trouble telling that he was embarrassed. *As well he might be,* she thought.

"Well, frankly, Detective Inspector, despite your admonition, I must admit I have given this case quite a lot of thought," she said. "At first, I thought it might be Jake Powers."

"The tinker?" White asked, flipping open his notebook and studying it before he continued. "What made you consider him?"

"His temper, his quarrel with Mr. Ward, which half the village witnessed. The fact that Jake thought Ward was responsible for his not being the only winner of this year's art contest."

"But?" White said. "You sound as if you have a 'but.' "

"But." Mary Helen smiled, feeling a bit foolish. "He denies doing it, and I believe him."

Detective Inspector Brian Reedy shifted uncomfortably in his chair. "Maybe the man is just a splendid liar," Reedy said, running his fingers through his short red hair.

"Maybe," Mary Helen conceded, "but I think not. Then, I thought about Zoë O'Dea," she continued. "When we first arrived in Ballyclarin I overheard Mrs. O'Dea talking to Mr. Ward. And I distinctly heard her say, 'It's a wonder someone hasn't killed you already.' It sounded innocent enough at the time, but in view of what has happened . . ."

"Meaning you think she could have?"

"Not necessarily, unless she had reason. It could have something to do with her daughter Tara's being the Oyster Festival Queen."

"Tara," Reedy spoke up again, this time sounding a little defensive, Mary Helen thought. "She's a beautiful girl. Why wouldn't she be chosen?"

"That's not the point." Apparently Eileen had been quiet too long. "You're right. Tara is a beautiful girl. And this whole tragedy seems somehow tied to the Oyster Festival, now doesn't it?"

A surprised White turned toward her, looking as if he had forgotten she was in the room. "What's that?" White asked, as if he hadn't quite heard her.

"Well." Eileen smiled. "I just mean Tara became queen and not Carmel. Jake did not win first prize. Who could have enough power to make both these things happen?"

"Only the chairman, Owen Lynch," Mary Helen answered, delighted with her friend's logic.

"Of course, old dear," Eileen said. "Only Owen could make those things happen, and who has power over him?"

"Willie Ward, of course."

"Are you saying that Owen Lynch is responsible?" All the color drained from White's face. "That he is the one who murdered Willie and attacked Tommy and Oonagh?"

"No, I'm not saying that he is our villain," Eileen said sweetly. "Only that he bears looking into."

The small room became suddenly quiet. The only sound was the rain tapping playfully against the windowpanes.

"Then, we had best do that," White said at last. "And if you think of anything else, Sisters, please let me know."

"That surely was a change of heart," Eileen said, watching the two detectives run across the wet backyard.

"The man is as changeable as the weather," Mary Helen said, gathering up the teacups.

"And just like they say about the weather," Eileen quipped, "'Twill never last."

Liam O'Dea sat in the small office in the back of the Monks' Table listening to the rain hit against the roof. He felt as if he had been sitting there for hours. When he checked his wristwatch, only fifty-five minutes had passed. He shook it to make sure it was still running.

In the distance he heard laughter. It must be the crowd in the pub. Now, there was a good life, being a publican. Everyone was always happy to see you. Not like being a policeman.

Maybe that's what he should do with himself. Open a pub somewhere. He wondered how Carmel would like to be the wife of a publican.

What was he thinking? He felt his face grow warm. *I must be daft. A doctor's daughter settling for being a publican's wife!*

He checked his watch again. Fifty-seven minutes since White and Reedy had left. What were they doing over there?

What should he be doing, besides listening for the telephone, which was strangely silent? Was it working? He picked up the receiver and listened for the dial tone. It was.

He replaced it and leaned back in his chair and closed his eyes. His neck and shoulders ached from hurling, but then, there was Carmel's kiss. Maybe he should take up hurling. Too bad it was an amateur sport and not one of those high-paid American games like baseball and football. Imagine making a small fortune for having fun!

He wondered where Carmel was right now. Probably visiting her mother in hospital, or maybe bringing her home. Liam's nose itched, and he scratched it.

Who could have sent Mrs. Cox such a note? A cheeky bastard, for sure. Someone who didn't think he'd be caught. Well, he would eventually, Liam knew, getting up and stretching, wishing he could join the lads in the Monks' Table for a pint. He checked his watch again. Nowhere near time to eat.

He had just about given up hope of anything happening anytime soon when the telephone gave off a shattering ring. Liam grabbed the receiver as if it were on fire.

"Tech team here. Is that you, Ernie?" the voice asked.

"No, sir," Liam said, explaining that he had been left to receive the call.

"Be sure to tell him we did the tests as fast as we could, will you now, lad?" the voice said and then went on to report that all they had discovered of any significance was a small thread, most probably from a piece of heavy linen, possibly a bedsheet.

A bedsheet! Liam could not believe it. *Those bloody bedsheets again,* he fumed, thanking the man, then ringing off and placing the receiver back in its cradle.

Would he be going through the search yet another time? What new could he discover? The sheet in question was probably two counties away by now.

Collapsing back into his chair, he stared up at the ceiling, the way he had seen White do when he was trying to figure something out. And he usually did. Maybe there was something to it, after all.

Liam stared up and listened to the rain tapping steadily on the roof. It was fortunate that the village women had done their laundry yesterday instead of today, he thought, noticing a small spiderweb in the corner of the office.

And wouldn't you just know that his Auntie Zoë would report him to Detective Inspector White. *More's the pity for poor Reedy if he wants to get serious about Tara,* Liam thought. *He'll have his work cut out for him.*

Realizing that his neck was beginning to feel stiff from staring up at the ceiling, he looked down at the floor. There didn't seem to be anything more there than he found on the ceiling, but you never knew.

Liam felt his cheeks grow hot at the thought of Zoë and her knickers. What in God's name had gotten into him? It must have been the sheets. Was there some kind of sheet sickness, he wondered, that can affect a person after checking too many of them? Did a man start seeing things? Like water and an oasis appearing to a person who's been too long in the desert sun? He shrugged. Could be.

By the time he'd come to the Lynches' clothesline, he'd even noticed that the twins had flowered sheets. He wondered idly if Carmel did too, not that he'd ever know.

And he had started counting, too. There were seven sheets on Patsy Lynch's line.

All at once, Liam felt the blood rush to his head. His thoughts began to pop and crackle like fat in the fire. Maybe there was something to this staring business after all.

But wait now, he cautioned himself. What was it his mam always said? "A wise head keeps a shut mouth."

He didn't claim to be wise, but he wasn't a fool either. He'd wait till Detective Inspectors White and Reedy came back, then test his thought out on them.

What was taking them so long? he wondered impatiently, checking his wristwatch again. When had fifteen minutes ever gone so slowly?

Detective Inspector Ernie White pulled up the collar of his raincoat around his ears, hunched over, and hurried down the road toward the Monks' Table. He knew his partner, following close behind him, was saying something, but he couldn't for the life of him make out what.

"What is it now, Brian?" White asked, pulling back the door of the pub.

The place was packed with people and the noise level was earsplitting. Hugh Ryan looked as if he had just won the Irish sweepstakes.

Reedy tried to speak again, but it was still impossible

to make out what he was saying. "In the office," White mouthed, and the two men hurried through the pub.

At last, Liam O'Dea thought, relieved. The moment they stepped through the door, he rose to his feet.

"Did we hear from the tech team?" White asked, taking off his wet coat, shaking it, and hanging it in the corner. Reedy followed suit.

"Yes, sir, we did," Liam said.

"And?" White asked impatiently.

"And they wanted you to know that they did the test as quickly as they could."

"Yes, yes." White rubbed his cold hands together. "Is there no heat in this room?"

"No, sir," Liam said.

"Did they find anything?" Reedy asked.

Liam wished either one or the other would ask him questions. He felt like a Ping-Pong ball with the two of them going at him.

"Only a piece of string, which they thought could be from . . ." Liam paused. The collar of his shirt felt tight, and he was afraid he might choke on the word. "A sheet," he managed.

Reedy chuckled. "Sheets, again," he said. "Be Jaysus, it could be worse. It could be knickers."

Will I ever hear the end of it? Liam wondered, feeling the heat start at his clenched jaw and slowly crawl up his cheeks until it touched his hairline. His face must be blazing, he thought, trying not to look at either of the detectives. He speculated for a moment on what would happen to him if he grabbed Reedy by the throat and throttled him. Best not to find out.

"Leave the lad alone," White said.

Liam could not believe his ears, which had to be bright red by now. "I had a thought," he blurted out. "After the tech team called and while I was waiting."

White blew on his fingers. "We could use as many thoughts as we can get, lad. What is it?"

Liam swallowed. His Adam's apple seemed to have swollen.

"Well?" He felt White's sharp eyes on him. "What's your thought? Out with it," he said, sounding more like himself.

"I'm not sure, sir, but something is bothering me about looking at the sheets yesterday."

"Get on with it," White said. "What is bothering you?"

"One of the clotheslines had seven sheets."

Both detectives stopped and looked at him. "And?" Reedy coaxed.

"If I'm not mistaken, beds have two sheets, so there should be an even number. Unless there is another reason for using just one. Which, of course, there could be," he added quickly.

Detective Inspector White studied him for a moment. "And where exactly did you see this odd sheet?"

Reedy chuckled. "The Case of the Odd Sheet," he said. "Sounds like a title for a thriller."

White shot him a look that could have soured milk. "Where?" he repeated, more gently this time.

"On the clothesline at Lynch's house."

"Lynch again, is it?" White seemed to be chewing on the thought. He took his notebook from his jacket pocket and jotted down something. Then he turned toward his partner. "And what was it you were trying to tell me, Brian, when we left the nuns' mews?"

"Just that." Reedy ran his fingers through his short red hair. "It's Lynch's name, again," he said with a half smile. "I was wondering if we shouldn't have a little meeting with our chairman. Ask him a few questions about his relationship with Mrs. Cox."

Reedy sat on the edge of the desk. Liam heard it creak.

"Wouldn't that be the limit?" Reedy said, thinking aloud. "The Oyster Festival chairman turning out to be a murderer."

"Stranger things have happened," White said philosophically.

Liam couldn't help wondering when.

A sharp rap on the front door of the mews startled Sister Mary Helen.

"Who in the world can that be?" Eileen whispered. "Were we expecting anyone else?"

Mary Helen shook her head. The rap came again, this time more insistently.

"Whoever it is wants in," she said, moving quickly to the door and opening it a crack.

At first glance she did not recognize the person standing outside. Whoever it was stood tall and wore a hooked fleece jacket, which covered his face and most of his hair. What the jacket didn't cover was wound in a green tartan scarf. Under his arm he carried a large rectangular package carefully wrapped in brown paper and covered with plastic. Only when she saw his enormous blue eyes did she recognize Jake Powers.

"Come in, Jake," she said, standing back to make room. "What brings you out on such a wet day?"

"Let me have your coat and I'll hang it by the heater," Eileen said before he had a chance to answer.

Once his coat was hung and his scarf draped over a chair, Jake settled down on the couch, the wrapped package beside him.

Without even asking, Eileen brought him a cup of hot tea that he cradled in his blue-tipped fingers. "Can I bring you a little biscuit to go with that?" Eileen asked.

Mary Helen could not get used to calling a cookie a biscuit. Maybe if she stayed longer. . . .

"Ah, no. This is grand," he said after the first long swallow and closed his eyes.

Mary Helen shot Eileen a quick inquisitive look. Was he just visiting, or was there some real purpose for his coming?

Eileen simply shrugged and sat quietly.

Finishing the hot tea in five big gulps, Jake put down the cup. *Poor man's throat must be on fire,* Mary Helen thought.

But if it was, Jake wasn't letting on. "Now," he began after several moments of tense quiet in which everyone seemed to be searching unsuccessfully for an opening sentence. "You must be wondering why I'm here," he said and reached for the package beside him. With a self-conscious grin, he handed it to Sister Mary Helen and waited expectantly for her to open it.

From its size and feel, she was sure it was a framed photograph. Carefully she removed the plastic and then the brown paper. She caught her breath. She had never expected anything so beautiful.

Jake's camera had captured a small piece of a rock garden with all its swirls and hollows. In shades of gray, he had caught the beauty of its deep, ragged cracks and its polished surfaces. Nestled in a crevice, as if it were placed carefully in a vase, was one delicate bloom, its petals stretched wide.

"That's a *bloody craneshell,*" Jake said softly, pointing to the flower. "If it were colored film, the bloom would be a bright magenta." He leaned back on the couch. "The Burren is alive with color and fragrance at this time of year," he said, clearly enchanted with the place. "The sight is stunning. I'm sorry you missed it."

"Paul, he's our driver," Mary Helen explained, "told us that his wife loves the perfume that is made from the flowers that grow there."

Jake nodded. "At the Burren Perfumery, no doubt. It was the first in Ireland, it was. They claim to capture the mystery of Ireland." He gave a short, hard laugh. "More to the point, if you ask me, they're out to capture the money of the new Ireland."

"Jake, this is truly beautiful." Mary Helen's eyes went back to the photo. "Absolutely beautiful." She turned it so that Eileen could see it.

"Lovely, indeed," Eileen said after a few moments. Her voice was filled with awe. "It's as if I could actually reach out and touch it."

Mary Helen wasn't sure, but she thought Jake's face colored. Was he blushing?

"I thought you might want to bring a piece of the Burren back to San Francisco," he said, obviously pleased that they liked his photograph so well.

Mary Helen's heart dropped. He was right. She had wanted to bring one of Jake's photos back to the convent, but she had no clue of how expensive his pictures were.

Could she actually afford one? And if she couldn't, how in the world would she tell him without either sounding as if she didn't like his work or, worse yet, that she wanted it free?

"It would be a perfect gift," she heard Eileen say.

"A perfect gift," Jake repeated, sounding pleased. "It's a rare day anyone calls anything I do perfect."

Wildly, Mary Helen wondered how Eileen was going to approach the price of Jake's work.

"To be really a perfect gift," Jake was saying, "I'll have to give it to you."

"Oh, no," Eileen demurred. Jake insisted. Eileen protested one more time, happily not too vehemently. And Jake placed the picture in her hands. Then, refusing another cup of tea, he bundled up and left.

"An odd duck, indeed, that lad," Eileen said as the two nuns watched Jake Powers go out into the rain.

"But a very talented odd duck, you must admit," Mary Helen said, closing the front door.

"Did you see this?" Eileen asked, turning the framed photograph over she pointed to a small tag on the back of it. "The price is . . ." She paused as if to check to make sure she was reading it correctly. Her gray eyebrows shot up. "Two hundred and fifty euros."

"Oh my," Sister Mary Helen said as soon as she caught her breath. She studied the picture again. "And worth every cent of it," she said.

Liam O'Dea couldn't help wondering if it was his imagination or if the two detectives were stalling. Not that he blamed them. To confront Owen Lynch, the chairman of the Oyster Festival and a prominent local businessman, was not an easy thing to do, especially if it turned out that they were wrong.

Detective Inspector White seemed to be memorizing today's activities' schedule for the festival, while his partner checked and rechecked the weather outside the window to see if the rain had let up. It hadn't.

Both men seemed relieved when, after a gentle knock, the door opened and Hugh Ryan, a happy grin on his flushed face, stood there with a tray of sandwiches, several bags of crisps, and three pints of Guinness.

"Thought you lads might need a little something," he said, putting the food down on the desk. "Enjoy."

Without a word, the three men sat down to eat. "We'll

work much better after a little nourishment," White said, biting into his ham and cheese sandwich.

"Indeed," Reedy agreed. *"Sláinte!"* he said, raising his glass and taking a swallow of Guinness. "Didn't Napoleon say something about an army marches on its stomach?"

His mouth full, White nodded.

Liam didn't add anything to the conversation. He just chewed and swallowed as if this might be his last meal, and indeed, he felt that way. Lynch would be furious when they confronted him. Sure, he'd want to know which *eejit* told the detectives. He'd demand to know where they had gotten this information. Liam took a swallow of his Guinness.

What would happen to him? he wondered. Maybe this really was a good time to go to America. Not to stay forever, but for a year or two, until the whole thing blew over. Who was he kidding? The Irish held grudges for decades, long after they had forgotten what the fight was about.

"That hit the spot," White said, crumbling up his serviette. "Now, lad"—his dark eyes focused on Liam— "give Lynch's a ring." White checked his wristwatch. "With any luck we'll catch him having a bite."

"Unless he's taken the ride to the Burren," Reedy inserted.

"Which is very unlikely," White said.

"What shall I tell him, sir?" Liam asked. What he really wanted to ask was, "Why me?"

"Tell him to meet us here as soon as possible," White said. "There is no bloody use in dragging this thing out."

Liam's stomach rode up and down, and his hand felt hot and clammy on the receiver as he listened to the empty ring of the telephone. When he was just about to hang up, someone picked up. "Yes," a voice said. Liam did not recognize it. Had he dialed the wrong number?

"Sorry," he said. "Have I the Lynch residence?"

"Yes," the voice said again. It sounded thick and far away. "This is Mrs. Lynch."

Patsy! Liam couldn't believe his ears. Her voice had none of its usual strong, cheerful sound. Had he awakened her? Or was something wrong?

"I'm calling for Owen," Liam said, after identifying himself. "Is he in?"

"I'm sorry, Liam," she said, beginning to sound a little more like herself. "He's just left. I believe he said he was going to Bon Secours to see how Oonagh Cox is doing today. Maybe you can catch him there." With that, she rang off.

"To hospital it is, then," Detective Inspector White said when Liam related the message.

The rain had stopped, at least for the time being, and Liam spotted a rainbow on the horizon. *A good sign,* he thought, watching White and Reedy bundle up in their raincoats, just in case.

"It could still be raining in Galway City," Reedy said.

Liam followed the two men out to the road. "Shall I stay here, sir?" he asked, hoping he didn't sound too eager not to be present for the meeting.

"No, no, lad," White said, holding open the door of the police car. "Come along. It will be good experience. Besides, it is your lead." He gave Liam a rare smile. "This might be all we need to solve the case. You'd want to be there for that, wouldn't you?"

At the moment, Liam wanted to be anyplace but, although he didn't dare say so.

After Jake Powers left the mews, Sister Mary Helen couldn't relax. She felt as if she had an itch just out of reach.

"What is it?" Eileen asked, noticing her fidgeting. "What is bothering you?"

"I'm not sure, really," Mary Helen said, and she wasn't. "I've been looking at Jake's lovely picture with that delicate little flower and thinking about Paul's wife and the wonderful fragrance she wanted him to bring back for her from the Burren, and . . ." She paused.

"And what?" Eileen asked.

"And, I don't know," Mary Helen said, frustrated, "but I do remember detecting a fragrance when I found Mr. Ward in the ladies'. Not a familiar one, for sure, but one, nonetheless."

"And you told that to Detective Inspector White, didn't you?" Eileen asked.

"You know I did."

"So, what is bothering you?"

"He seems to be ignoring it, or maybe he has just forgotten," Mary Helen said, "and it could be important."

Eileen looked at her quizzically. "How so?" she asked.

"I just assumed the fragrance was from soap or some air freshener, but it could have been on a person."

"Do they make men's perfume, as well?" Eileen wondered aloud.

"I don't know, but we should find out."

"Stop right there," Eileen said. "Tomorrow we are leaving, so even if Detective Inspector White wanted you to, there wouldn't be time."

"Now you know what has me fidgeting," Mary Helen said, momentarily distracted by the glorious rainbow stretching across the sky. "We really should remind the detective inspector."

"Then, let's," Eileen said, much to Mary Helen's surprise. "I cannot bear to see you fidget the whole rest of the time we're here, even if it's only a day."

Handing Sister Mary Helen an umbrella, Eileen

dropped the key to the mews in her pocket. "He can't have left the village already, can he?"

"Hello, Sisters," Father Keane's voice called out across the road. "Can I give you a lift somewhere? You look to be in a hurry."

Checking both ways for traffic, the two nuns crossed over quickly and joined the priest in the car park of the church. There was no sense shouting out that they were looking for the inspector. It would be all over the village in seconds.

"Have you any idea where Detective Inspector White has gone?" Mary Helen asked, looking up at the priest. She had forgotten how tall the man was.

"I just saw his car going down the road out of the village," Father Keane said. His gray curly hair was damp with rain. "He said he was on his way to Bon Secours to see Oonagh. I'm on my way there myself to make a few sick calls. I'd be happy to drive you. And bring you back," he added. "If you can wait until I'm done. I shouldn't be long."

Without further discussion, the two nuns climbed into the priest's black Mazda.

Even before they were halfway to Galway City, Mary Helen felt better. She'd done the best she could to help solve this case, and, as the old saying went, angels can't do more than their very best.

Father Keane left them in the lobby of the hospital and was led away by a Sister in a white habit to do his spiritual rounds.

It was only in the elevator that Mary Helen had a second thought. "What do you think Detective Inspector White will say when he sees us?" she whispered to Eileen.

"There's no telling," Eileen said, "but if he has any sense, he'll be glad to have the information."

"You're right," Mary Helen agreed with more assurance than she felt.

The elevator door opened and the nuns hurried down the hospital corridor to Oonagh Cox's room. They paused in the doorway and listened. The room was so quiet that, at first, it seemed empty.

"Maybe we've come on a wild goose chase," Mary Helen whispered. "Could Oonagh have been sent home?" She peeked in, half expecting to see an empty bed.

Instead, she was met by five frozen sets of eyes staring at her. Tension hung like fog over the little group.

"Who's that?" Owen Lynch demanded, his red face twisted into an ugly scowl. He squinted at them through his horn-rimmed glasses.

Mary Helen smiled sheepishly. "Sorry," she said. "We didn't mean to disturb anything. We just needed a word with Detective Inspector White. Tomorrow is our last day and . . ." She stopped, feeling as if she were babbling.

"Now is not a good time, I take it," Eileen said, stating the obvious.

"Not at all." Oonagh was the first to recover her poise. "Of course you can speak to the detective inspector. After all, you were the ones who found me. We'll be sorry to see you go." Her blue eyes were damp, as if she'd been crying.

All at once, Mary Helen realized what they had stumbled in on. "We can wait," she said, trying to back out of the room.

Oonagh smiled sadly. "No need." She reached out to Owen. "I'm sure you've heard, or maybe you've even noticed that Owen and I are more than friends. We didn't want to be, but—"

"Stop, Oonagh," Owen commanded angrily. "Is nothing sacred?"

"Not when it involves a murder, my darling." She studied the nuns as if she was trying to decide just how much to tell them. Swallowing, she closed her eyes and began. "You see, Willie Ward knew of our affair. Somehow we hadn't been careful enough. And for all practical purposes, he was blackmailing Owen. Threatening to tell Patsy." Her voice softened. "Neither Owen nor I wanted to hurt Patsy, so Owen gave in to his demands."

"His demands?" Mary Helen said, looking over at White. His face could have stopped Big Ben. "Sorry," she muttered.

White acted as if he hadn't heard her. "What demands?" he asked, turning his full attention to Owen. The chairman sank like a deflated rubber toy into the chair by Oonagh's bedside. "Such as choosing Tara over Carmel for the Oyster Festival Queen," he said.

"Why?" The question was out of Mary Helen's mouth before she even thought. She avoided looking at either detective.

"For no other reason than to hurt Oonagh." Owen swallowed, again. His mouth seemed dry. Mary Helen looked around for a glass of water. She pointed to one on Oonagh's bedside table.

Owen shook his head. "I'm fine," he said. "He also made sure Jake Powers didn't win the art award again, although Jake is clearly one of the best photographers we have in the county. For that matter, maybe in the whole country. I made sure that my twins' work was chosen—the poor angels can hardly draw breath, let alone a landscape—to show how ridiculous it was having a second winner." Owen took a deep breath. "Willie hated Jake, you know, and he threatened to tell Patsy if I let him be the lone winner."

An uncomfortable silence settled over the small hospital room. "But I didn't kill the man." Owen Lynch sounded pathetic. "Honestly, much as I would have liked to, I didn't."

"Can you prove that?" White asked gently.

"I can," Oonagh said. "We were together."

White frowned. "Come on now, Oonagh! How do you know you were together when you don't even know what time he was killed?"

Oonagh's face went white, and then turned a brilliant red.

"Best we stick with the truth," White said.

"Sorry," Oonagh said. Her eyes welling up with tears, she reached for a tissue.

"You say Patsy has no idea about you two?" Reedy asked, handing her the box.

"None that we know of," Oonagh said.

Ernie White cleared his throat and turned toward the nuns, as if seeing them for the first time. "Sisters," he said formally, "maybe we should step outside."

"Of course." Mary Helen followed the man into the corridor.

"Now then," he said when he had shut the door for privacy. "What is it you want to see me about?"

Mary Helen was so taken up with what had gone on in the room that it took her a moment to remember. "Oh yes, Detective Inspector," she said, "the smell."

He looked puzzled.

"Don't you remember? I told you I smelled something that I didn't recognize in the ladies' room when I found Willie Ward's body."

He nodded.

"I was wondering if the fragrance could be from the Burren Perfumery. It's quite unusual and maybe a person who wears it . . ." Her voice trailed off.

Detective Inspector White's dark eyes studied her. "You mean that the killer might have been wearing the scent?"

Sister Mary Helen nodded.

"Would you recognize it if you smelled it again?" White asked, taking his notebook out of his suit jacket pocket.

"I think so," Mary Helen said. "In fact, I'm sure I smelled it when I found Oonagh on our lawn. And I think I saw a small bottle of the cologne on the window ledge when we came to visit her in the hospital. She must wear the same fragrance."

Mary Helen watched as he jotted down a few words in his notebook. She wished she could read what he was writing.

"Are you ready to go, Sisters?" Father Keane's voice floated down the corridor. "Sorry!" he said when he realized that they were talking to the detective inspector. "I'll just stick my head in to Oonagh," he said, and before anyone could stop him he was in the room.

Detective Inspector White ran his fingers through his dark hair, which looked as if it hadn't seen a comb or brush for at least a week. "This is no way to conduct an investigation," he muttered to himself. "Father," he called after the priest, but there was no need. Father Keane came right out.

"Ready, Sisters?" he asked again.

This time Detective Inspector White answered for them. "They are, Father," he said. "They definitely are!"

Liam O'Dea could hardly believe his eyes when Father Keane popped into the room. Owen Lynch's face became so red that Liam feared the man might have a stroke.

"Father, what are you doing here?" Owen blurted out rudely.

"I just came to check on Oonagh," the priest said, seeming to take no offense. "But I can see she is being well cared for."

Then, appearing to be a little uncomfortable, he gave the woman a quick blessing, made the sign of the cross on her forehead, and left the room.

What, Liam wondered, watching relief flood Owen's face, *was that all about?* Could it be that the priest knew something that Owen was afraid he'd tell? Owen would have to know that if Father Keane heard it in confession, he'd be forbidden to reveal it. Or had the priest seen something?

Oonagh reached out her hand. "What is it, Owen? What is the matter?"

Before he could answer, Detective Inspector White reentered the room, stopped, and locked the door.

"What are you doing?" Oonagh asked. She sounded frightened.

"I need a few uninterrupted minutes is all," White said. "I want to ask you some questions without some visitor or other popping in."

White studied the notebook in his hand for several seconds. Liam shifted from one foot to the other while they waited.

"First of all, Mrs. Cox," he began, his mouth tightening, "what kind of perfume do you wear?"

"I beg your pardon?" Oonagh asked, as if she didn't understand the question.

Who can blame her? Liam thought. It seemed to come from nowhere. For a moment, he wondered if he had heard it correctly himself.

"What kind of perfume do you wear?" White repeated.

Oonagh frowned. "Do you mean the brand or the fragrance?"

"Both," White said. His dark eyes never left her face.

"Well, Detective Inspector," she said, "I favor Ilaun, and it is from the Burren Perfumery."

"Can you describe its fragrance?" White asked.

"Better than that," Oonagh said with a shy smile. "Owen bought me some as a get-well gift, although he shouldn't have. It is very dear." Her bright blue eyes caressed him, and Owen, a boyish grin on his face, actually seemed to blush.

How in the world did they think to keep their affair a secret, Liam wondered, *looking at one another that way? All you need is two eyes to see.*

Oonagh stretched out her arm so that the detectives could sniff her wrist. Liam felt like a perfect *eejit* when it was his turn to smell Mrs. Cox. Thanks be to God, the hospital room was locked. He'd die if Carmel came in on it.

The perfume was so light he had to smell twice. If anyone asked him—and he was hoping no one would—he'd say it smelled faintly of flowers and maybe fern.

"Do you smell the orchid?" Mrs. Cox asked.

Liam felt his face flush. He'd never in his life smelled an orchid. How would he know one if he did smell it now?

"Carmel likes this, too," Mrs. Cox said coyly.

Wouldn't you know it, Liam thought, wondering if he could afford it on a garda's pay.

"From the Burren Perfumery, is it?" Liam asked, for lack of anything better to say.

Oonagh Cox nodded. "Now, may I ask you something, Detective Inspector White? What's your sudden interest in my perfume?"

White acted as if he hadn't heard her. "One more

question, Mrs. Cox. Were you wearing that same perfume the night you were attacked?"

"Yes," she said without hesitation, "I was."

"What was all that goings-on about perfume?" Detective Inspector Reedy asked as the three men rode in the police car back to Ballyclarin. "Didn't you feel a bit foolish sniffing her arm?"

How could you not? Liam thought, leaning forward in the backseat to catch White's answer.

"The American nun," White explained, "remembered an unusual smell in the ladies' when she found Willie's body."

"That could have been air freshener, or soap, or anything," Reedy said.

"Right you are, but at the moment we are desperate for a clue, any clue that might lead us to our killer."

The traffic was light on the dual carriageway as Reedy sped along. "Wouldn't you say that this clue is a little slim?" he asked.

Mentally, Liam agreed with him.

"Even if it was the same fragrance she smelled, how many women in the village wear it?" Reedy continued.

"How are we going to find that out?" Liam asked and then wished he'd kept his gob shut.

Turning halfway around in his seat, White's dark eyes fastened on him. "Are you going to the jamboree tonight, lad?" White asked.

"Yes, sir," Liam answered, looking out the window at the green fields to avoid his superior's eyes.

"I'll bet the entire village will be there," White said, thinking aloud. "I'd go myself, but I promised my wife I'd be home for supper tonight. It's her mother's birthday and my life will not be worth living if I don't make it." White paused. "And you've smelled the perfume."

Liam's stomach dropped, and for a moment he felt as if he couldn't catch his breath. *Here it comes,* he thought.

"While you're there, see if you can locate the fragrance on any other women."

"But, sir, how do we know it's the same smell?" Liam asked, clawing for any excuse to get out of what seemed to be the inevitable.

"We don't. But we'll have to give it a try. The American nun says she thinks it was the same fragrance in the ladies' that she smelled on Oonagh Cox."

"So I just go around during the jamboree, smelling women? Sir." Liam tried to control his temper.

"Now, there's an assignment for you," Reedy said, grinning like a hungry alligator.

I swear, if he makes one remark about the knickers, Liam fumed.

"Liam, my lad, some men would kill for that assignment," Reedy joked.

At that moment, Liam could have gladly killed Brian Reedy with his bare hands.

"It's a long shot," White admitted, "but one of the only concrete things we have so far."

If you can call a smell concrete, Liam thought.

"That, and the bit of sheet from the tech team and, of course, the affair, which seems pretty obvious when you're around it."

"You don't have to be much of a detective to see something is going on," Reedy agreed. "The amazing thing is that they were able to keep it a secret."

"If, indeed, they were able," White said. "I guess we should be grateful to the American nuns for telling us."

I'll be glad to see the backs of both of them. Liam fought down the urge to scream. *Tonight promises to be one of the longest nights of my life,* he thought, staring out at a lone cow in a field, chewing her cud. *Sniffing like a drug-smelling dog! What have I come to? And what will Carmel think? She wants to dance every dance.*

Could he sniff and dance simultaneously? Time would tell. And would it all start to make sense? Who killed Willie Ward and why?

He couldn't wait to find out. Unfortunately, he was one of the ones who had to come up with the answer. *Heaven help us,* he thought, *the answer can't come soon enough.*

Sister Mary Helen and Sister Eileen had no sooner stepped inside the mews than the telephone rang. It was Paul Glynn, ever on the job.

"Shall I pick you up at half five for the jamboree?" he asked. "You won't want to miss a thing. There's entertainment, and you'll want to get a good seat."

"Do we need to bring anything?" Mary Helen asked. "Besides our tickets?"

"All you need is stamina and a good liver," Paul said.

The liver is not a problem, Mary Helen thought, *but the stamina?* If they were lucky they could get in a short nap before Paul arrived.

When Paul arrived at 5:30 sharp, his lovely redheaded wife was with him, looking quite glamorous in a bright green silk dress. Paul, too, was more dressed up than she had ever seen him.

Eileen and she climbed into the backseat of the car, and Paul slammed the door behind them. *Mrs. Glynn not only looks lovely but she smells good, too,* Mary Helen thought, catching a whiff of her fragrance. The nun's heart began to race. Was it the same fragrance she had smelled on Oonagh Cox and, God help us, in the ladies' when she found Willie Ward?

Mary Helen was almost certain Mrs. Glynn's perfume had come from the Burren, since Paul had mentioned being saved from bringing her more. Surely Paul's wife was not the murderer, but someone was, someone who wore that same perfume.

Stop! Stop! Mary Helen thought, shaking her head. She'd have to stop or she'd spend her last hours in Ireland preoccupied with who had killed Willie Ward. She had done all she could to help the detectives, more than they actually wanted her to do. And now she'd just have to let it go.

The streets of the village were packed with people who paid no attention to the traffic. They could have walked to the jamboree faster than Paul could drive them, but it was nice not to have to battle the crowd. Paul and the missus dropped them at the entrance, telling them that they'd see them inside. If for some reason they didn't, Paul said, he'd collect them for home outside the front door of the tent at nine o'clock.

The inside of the tent was already full of partygoers talking and laughing. A band called the American Drifters was playing, and the dance floor was literally packed with dancers of all ages.

Mary Helen spotted the young garda, Liam O'Dea, dancing with Carmel Cox. Did he appear to be a bit uncomfortable, or was that her imagination?

And Detective Inspector Reedy was here, too, dancing with Tara O'Dea. Neither of them seemed to be worrying about who killed Willie Ward, she noticed. Why, then, should she?

If Tara is here, then Mama Zoë can't be far away, Mary Helen thought. Her gaze swept the floor. Sure enough, Zoë was in the tent, sitting with Patsy Lynch. The two women were so deep in conversation, they didn't seem to notice the partying around them.

"Hello again, Sisters." Mary Helen jumped as Father Keane came up behind them. "Sorry," he said. "I didn't mean to startle you."

"Hello again, Father," Mary Helen said. "I was so busy looking around, I didn't hear you."

"Would you believe," he said, taking in the crowd, "that the first time they held this festival in 1954, only thirty-four people came?"

The priest bent forward so that they could hear him. "They've a table reserved for me," he said. "Won't you join me?"

The two nuns followed Father Keane across the crowded room to his table. *Thank goodness he's tall,* Mary Helen thought, *or we would have surely lost him in the crowd.*

"How about some oysters?" he offered, once he had them seated. "Our oysters are justifiably the best in the world. They are wild, you know, and sit at the bottom of Dumbuleaun Bay where the Clarin and Dunkellin Rivers both empty into the sea. That's what gives them the mild flavor, which is positively addictive."

"He should be a salesman," Eileen said, watching the man cross the floor toward the refreshment table.

"He is one of sorts, I guess," Mary Helen said.

In minutes, Father Keane returned with a tray containing a large platter of oysters, three small knives, and three glasses of rich, creamy Guinness.

The nuns watched as Father Keane pried open the shell and ran the knife under the oyster to loosen it. "Now's the time to check for a pearl, if you're feeling

224   *Sister Carol Anne O'Marie*

lucky," he said. Then, he threw back his head and tipped the contents of the shell into his mouth. He savored it for a moment, and then let it slide down his throat. "Ah-h-h," he said, sounding satisfied, and took a mouthful of Guinness.

"You can have lemon or Tabasco sauce if you'd like," he said, waiting for them to try an oyster.

Eileen went at it like a connoisseur, and Mary Helen followed suit. After the initial shock of the texture, she had to admit it was delicious, especially if you didn't think about its being alive. After the second one, however, she decided to give up following it with a swallow of Guinness. After all, they had to be up early tomorrow.

Sister Mary Helen was wondering what to do with the oyster shells that were quickly forming a mound on the table when Zoë O'Dea came by with a plastic bag in which to dump them. "Good evening, Father, Sisters," she said, eyeing the Guinness glasses. "I see you're enjoying yourselves." Her dark eyes fastened on the priest. "Too bad Oonagh is still in hospital," she said. "She enjoys a party so." Without missing a beat, she went on. "How is she?" she asked. "I understand you went to see her today. Nothing serious, I hope."

Mary Helen could scarcely believe her ears. Was there anything this woman didn't know?

"She seems to be coming along, Zoë," Father Keane said evenly. "I'm sure she'll be home in a couple of days." The priest turned to the nuns and asked, "Can I get you some dessert?" He looked so desperate to escape from Zoë O'Dea that Mary Helen didn't have the heart to say no.

"That would be nice," she said, figuring that once the priest was gone, Zoë would be on her way. Unfortunately, she was wrong.

"And you Sisters are on your way home to America tomorrow?" Zoë asked, as if she didn't know the exact time and number of their flight.

Eileen, who was busy wiping oyster juice from her hands, simply nodded.

"What must you think of us?" Zoë asked, shaking the tight curls that covered her head. "A murder and two attacks! Have they ruined your stay?"

Mary Helen wondered how to answer. "Yes," she knew, was not right, and "no" sounded too callous. She was relieved when the band gave a loud drum roll and Chairman Owen Lynch reached for the microphone.

After welcoming everyone and thanking them for coming, he introduced the lead singer, a street theater group that was to perform, and a local group of Irish dancers. The young step dancers filed onto the floor first for a reel. The crowd cheered them wildly as the music began and before they had taken a single step.

Blessedly, Mary Helen could hardly hear herself over the music, let alone hear what Zoë was saying. After a few minutes of fruitless shouting, Zoë moved on.

Father Keane returned with an assortment of desserts. Although he said nothing, Mary Helen thought that he looked relieved that Zoë had gone.

Even though she was enjoying the entertainment, Mary Helen stifled a yawn. The tent was warm and the music was loud. She would really have liked to slip out for a breath of fresh air, but she was a little gun-shy. The last time she had stepped out, she'd overheard Oonagh and Owen Lynch.

She yawned again, trying to decide what to do. Wasn't there an old saying about lightning not striking twice?

"Getting sleepy?" Eileen asked, putting her mouth close to Mary Helen's ear.

Mary Helen shook her head. "Just need some fresh air," she mouthed.

"Me, too," Eileen replied. Motioning to Father Keane, who seemed totally absorbed in eating a large helping of trifle, the two nuns slipped out the side door and moved just far enough away that they didn't need to shout to hear one another.

The night was crisp and clear. Thousands of stars shone like diamond chips scattered across a black velvet sky. The air smelled fresh and clean. A gentle breeze rustled the leaves of a nearby chestnut tree, waking a bird who gave a soft coo.

"This is so beautiful," Mary Helen whispered, not wanting to disturb the tranquil scene. "I hate to leave. Where did the week go?"

"Maybe we'll come back again someday," Eileen said.

"Maybe," Mary Helen agreed, although she knew that neither of them really thought they would.

"Perhaps we should wish upon a star," Eileen, ever the optimist, suggested. She pointed to one that seemed larger than the rest.

Mary Helen stood quietly, savoring the moment. Tomorrow they would be on their way back to San Francisco. Ballyclarin would be just a pleasant memory. She sighed.

All at once, she smelled something. Was it her imagination, or was that the same fragrance she had smelled in the ladies' the day she discovered Willie Ward? It was hard to describe—flowery, yet woodsy.

Eileen turned to face her. She must have smelled it, too. Mary Helen put her finger up to her lips, and the two nuns moved farther back in the shadows.

"Ah, Patsy, you can't mean it. How could you?" Sister Mary Helen recognized Owen Lynch's voice. The poor man sounded desperate.

"I did it for you, love," she said. "I'd do anything for you. You know that. I wouldn't let that awful man talk about you. You are my husband. I couldn't let him break up our marriage, now could I? I had to, don't you understand?" It was Patsy's voice, clear and logical.

"You had to murder the man?" Owen asked breathlessly. "There was no other way?"

"He wouldn't stop otherwise, now would he?" she said, quite sure of herself. "I had to stop him."

"Patsy."

Owen must have grabbed her because his wife said, "Ouch! You are hurting my arms."

"Sorry!" he said.

"What's the matter, love?" she coaxed, sounding quite mad. "We had a problem and I fixed it, just like I always fix our problems. Right, my love? That is what a wife is for."

"Oh, Patsy." Owen's voice choked. "This is all my fault," he said miserably. "I'll call Detective Inspector White after the jamboree is over and tell him I did it."

"But you didn't," Patsy said. "That would be a lie. I did it and I'm not a bit sorry. He was an awful man, really."

"But, Patsy, the twins. Who will take care of the twins? Have you thought of them? They need a mother."

"Oh, the twins." Patsy hesitated. "Maybe what we should do, love, is not tell anyone. If the detectives from Galway have not figured it out by now, my guess is that they never will. And Liam O'Dea is hopeless." She gave a high-pitched snicker, which sent shivers down Mary Helen's spine.

"I'm afraid that Zoë suspects. But she won't say anything. She's my best friend. Besides, she hated the way Willie treated her Tara. Don't you remember?"

"Patsy, have you taken leave of your senses? You can't just murder a man and think it will all go away."

"Why not?" Patsy asked. "I used Death's costume as a disguise. It was just an ordinary old sheet. And, by the way, how much did they charge the festival for that? Some people have no conscience," she said testily. She thought a moment. "I should have washed our butcher knife, as well, and put it back in the kitchen drawer where it belongs. That was a good knife."

"You killed the man with our butcher knife?" Owen gagged.

"Yes, love." She giggled. "Silly man, you have such a weak stomach." She paused. "My only mistake, I think, was that I forced him into the ladies'. I am so used to using the ladies' myself. I didn't think of forcing him into the men's. I should have killed him in the men's, shouldn't I have?"

"And what about Oonagh?" Owen asked softly.

"Oonagh should be ashamed of herself," she said primly, "flirting with other people's husbands. But I think she's good and sorry now, don't you?"

"I do, Patsy." He sounded as if all the air had been knocked out of his body.

"So then, love, do you want to dance? Listen, I just love this song."

Strains of "Sentimental Journey" floated out of the tent and into the starry night.

"Patsy," Owen said gently, "listen to me. You need help."

Patsy's voice was strong. "God helps those who help themselves," she said with a high wild giggle that made Mary Helen's blood run cold. "Come on now, love. Hurry or we'll miss this dance."

"God have mercy on us," Eileen whispered once the Lynches were safely out of earshot.

Sister Mary Helen let out her breath. "The poor woman is mad," she said.

"Mad or not," Eileen said, "we have to tell someone. And the sooner the better. There is no telling what she'll do next. But who?"

"That young garda is here," Mary Helen said. "I saw him dancing with Carmel Cox."

"Good idea." Eileen turned on her heel. "I'll go get him, you stay here."

Within minutes, Eileen was back with Liam O'Dea in tow. Quickly and succinctly they told him what they had overheard.

Liam stared at them, openmouthed. "Are you sure?" he asked not once but twice.

And who could blame him? Mary Helen thought. It was bizarre. "We are positive," she said, "and I suggest you call Detective Inspector White as soon as possible."

Back in the tent, the two nuns made a pretense of watching the dancing and the entertainment. Both of their minds were somewhere else.

"Are you all right?" Father Keane's dark eyes studied them. "You're so quiet. Is something wrong?"

"No, Father," Eileen answered brightly.

"You are sorry to be leaving, I guess," he said, and they let it go at that.

Liam O'Dea stood for several seconds outside the jamboree tent. He felt as if his two feet were growing into the lawn. What should he do? he wondered. He'd have asked Reedy's advice, but a while back he had noticed Brian slip out of the tent with his arm around Tara and a lovestruck look in his eyes. You needn't be a great detective to figure out what those two were up to.

He gazed up at the starry sky, glad that he was out here alone. Thank goodness, Carmel had gone to freshen up, whatever that meant, when the nuns came for him. How could he explain that he'd found the killer, not by clever deduction, as it is supposed to be done, but by eavesdropping? A simple case of eavesdropping!

Not even his own eavesdropping, but a confession overheard accidentally by a couple of old nuns. He had never expected that the murder would be solved this way.

He wondered what Detective Inspector White would think. Quickly he slipped into the empty pub and made his way to Hugh Ryan's office to call the detective inspector at home.

Liam could hear White breathing as the young garda repeated the story. "That explains the extra sheet on Lynch's clothesline," White said.

Liam had completely forgotten about that.

"And why he was found in the ladies'," the detective went on quietly. Liam wasn't sure if White was talking to him or to himself.

"Yes, sir," Liam said, hoping that would cover either scenario.

"Good work, lad," White said. "You'll make a fine detective some day."

Liam could hardly believe his ears. A fine detective indeed!

"Sir," he said, "I've been thinking."

"Yes." White sounded impatient. "Keep that thought until I get there," he said and hung up.

Liam scarcely had time to get his speech in order, let alone summon up the courage to give it, before White arrived. Quickly the detective outlined a plan to take Patsy Lynch from the tent to Galway City with as little commotion as possible.

"Now, then." White turned his attention to Liam. "You said you had a thought?" he asked.

"Yes, sir." Liam felt the blood drumming in his ears. "I did, although I'm not sure this is the time for it."

"Let's hear it, then," White said, not unkindly.

Closing his eyes, Liam blurted out, "I don't think I'm cut out to be a garda, sir." There, he'd said it!

He heard White sigh. "And why do you say that, lad? You've certainly helped me in this case."

"That was an accident," Liam said miserably. "Detective work had nothing to do with it. In fact, it was worse than an accident. It was eavesdropping, pure and simple, and not even my own!"

Detective Inspector White sat on the edge of the desk, and for a few moments Liam watched him stare at that blasted spot on the ceiling. "You have the one thing that any good detective needs," he said at last.

Liam waited to hear what exactly that could be. When he could stand the silence no longer, he asked, "And what is that, sir?"

"Luck, lad," White said. "Dumb luck. 'Tis better to be lucky, they say, than to be wise."

"Thank you, sir," Liam said. "I think." He could feel his face burning. Detective Inspector Liam O'Dea! He threw his shoulders back. There was a nice ring to it, he had to admit as he followed his superior officer out of the office.

Almost no one seemed to notice Detective Inspector White arrive, nor did anyone see him leave with Liam O'Dea and Patsy Lynch. *So sad,* Mary Helen thought, watching the trio exit quietly by the side door.

"Are you ready to go home?" Father Keane asked above the music. Mary Helen smiled wearily. "Paul said he'd take us."

Father Keane pointed to the dance floor. "He and the

missus are having a wonderful time. Let me tell him I'll take you home."

"Paul wasn't too disappointed?" Mary Helen asked, climbing into the priest's black Mazda.

"Not a'tall," Father Keane said. "He said he'd pick you up at half ten tomorrow for the plane."

They rode the short distance in silence. "I saw Detective Inspector White come for Patsy Lynch," he said.

"Yes," Mary Helen said, wondering just how much Father Keane knew and what he had been doing in the field the night they found Tommy Burns. These were two things, she realized, that she would probably never know the answers to.

"I feel as if I've just awakened from a nightmare," Eileen said, making sure the door of the mews was closed and locked behind them.

"Don't you wish?" Mary Helen collapsed on the couch. As soon as she did, she knew it was a mistake. All her energy seemed to leak out, and she wondered if she could ever get up.

"I can't believe the week went so quickly." Eileen sighed. "And tomorrow we leave for home." She studied Mary Helen.

"What is it?"

"I was just wondering what we should say about the Oyster Festival when the nuns ask us?"

"That it was an experience we will never forget," Mary Helen said. "And you must admit it was."

"No mention of the murder?"

"What's the point? It would only upset them. And the truth is, we will never forget it."

"Are you packed?" Eileen asked.

"Almost," Mary Helen said.

"Do you think you'll be able to sleep?"

"I hope so. How about you?"

"Shall I make us some hot chocolate and maybe put in a drop of brandy? That ought to help."

Eileen had just served their drinks when the telephone rang. "What now?" she said, picking up the receiver. "Oh, hello!"

Whoever it is, Mary Helen thought, *she sounds happy to hear from him or her.*

"It's my niece," she mouthed to Mary Helen. "Yes, love, we had a grand time. Thank you so much. I was going to call you in the morning. The Oyster Festival was an experience we'll never forget." Eileen rolled her eyes at Mary Helen.

True enough, Mary Helen thought, blowing on her hot chocolate. *And what's more, this Oyster Festival is one that no one in the village, no, the whole county, is likely to ever forget.*

Friday, September 5

The Final Blessing

True to his word, Paul Glynn arrived at the mews at 10:30 sharp, in plenty of time to drive the nuns to the Shannon airport.

"Have we everything?" Paul asked, about to close the boot of his car. "Two suitcases, two carry-ons, and one wrapped package."

"That's Jake Powers's wonderful photo of the Burren," Mary Helen said.

"Maybe we should keep it in the car with us," Eileen suggested. "We don't want anything to happen to it before we get it home for the other Sisters to enjoy."

Mary Helen agreed.

"Fine," Paul said, moving the package. "That's it, then?" he asked.

Eileen nodded, and Paul gave the boot a confident slam.

Sister Mary Helen stood on the cobblestone sidewalk, drinking in all she could of the picturesque village. The acrid sweet aroma of peat was in the air. A wafer of sun rose over the clouds, gilding the chestnut trees and the rooftops.

Save for a host of sparrows dropping onto the village square in search of worms, the place seemed deserted. The jamboree tent had been dismantled, and oddly, no cars were in the church car park or parked along the road. It was eerie.

Frowning, Mary Helen turned to Paul. "Where do you think everyone is?" she asked.

"Gone to the funeral at the cathedral in Galway City. This morning they are giving Willie Ward a grand send-off."

Mary Helen was surprised. "I didn't know he was so popular," she said.

"Oh, he's not." Paul shook his head. "As the old saying goes, 'There will be many a dry eye at his funeral.' I'd say most are there to make certain that he's dead and buried."

"May he rest in peace," Eileen said as the two nuns climbed into the backseat of the hackney.

"Amen," Paul answered piously. "And did you hear about poor Patsy Lynch?"

Fortunately, he did not wait for an answer. "They say that she was the one who killed him."

Without so much as a backward glance, Paul turned on the ignition, put the car in reverse, and pointed it toward Shannon.

"Nobody is saying why, but someone told my missus at the post office this morning that Patsy had her reasons. I'd have put my money on Jake Powers, but Patsy, never." Paul was quiet for a moment. "You never know. As my old mam used to say, 'There's so much good in the worst of us, and so much bad in the best of us, that it little behooves any of us to talk about the rest of us.' "

"Isn't that the truth," Eileen said.

As the hackney started down the road, Sister Mary Helen felt a sudden sadness. She wondered what would happen to those she had met on her short visit to this lovely village.

Fat raindrops, like so many tears, bounced off the roof. Turning, she gazed out the rearview window, watching the Monks' Table grow smaller.

The familiar words of the old Irish blessing tumbled through her mind. "Until we meet again, May God hold you in the hollow of His hand. May God hold you in the hollow of His hand."